KT-501-995

Too close To Home

Also by Aoife Walsh

Look After Me

Too Close To Home

AOIFE WALSH

ANDERSEN PRESS • LONDON

First published in 2015 by
Andersen Press Limited
20 Vauxhall Bridge Road
London SW1V 2SA
www.andersenpress.co.uk

2 4 6 8 10 9 7 5 3 1

All rights reserved. No part of this publication may be reproduced,
stored in a retrieval system or transmitted in any form, or by any
means, electronic, mechanical, photocopying, recording or
otherwise, without the written permission of the publisher.

The right of Aoife Walsh to be identified as the author
of this work has been asserted by her in accordance with
the Copyright, Designs and Patents Act, 1988.

Text copyright © Aoife Walsh, 2015
Illustrations copyright © Kate Grove, 2015

British Library Cataloguing in Publication Data available.

ISBN 978 1 78344 300 0

Typeset in Adobe Caslon by Palimpsest Book Production Limited,
Falkirk, Stirlingshire
Printed and bound in Great Britain by CPI Group (UK) Ltd,
Croydon CR0 4YY

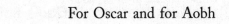

For Oscar and for Aobh

WHO'S AT HOME?

The Molloys

Minny, 14

Aisling, 15

Selena, 7

Raymond, *their baby brother*

Nita, *their mum*

Babi, *their grandmother*

Guts *the cat*

Gil, *Babi's boyfriend*

Dad's flat

Des Molloy, *the girls' dad*

Harriet, *his girlfriend*

The Greys

Penny, 14

Cora, *her mum*

Alison, *Cora's girlfriend*

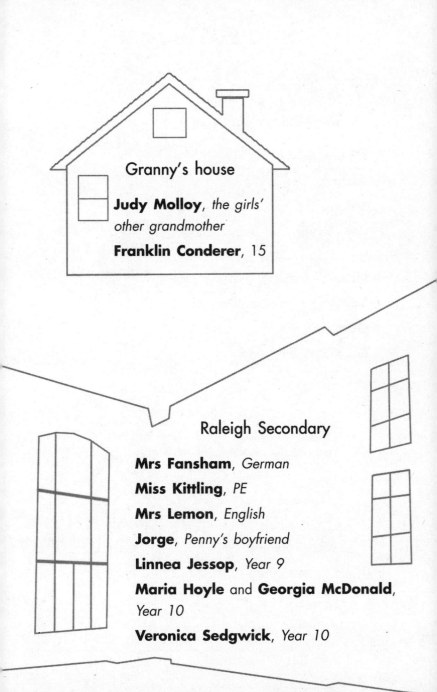

Granny's house

Judy Molloy, *the girls' other grandmother*

Franklin Conderer, 15

Raleigh Secondary

Mrs Fansham, *German*

Miss Kittling, *PE*

Mrs Lemon, *English*

Jorge, *Penny's boyfriend*

Linnea Jessop, *Year 9*

Maria Hoyle and **Georgia McDonald**, *Year 10*

Veronica Sedgwick, *Year 10*

ONE

All year Minny had endured having PE last thing on a Friday. It was hateful in winter but at least everyone else thought so too. It hit new lows in the summer term when most people apparently loved running round in an astro-turfed cage, swinging tennis rackets. But it reached the absolute depths on this particular Friday when, after a horrible English lesson, she was informed that they were all playing rounders together, girls and boys. Rounders. Minny had loathed it since primary school.

Of course, it was funny to see how playing a team game with boys affected the girls. 'Look at that,' she said to her best friend Penny, as they lurked as far away from the action as they could get. 'Juliet's gone all weak and feminine. Oh, look – straight at Andrew, that one.'

'She wasn't weak or feminine when she stamped all over me in football last term,' Penny remarked. 'I've still got that lump on my shin.'

'No.' Minny watched Emma Daly drop a hit from Michael, who was batting after Juliet. 'And Emma didn't fumble that hockey stick she ground into my ear either, that time I fell over in front of her.' It was strange to be talking to Penny during PE – since spring she'd been all into tennis, running away from Minny at the start of lessons so as to get put in a group with the good people.

Then of course they had to go up to bat. Minny's heart pounded as she stood in line; she didn't know what was scary about it really; it wasn't as if she wasn't used to looking stupid in PE. She missed with the first swing. 'Keep your eye on the ball,' Miss Kittling barked. Minny had no idea how to keep her eye on the ball. Her eye didn't want to stay on the ball, at least not while she was also swinging a bat. She was happy not to hit it; all she wanted was to be able to run to first base without getting anyone else out. After her third air shot, Miss Kittling blew her whistle.

'Look, Minny,' she said, polishing a ball of her own on her thigh, 'there's no point in coming to these lessons if you're not even going to try.'

'I couldn't agree more, miss.'

'That's enough of that. Honestly. Just watch the ball.' She tossed it at Minny, who swung and missed. 'Right, we'll try one more time. This enthusiasm for sport must run in your family.'

Minny missed again.

'Apparently I can't make your sister Aisling come out here and join in a team game any more, but I'm not having you wriggling out of it as well. Is that clear?' Minny swung in desperation and connected; Michael Dearbourne caught her out straight away but at least she could drop the bat and get away from the situation. She only overheard a few sighs from her own team, and Penny saying supportively to Nathan, 'It's not her fault she's crap at sport.'

'What are you doing this weekend?' Penny asked as they changed back into real clothes in the sweat-drenched cloakroom.

Minny brightened up a little as she threw her T-shirt into the bottom of the locker; at least school was over for the week. 'I don't know yet, no plans. What about you?'

'I can't meet up tomorrow, anyway. Jorge is in that tennis competition.' She finished dabbing a fresh layer on the caked concealer between her eyebrows. 'See you later, have a good one, byeee.'

Minny slammed her locker shut and trudged through the school. The main door was a rectangle of golden light, promising a couple of days' freedom, even if it was friendless freedom filled only with her family. She was almost there when Mrs Fansham stampeded out of her classroom and grabbed her, literally and damply. Mrs Fansham was a German teacher. Minny had never even taken German, but they had spoken several times before because Aisling, Minny's sister, was in her form. 'Oh, Minny –' she towed her into the classroom – 'I wanted a word about Aisling.'

''Kay,' Minny said, non-committally.

'She hasn't had a very good day, to be honest with you.'

She put her hand on her fat chest. 'I don't know what was wrong, do you?'

Minny shrugged.

'She wouldn't say. Anyway, I saw her leaving a few minutes ago and she looked upset.'

The fact was Mrs Fansham was just stupid. Minny had to work hard to stop her face saying so. Ash had chemistry on a Friday afternoon, and Minny knew for a fact that their mother had explained, in short words, why Aisling found science stressful. Bustle, open flames, being expected not to spill things; plus long benches all joined together and distracted teachers – open season for bullies and hell on a stick for an autistic person. Besides, all Mrs Fansham was achieving by rabbiting on in her steaming-hot classroom was that Ash was getting further and further away from school and it would take longer for Minny to catch her up.

Now she had to hurry most of the way home, getting hotter and crosser all the way, until the last stretch of shops when Aisling was in sight. Also just about within earshot; Minny caught the odd squeak. Her sister got louder and shriller the more stressed out she was.

'Minnyminnyminnyminnyminnyminnyminnyminnybatman. Aisling Molloy! You know very well . . .'

Ash was crossing the road now, skipping irregularly the way she did. There was a group of boys up ahead, on the corner of Whitsun Road where the big puddle always was; there was a leaky pipe there or something. Minny speeded up. Aisling, crossing, stretched carefully over the water. One of the boys bustled her so that she stepped right back into it. There was a roar of appreciation.

Minny half ran, half power-walked up towards them with her hardest face on. Ash was just standing there, squeaking in a voice that only bats could have heard. The boys were still sniggering but had stepped away. 'Idiots,' Minny muttered, taking Aisling's arm. 'Come on, let's go home.'

'But I can't NOW,' Aisling said shrilly.

'Yes, you can, we're nearly there.'

'My feet.'

'Try not to think about it.'

There was a boy pelting towards them from further up the road that she'd been half aware of. She stood back to let him go past, only he stopped instead.

'Are you all right?' he asked. Aisling looked at him as if she wasn't sure he was speaking to her. 'I saw – are you soaking?' They all looked down at her feet. She sidestepped, and squelched. 'Morons. Yeah, well done,' he shouted at the boys.

'Yeah,' Minny said, to make herself known. 'You're OK though, aren't you, Ash?'

'Good.' He fidgeted. 'Hi.'

'Hello,' Ash said.

'Hi,' Minny said. 'Oh. Hi.'

The profundity of the exchange was because she had recognised him. His name was Franklin Conderer and she hadn't seen him since she was eight years old when he had moved to the other side of London.

'What are you doing here, Franklin?' Ash asked him in her small-talk voice, which was the most normal one she had. Minny wasn't sure how they had both recognised him; he looked really different. He hadn't been at their primary school very long, only while he was living with his aunt, but she remembered him as the kind of little boy who did things like running into other kids at full speed and hurling them down on their faces. He never touched the Molloys, but Penny got a kneeful of black gravel once. He was supposed to be in Ash's class but he got sent down one to Minny's; their mother said it was because Minny's teacher that year was a man, and was therefore supposed to be able to handle him. Back then, Franklin had had one of those sad super-short haircuts some little boys got with a separate fringe, as if they didn't deserve to have hair, and always looked miserable and out of place. He had good hair now. He was thin and pale.

He looked surprised. 'Well, I'm . . . I'm living with Judy for a bit.'

'What?'

'Judy Molloy?' Aisling enquired. 'Our granny?'

Their granny, Judy Molloy, lived less than two miles from them. Since their dad had left, the time they spent with her had been gradually whittled down – first they had all moved in with their other grandmother, Babi, whom Granny couldn't stand, and then they started getting so much more homework, and the baby came, and they just didn't go round to her house as often. Still, Minny would have expected to know that she had adopted a teenage boy.

'Yeah.' He put one hand behind his neck. 'I got in a bit of trouble, a while ago now, and anyway no one seemed to think I should stay at home, so Judy said she'd have me for now. See how it goes.' He shrugged at them. He was really thin. 'I only came yesterday. I suppose that's why you didn't know or anything.'

'Yeah.'

He was looking all around them. 'I was at the school to talk about starting there, you know. I was just waiting for the bus.' He pointed at the bus stop.

'You're starting at Raleigh?'

'Yeah. On Monday.'

'That's where we go,' Minny said.

'I know.' He hesitated. 'Is it all right?'

'Er. You know.'

'We're coming to Granny's on Sunday,' Aisling said brightly.

'Are we?' Minny said.

'Yes. I said to Mum the day before yesterday that we hadn't seen Granny since the twenty-second of April.'

'What happened on the twenty-second of April?' Franklin asked.

'That's when we last saw Granny,' Aisling explained. 'And

7

we agreed that was a long time so Mum said she'd phone Granny up and ask if we could go round this Sunday.'

'Right.' Minny looked at Franklin. 'So I guess we'll see you then.'

'Cool.'

'Or not.'

'Or not,' he agreed.

'Why not?' Ash asked. 'We're going round on Sunday.'

'Come on, Ash,' Minny said, rolling her eyes. 'See you, Franklin.'

'Yeah, see you.'

When they'd left the bus stop safely behind, Minny glanced at Aisling. There were tear marks, but only at the sides of her eyes as if meeting Franklin had distracted her in time. 'Don't pay any attention to those idiots.'

'No. My shoes are wet.'

'We'll dry them.'

Ash snuffled a bit. 'Will Mum be at home?'

'She's got a staff meeting. She said she'd be back for dinner.' They trudged on. 'That's a bit weird, about Franklin.'

Aisling was looking at her shoes.

'I mean, you'd have thought we'd know. It's not that long since we've seen Granny.'

'It was the twenty-second of April.'

'You said.'

'That's six weeks . . .'

'Mmmm.'

'And five days. Which is closer to seven weeks really.'

'Oh, shut up, Ash. I almost didn't recognise him.' She paused. 'He's taller than I thought he'd be.'

'He's not very tall.'

'He's got better hair. He used to have terrible hair. I liked his T-shirt.' It was always like this. They wandered along side by side and one of them talked. Usually it was Ash, spouting complete gibberish, while Minny let her get on with it; sometimes, like now, Minny would just think out loud. She assumed that to Ash it meant about as little as the details of the 1972 Congressional US election, or as endless sung renditions of 'There's a Hole in My Bucket' meant to her. They didn't actually converse. That was fine; they never had, except when they were younger, if they were ever doing the same thing at the same time, like playing a computer game or constructing a fantasy football cup draw, they might have talked more co-operatively then. The only thing now was you had to be slightly careful to say: 'Ash.'

'Mmmm.'

'Don't repeat any of that, OK.'

'Don't repeat it to who?'

'To anyone.'

She was normally pretty safe, but because their stupid parents had always played stupid parental games about 'don't you dare do this or I'll tickle you', you had to look solemn and serious and right in her eyes when you were telling her.

The December before last she'd announced to the front room, where Babi was having a cocktail party, that Minny was expecting her second period any day now, she'd had her first at Halloween! with a mischievous glimmer that showed she was expecting some roughhousing.

'Look,' Ash said, pointing. 'There's Selena.'

They crossed the road. Their other sister was leaning on the sign at the corner of their street. 'I've been waiting for you.'

'Why?' Selena always got home first; normally Babi picked her up after her afternoon Weight Watchers meeting. Today though, Greengrocer Gil had rung her just as they were getting home, and she'd strolled off down the street, refusing to open the front door first for Sel. Selena was seven. Their grandmother was a liability – Sel should never be left hanging about on a corner by a main road on her own; even Minny could see that. Sel looked like Aisling, except less dreamy, and like their mother too: lots of cloudy blonde curls and a wistful luminous face. Minny was inclined to put it down to nomenclature. Aisling meant a kind of poetry, or dream or vision, or a woman you see in a dream or a vision. Selena meant the moon. But she, she was Minny. All that made you think of was words that were insults or at least very basic, like skinny or tranny or dunny. They weren't even real words.

Babi had returned to the house without bothering to fetch Selena; she opened the front door as Minny stuck her key into the lock, said nothing, then glided back up the hall as if there were wheels under her very long black trousers. They had been living in Babi's house for nearly two years. Minny was so used to it that she got resentful about Babi being there, even though it was her house, and blamed her for it being so crowded. She supposed in fact their old flat must have been smaller, but at least it was *theirs*, and there was room for their stuff. This house was too full. Minny knew her sisters, brother, mother and grandmother weren't actually evil, not even her grandmother; they just didn't all fit together properly. Like the games and jigsaws which had been stuffed together over the years and come spilling out of their boxes. And like those boxes, it sometimes felt as if the top of the house was going to come off, or the side might split, or a giant foot would come down out of the sky and casually squash it so that even masking tape couldn't fix it.

They squeezed through the porch, between the pushchair and the big tippy pile of shoes. Ash normally just stepped out of her trainers and chucked them in the direction of all the others, but now she stood there awkwardly holding them. 'Stick them out the back in the sun,' Minny suggested. 'And put your socks in the washing machine.'

'I want to wear my socks.'

'They're soaking wet.'

'No, they're not.'

'Ash, you're leaving footprints on the carpet.'

'But I like these socks.' She took them off in the end,

looking resentful as if the whole thing was Minny's fault. Minny sat down to unlace her high-tops properly because they were coming to pieces, and then got her books out of her bag, balancing her real book on top.

'What are you reading?' Selena dusted her sandals off and placed them on top of the shoe pile.

'*Peter Pan*. What? It's a great classic of English lit-er-a-ture,' Minny said, dropping her pencil case so that all her biros fell out and rolled under the radiator. 'Mum reckons you can't appreciate any post-war novels if you haven't read this. Or something.'

Babi was passing through the hall again with an empty glass in each hand. She snorted. She refused to believe that anything good at all could have come out of Britain, since Shakespeare anyway, even though she'd been living here for about fifty years. English literature annoyed her because you couldn't really argue with it being good, compared to everything else English in the arts. She took the arts very seriously. A lot of her family had been arty, intellectual types who died in Czechoslovakia when the Nazis came. Then after that it was the Communists, and she and her parents had fled, more or less, and ended up in London. Later on she'd met their grandfather, who was a writer from South Africa who didn't get on with the government and so he'd left there and come to England as well. It all seemed to mean that Babi couldn't take any kind of creativity seriously unless it could get you thrown in jail.

Minny started to get up, but just then there was a thumpety thump from the back room and the baby came bustling round the corner, crawled up to her and grabbed her hair so he could get up on his feet to kiss her. She picked him up, wiping snot off her jaw, and carried him into the front room. At least it was Friday and her mother would be home soon.

The front room was misleadingly subtle and sophisticated, at least when you looked in from the street outside and if you ignored the green plastic highchair. There was no TV because that was in the back room: instead it had the real-wood bookshelves and the walnut table and chairs; the carved mantelpiece with ceramic tiles and the big old-fashioned wooden globe their mother had bought on her honeymoon in Italy. You couldn't see the baby toys from outside, stacked underneath the window, alongside the piles of books that had never fitted on to Babi's shelves. Also it wasn't mouldy, like most of the other rooms were in the corners, except when their mother had just been on one of her cleaning binges. Minny was up for playing cars with the baby for a while, but he'd already heard the *Countdown* music and was crawling next door, to Aisling.

'You can go and do your homework,' Babi announced, suddenly appearing in the doorway with a giant metal spoon and stepping over the baby. She had her house shoes on now, which were incredibly shiny, just like her outside shoes, but without the four-inch heel that could kill a horse.

'I will look after him till five thirty.' Five thirty was when their mother was meant to be home.

'It's Friday.' She never did homework on Fridays.

Babi shrugged. 'Suit yourself. But I don't have to cook till then. So . . .'

Minny trailed upstairs. She didn't get so much time free of sisterly duty that she could turn it down. Summer holidays soon though; her mother would be off work, more or less, so there wouldn't be nearly so much for Minny to do in the house. Of course that all meant more time listening to her sisters babble. Sel just banged on and on about all this crazy Bible stuff she insisted on reading at the moment; Minny felt like she was sharing a room with all of them as well: Moses and Hagar and Jephthah and their nasty habits. And Ash lived in a world of her own, people were always saying it – with varying degrees of indulgence. Took up plenty of space in the real world as well though.

It still seemed unnecessary to do homework on a Friday evening, so she went into her mother's room and flipped open her laptop. It wasn't supposed to be up here. Computing was meant to be done downstairs to ensure that no one happened on anything unsuitable. Still, whenever anyone said they had serious homework to do they were allowed to take the laptop to wherever it was quiet, and then no one ever remembered to bring it back. Sometimes all Minny wanted was a couple of minutes to talk to someone, an adult who wasn't talking to someone else at the same time. And then email was the best thing on offer.

'*Howzaboy Kevin,*' she typed. Sometimes they addressed each other as if they were drunken American characters from P.G. Wodehouse books. '*I had a triple-suck day today, having to listen to Penny gloat all morning and all through lunchtime about how much she snogs Jorge, and then horrible bitter Mrs Lemon said she couldn't give back everyone else's creative-writing homework from last weekend because she had to spend so long reading mine because it was twenty-two pages. And she said some of my sentences were nearly a page long too.*' She wouldn't reread it now to check if that was true. She didn't particularly want ever to reread it. '*Like I was just a show-off and a suck-up. Like I'd ever try to show off to her, as if I didn't know better. Everyone looked at me like I was the worst geek in the world.*' If only they knew; she'd had lunchtime detention on Monday because of the maths homework she should have been doing instead of writing the last ten pages, and failed a French test the same day. '*Can't WAIT till next year when I get a new teacher, though she'll probably have put me down a set. Mum says she won't, but I bet she does.*'

She never felt she had to think about what she was writing with her Uncle Kevin. He was all piled-up sentences and missing commas himself, so there was no great stylistic pressure, and she never worried that she was boring him because he remembered the tiniest things. He said her emails were like a soap opera set in a school, and that he loved

15

hearing about teachers and about evil girls like Juliet and Emma. Mostly she resisted the temptation to make things up to please him. And he only asked the most general questions about Aisling or Selena so she didn't feel like she had to keep him up to date on how school and Ash were getting on with each other. Which was good because it was depressing enough having to answer her mother's questions.

Also you could talk about books to him, stuff you'd read and stuff you might read, without feeling like an idiot. He had time and he was interested. The day Minny had learned to read and knew she had, they ran all the way home from school so that Ash had to ride the last quarter-mile on their mother's back, and as soon as they were in, bundling up the stairs to their flat, Nita had phoned Kevin at his bar in Ireland and got her, Minny, to read out two verses of a poem. Dylan Thomas, it was. And Uncle Kevin burst into tears. Minny missed him, not that they'd ever seen much of him, but he'd always been on the phone to one or other of her parents, and sometimes he'd visited, laden down with bags of chocolate bars. Now her father was gone it was only emails.

Anyway he already hated Mrs Lemon and he'd be sympathetic. English was supposed to be her favourite subject, not the one she dreaded only slightly less than PE. It was her thing, reading books and writing stories, what she had always been best at, not just compared with how she did at other things but compared with the rest of the class. Only

Mrs Lemon hadn't given her anything higher than a B all year, and mostly B minuses. '*Don't know what to read next. Mum says it's time for Jane Austen but I'm not sure.*' She might just spend the weekend on Malory Towers or *The Railway Children*, but that wasn't something she would tell Kevin.

She was thinking of a sign-off when she heard Selena's squeak and the scuff-thump of the baby climbing the stairs. The stair gate clanged against the wall and then the door flew open.

'Babi says she's got to cook now and you've got to have Raymond!' Selena announced, puffed from carrying the cat and circling the baby.

'Why me?' Minny pulled him onto her lap. He was a devil with the computer. It was just like her grandmother to offer so aggressively to look after him, so that you would start doing something, and then ditch him on you before you'd finished. 'Couldn't you watch him just till Mum gets home?'

'No. He was crying to get up the stairs.'

Minny wasn't really cross. She loved him. He was her favourite and she was his – after their mother, which didn't count. She fluffed up his hair and batted his hands away from the keyboard. 'Well, can you just play with him till I send this?'

There was no room for them to sit on the floor – their mother even had to keep her knickers in a plastic bag at the bottom of the wardrobe, so Selena got the jewellery box from the dressing table and she and Raymond got stuck into it on the other end of the bed. It was even smaller than Minny's room, which had bunk beds for her and Sel; only Aisling's was more tiddly. Ash had to have her own room because she got up at five o'clock in the morning. Her stuff was so wedged in there that the door didn't open properly and you had to climb over the bed to get in.

Minny finished her email, knees drawn up to protect the laptop from Raymond. *'I've got to go now because the baby's going nuts and there's no one to look after him as usual except me. Babi's too busy making Czech fish stew, which smells completely ram and will probably make us all violently ill – but I thought I'd tell you so you can start thinking of books for me and ways to murder and dispose of Mrs Lemon and think of me when you're having a NICE dinner this evening with no fish heads . . . Minny.'* She turned round to find that Sel was checking out her reflection in two necklaces against her school jumper, with another in her hair and four rings on her wiggling fingers, while the cat purred in her lap with a bracelet around his ear, and Raymond looked gravely disgusted and had two strands of a beaded earring dangling from his mouth.

'Selena! He could choke on this kind of crap! Have some sense, will you.' She put her little finger into the corner of his mouth and he opened it unwillingly. She pulled the earring out. It looked intact, although with her mother's jewellery it was hard to tell.

'Well, it wouldn't have been my fault.' Sel threw all the necklaces down. 'I'm only seven.'

'Oh, and I'm sure that would have been a great comfort to you as he breathed his last,' Minny snapped. 'Now tidy that stuff up.'

'You tidy it up.' She stropped out, banging the door behind her. Raymond reached for another earring.

'No no no. Give it to Minny. Listen, there's the front door. Mummy's home. You go and find Mummy. No, leave Guts alone.' She tried to keep him away from the fleeing cat with her knee while she bundled all the jewellery back into the box. Her mother would probably never be able to unravel a single necklace from the clump.

When she came downstairs with Raymond under her arm, her mother, Nita, was still in the hall, taking everything out of her shoulder bag and spreading it all to the corners they lived in. 'Hello, sweet angel,' she said, rescuing Raymond as he tried to dive head first over the banisters to get to her. 'And hello, other sweet angel.' She aimed a kiss at Minny. 'Good day?'

'No, rubbish.'

'Oh no. I smell fish stew though.'

'I know.' They both squeezed their faces up. What Minny had said to Kevin had only been for effect, and because you couldn't say you loved fish stew; actually it was one of Babi's best, and though she said the stench would kill her, she often made it on Fridays. Friday was non-meat day. They ate so much dead animal that Minny's mother got fits of conscience about it and insisted on one day off; they'd picked Friday because they were usually out of meat by then anyway, and Selena still went to Catholic primary school and Friday was the day recommended there. Though that meant the weekly risk of some anticlerical feeling getting aired at the dinner table. Also, since they usually cheated and ate fish, Minny wasn't sure there was any point.

'Oof,' her mother said, bending down to pick up her mobile, which Raymond had dropped, then straightening up again. 'You are a big heavy tubby, aren't you? Where are the others?'

'Watching TV, I suppose. I had English today.'

'Oh yes? Was it good?'

'It's never good, I told you.' Minny came down a step. 'Mrs Lemon made me look like an arse for writing a long story. She said it showed bad judgement and she didn't have time to mark any of the others just because of mine, and that I was self-indulgent.'

'Oh, Minny.'

'She's a cow.'

'Of course she is. A big Friesian heifer. Don't worry about it – she was probably just having a bad day.'

'Good, she deserved to. It was embarrassing.'

Her mother was looking up, but she wasn't listening now. Aisling was calling her, monotonously, from the back room. She headed off. 'What's wrong, Ash? All right, I'm coming. Mama, when's dinner? And where's Selena?'

Minny would have liked to go back upstairs on her own, but it was all hands on deck between Nita getting home and dinner being dished up. She had to look after Raymond while her mother first spoke to Selena about kiddy stuff at school and let Sel drivel on about some project she was doing on Ancient Greece, and then started going through Ash's homework. Mostly the teachers emailed it to Nita because Ash never wrote it down properly. On a Friday the two of them always had to plan minutely when it was going to get done. Meanwhile Raymond kept shoving *The Very Hungry Caterpillar* in her face. Normally he liked Minny reading to him, but not on Fridays when he'd been at nursery all day and their mother hadn't come home till five thirty.

At ten past six Nita finally came running into the back room with the baby chewing the corner of his book, ditched him on the floor and flung herself onto the sofa. 'My *God*, that was a hard day. I need to lie down. You can all do what you want. I'm just going to lie here.'

Aisling, who'd been drifting around muttering about *The West Wing*, immediately went to lie on top of her. Nita groaned. Selena started bouncing up and down and shouting, till Minny took her cue and went to lie on Ash so that Sel could lie on her. 'Chaos, Minny,' Ash said from underneath, 'you brought chaos.' All-pile-on was a tradition. It put everyone in a good mood, unless you happened to get an elbow in your collarbone.

Dinner was usually when they were all together for the

first time. They weren't a picky family – they ate anything put in front of them while exchanging news and opinions so fast that food had been known to fly across the table. But not that day, because just as they were all rolling around on the sofa trying not to fall on Raymond, who was engaged in climbing on top, the doorbell went. Selena sucked herself off the heap and flew towards it as usual. No one else in the house had had the chance to open the front door for about five years. Even political campaigners and Mormons had learned to miss out their house now because they had to struggle through five minutes' really intense conversation with her before they got to see anyone else. Minny wasn't sure why Sel found the ring at the door so exciting, but it was a disappointment this time because it was Gil.

'Hallo, Selena,' he said in his fake jolly way, taking off his stupid hat. 'Am I on time for dinner?'

'I don't know.' Sel put her finger in her mouth as if she was four, and ran away. Babi came out of the steamy kitchen and hung his hat up for him.

'Darrrlink,' she said in her throaty voice, 'I am just serving up. Won't you go and sit down for two minutes till everything is ready?'

Their mother had to change Raymond's nappy before dinner, and Selena, being seven, could scamper wherever she wanted whether there was a guest or not. So that meant Gil watching *The Simpsons* with Ash, because Minny was reading. She didn't like him. He had a lot of virtually white hair which he swept in a puffy ring around his red bald patch, and he wore mossy jumpers. Babi was never polite to Minny's friends, in fact she went out of her way to blow smoke at Penny, so why should Minny be friendly to Gil?

'You watch this every day, Aisling?' She just nodded and hummed. She didn't like Gil being in the house either, because he was new, and a man. 'I've only seen it once or twice. Is it good?'

'Roger Ram is up and Roger Ram is down,' Aisling shouted suddenly.

'Christ!' Minny shouted too because she hated to be startled.

'Roger Ram is dancing all around the town.'

'Shut up, Aisling.'

'Why don't you like it when I sing that?'

'You don't sing it, you scream it.'

'And it makes your heart jump,' Ash added joyfully. Minny had made the mistake of saying that to her about eight years ago and she never forgot stuff that tickled her. Minny didn't like to say they had a pensioner with them and shocks probably weren't good for him. 'I sing about Roger Ram sometimes when I'm feeling stressed,' Ash explained to Gil.

'Oh dear, are you feeling stressed? And on a Friday night?'

Minny felt sorry for him in a way. They weren't the easiest family.

*   *   *

23

At dinner they all had to be polite instead of just eating. Gil had never come for a normal dinner before, and his arrival had always been announced. Babi refused to look at anyone. Minny was wondering if this meant he'd be popping by all the time now, and could see her mother was wondering it too. Nita was the world's most polite and friendly woman, it was sickening sometimes, but she struggled with Gil. Anyone would feel weird with someone dating their mother, particularly their sixty-five-year-old mother, and it was so hard to imagine what Babi could possibly see in this red-faced old man. Say what you would about their grandmother, she wasn't Minny's cup of tea, but she was sort of magnificent. She had a very sharp pure black bob, sticking-out cheekbones and deep hooded eyes, and she kept herself pretty trim.

Then there was their grandfather, who to be fair had died eight years ago – but he was supposed to be this extra-ordinary man. Minny didn't remember that side of him because she'd been too young, but she remembered looking forward to seeing him – he wasn't so much the kind of grandfather who took you to the playground; he'd taken them to theatres instead, or to museums, and then, when they were flagging, to beautiful restaurants for tea. Once there had been a cake with silver icing. And the carousel on the South Bank. And he was this great political writer and everything, and knew everyone in the world that was famous and interesting, and Babi had apparently worshipped him. She was miserable when he died. And now here she was doing whatever she was doing with the old bloke from the greengrocer's on Grenville Road. Minny wasn't the snob in the family, Babi was. So it all seemed a bit mysterious.

Nita tried to be nice, like she always did. She didn't have much chance to pay attention to him because she had to feed the baby and talk to Selena and Aisling, neither of whom had ever grasped that you were supposed to wait for a gap in the conversation before you started telling an irrelevant story. It all went much as usual: Selena tutted and sighed because there was chaos going on after she was ready to say grace. Then, when everyone had said amen, she immediately opened her eyes and said, 'Victoria got told off today because Lily and Fran were fighting over who was going to be her partner in baseball. It was really unfair.'

'Mmm, this is tip-top tasty,' Aisling said, at pretty much the same time Gil said, 'Nita, can I pass you the pepper?' Their mother had to accept it brightly while blowing on the baby's bowl to cool his dinner down, fastening his bib and listening to Selena. While she was telling her completely boring and structureless story about three girls in her class that no one else knew, Aisling was repeating 'tip-top tasty' at increasing volume because no one had acknowledged her. When their mother finally did get to say, 'That's great, Ash, good,' Aisling straightaway said, 'That's another thing that's wrong in *The West Wing*, you know, this man says that Franklin Pierce – you know, the president? – he says that he was his great-great-grandfather, only Franklin Pierce never had any grandchildren, so he can't have been.'

By the time there was a lull, because Selena and Ash were both chewing at the same time, Raymond had his fists twisted up in Nita's hair. 'It's good to see you here, Gil,' she said, turning her head from where it was resting sideways on the highchair tray. 'Is everything going well with the shop, and everything?'

'Oh, very well,' he said, sucking fish off his fork. 'I'm delighted to be here, Anita. Dining with not one, but five beautiful women – I'm the envy of every man in London.' It was so cheesy Minny felt her mouth go dry, and Nita practically shuddered. Minny could see Selena's eyes moving round the table, counting to make sure one of the five was her.

'Well, we're very pleased to have you. I'm sorry it's all a bit chaotic, but Fridays are always like this – I didn't get home till half past five, so Mama had to look after everything as well as cook.' She paused but he was busy eating. 'So – Minny,' she said, turning in desperation, 'tell me about this teacher. What's her name again?'

'Mrs Lemon.'

'Of course.'

Minny shrugged. She had no interest in talking about it in front of the whole world.

'No? Anyone got any plans this weekend?' She filled her mouth up with stew, looking as if she was in pain. 'This is really wonderful, Mama.'

'It had better be. The pan will smell of fish bones for a month, and so will my fingers.'

'Nonsense,' Gil said, stopping guzzling, swallowing a belch and reaching across Ash to pat Babi's hand. Aisling promptly dropped her fork, which clattered against her glass. 'There's nothing wrong with a woman's scent reminding you of the good food she's given you.'

'Oh my God,' Minny said under her breath. She saw her mother look down at her plate with round eyes.

'Anyway,' Nita ploughed on after a pause, 'something exciting happened to me today. It looks as if we might be asked to take the play to the Edinburgh Festival!'

'What's the Edinburgh Festival?' Aisling asked.

'Can I come?' Sel looked anxious. It had taken about a year for her to get over not being allowed to be in the play – their mother's drama group was for kids with disabilities and special needs, but Selena didn't see that as a reason why she shouldn't get the starring role in every production.

'When?' Minny didn't want to ask what would happen to them.

'What would happen to them?' Babi demanded.

'It's just an idea.' Sometimes their mother looked like she was going to cry; it was the kind of face she had. 'It'll probably come to nothing. And if it did, it would only be four or five days at most.'

Babi snorted. 'I can't help remembering what happened the last time you went away for a few days.'

27

Nita went scarlet.

'What happened?' Selena asked, tipping up her bowl to get the broth.

'Nothing,' Babi snapped. She shouldn't have said it, not in front of Gil. The last time Nita had gone away on her own she had come back pregnant with Raymond.

When the stew was all gone and they were eating boring Neapolitan ice cream, because the dairy-free stuff Ash had to have only came in dull flavours, Babi asked Gil to help her with the clearing away. 'No, Mama, you did the cooking,' Nita protested. 'The girls and I will take care of it.'

'No, no,' Gil said, all jovial. 'You've got enough to do, Nita. And I'm sure the girls would rather be painting their nails or something, eh? I enjoy being shut into a confined space with Milena.' Minny tried not to gag. She had an unwelcome memory of the day, around last Christmas, when he and Babi had only just got together and she turned round in the greengrocer's and they were smooching behind the counter. It was also the first time she had seen unpicked Brussels sprouts, sticking out alternately from sticks. She had found them disturbing.

'I don't paint my nails,' Selena remarked, mixing her ice cream up so it would turn into a weird sludge she could drink. 'I'm not allowed to use make-up till I'm older. But I'd like to go and read some of my Bible.'

'Still slogging away at it then, Selena? What do you think of that?' He nudged Minny.

Minny thought it was mental, obviously. 'I think it's up to Selena.'

'It's great literature, apart from anything else,' her mother said brightly.

'Well, so they say, but I could never get my head round that. Seems to me a little girl could find better things to do, playing with her friends or what-have-you. Still, it's not up to me, is it?'

'No,' they all said together.

He put an apron on, to clear the table. Over his horrible belly. It was the flowered apron their father used to wear when they made bread on Sundays. Minny couldn't relax until they'd finished stacking the dishes up and Babi had replastered her face and she and Gil had gone out; she never did proper homework on Fridays, but since they weren't allowed the TV on, because Ash was doing hers and Sel was drawing urns and daisies around the edges of her sums, Minny looked at some doctored Soviet photographs in her history textbook for a while. She thought she wouldn't mind a job like that, just rubbing people out. Then Ash had finished what she was doing and left the computer, so Minny glanced at her emails. She was about to shut it down when a new message flashed in from Uncle Kevin, with the subject 'Marvellous Minny'.

'*Minnymouse!*' it started, which was what she'd been called when she was little – all one word, like that, like lollipop or cantaloupe. '*You are a martyr to your own brilliance, and to this terrible woman who is obviously sexually unsatisfied in her marriage or perhaps never actually learned to read but has risen to the eminence of English teacher only through trickery and deceit. I'm speaking to Mam later if I can get hold of her and I'll have her on the rosaries for you every night that you get a decent teacher next year who might stand a chance of appreciating you. I loved the sound of Mr Fahey who took you to see* The Tempest, *he sounded just my sort of man. I'm guessing from what you didn't say about him that he's handsome and sad with sensitive hands and hair falling into his eyes. Am I right? Don't tell me if I'm not. Anyway it doesn't much matter as long as it's someone bright enough to be glad to have a pupil who can string a couple of clauses together and actually reads books that aren't about vampires. You should tell her all the Salinger books you've read, and Vonnegut – can you imagine? It might put an end to her. Your mother's right, you'd love Jane Austen. Also I was just thinking the other day, you're ready for Steinbeck. I introduced your dad to him when he was fourteen and it was love, it truly was. The time might be ripe.'* Sometimes Minny got a great urge to call her uncle, and *hear* him talking like that, even if she couldn't see him. He never even came to visit his own mother any more; it must be three years since he stayed at Granny's and probably more.

Actually, Minny realised, she missed her granny too. She wondered for a second if Nita was deliberately trying to stop them seeing much of her. Nita had always been driven a bit nuts by Granny, who filled them full of fizzy drinks and sweets whenever they went to her house, and did things like taking them out for milkshakes even though Aisling was dairy intolerant. They'd never rowed, but once when Granny was round, Minny had found her mother alone with her back to the kitchen door and her arms stretched out pressing against it, whispering things to herself. But no, unless her mother was playing a very long game, it couldn't be that; she used to get Granny round to babysit and everything. That would have been more awkward now, with Raymond and all, but anyway they were old enough not to need a babysitter any more. Since the baby came, and especially since she had to go back to work afterwards, Mum had chilled out a lot about them being home sometimes by themselves. Usually Babi was meant to be there, but it wasn't as if that made much difference, apart from the cooking.

After the baby was in bed Minny sat about waiting for people to come downstairs and start annoying her. In the end she turned the telly off and wandered upstairs. Ash was in the bath singing to herself. Her mother was drying Sel's hair while Sel brushed it, standing with her eyes shut. Minny waited in the doorway till Nita looked up. 'Shut the door, sweetie. I don't want to wake the baby.'

Minny did shut the door, with herself outside it. She heard the dryer being turned off, Sel yelp in protest and then her mother put her head around the door.

'Are you all right?'

'Fine.'

'Is there something you want to talk about?'

'Not really.'

'Is it about Ash?'

'No,' Minny snapped. Then she said, 'Well, Mrs Fansham told me to tell you she was upset in chemistry but wouldn't say why.'

Her mother blew a raspberry. 'That woman. Thank God the school year's nearly over. Look – never mind. You want to talk about something else, don't you? The thing is, I've promised to read to Selena before she goes to sleep.'

'Mum, Selena has been reading the Jerusalem Bible to herself for a year now.'

'I know, but she's only seven, I like to do bedtime stories when I can. And she's a bit sensitive at the moment. I'll be down soon. I promise.'

She wasn't especially. It stayed unusually quiet downstairs, and Minny started watching a film she didn't want to watch because her book was in her bedroom. It was the second ad break before her mother came in.

'Feel like helping me with the washing-up?'

'No.'

'Oh, go on. If I sit down now I'll never get it done, and we'll get up tomorrow feeling as if we live in a fish bin. Please. I'm extremely tired. You don't have to do anything, just stand in there and talk to me.'

Minny sighed and got up, because she had nothing better to do. Even though, as soon as they were in the kitchen,

32

Nita threw a tea towel in her face so that she could dry. Normally just one of them did all the tidying, because the kitchen was too little and two people got in each other's way; and usually the baby was still up and crawling around tripping you up, or throwing the magnetic letters off the fridge across the room. Most of them were missing now. Minny had arranged the remaining ones into rude words yesterday, and then Selena had come along and tried to change them into Biblical terms, but her concentration wasn't very good for things like that so now the fridge said 'vargin' and 'bullocks'. ('Bullocks?' her mother had asked her. 'Are you sure?' 'Oh yes, all the farmyard animals come up in the Gospel,' Sel said airily.) Minny got the giggles now, wondering if Gil had noticed them.

It was easier to have a conversation when you were doing something, and even with Carole King playing so her mother stopped talking to dance every few songs, she still got quite satisfactorily worked up about Mrs Lemon. 'Stupid woman. If she treats you like that, how's she teaching her non-gifted pupils?'

'Don't know.'

'I hope to God you get a decent one next year. You're so bloody-minded about the subjects you like, especially English, I'm always afraid they'll see your brains as a nuisance and shut you down, the way the maths teachers did with Ash.' Aisling didn't learn maths at school now; Nita taught her at home. The teachers said the way she learned was incompatible with the way everyone else in the class needed teaching. 'It's probably inevitable in any school, but it's so frustrating. I get really resentful about it. It's like those self-service checkouts in the supermarket that have signs on saying, "Sorry, no fifty-pound notes." Well, what if a fifty-pound note is what you have?'

Minny had finished drying the knives and leaned against the oven. Her mother's face was reflected in the kitchen window, lit up with her hair flopping around it. Minny told her about meeting Franklin Conderer that afternoon – she'd wanted to mention it earlier over dinner, but it was like an unwritten rule that you didn't talk about one grandmother in front of the other unless you absolutely had to. Too much like tickling a bear. 'Why has he moved in with Granny?'

Nita dashed her hand against her head. 'I was going to tell you that. It went clear out of my mind. I rang her just this morning and she told me he was staying. I think it all happened fairly fast as far as Judy was concerned – he's been in some trouble lately, and his mother's not in a great condition at the moment, and it came down to him having to go into care for a while because there was no one else to look after him, and then someone thought of Judy. Bless her heart, taking him in. She's always felt bad about him though, and especially since poor Lou died and he had no one. I mean, besides his mother.'

Minny digested this. Her granny and Franklin's had been

best friends back in the nineteenth century or something when they were both student nurses in London; that was the whole reason they'd known him. When his gran died, his aunt Lou used to bring him round to see Judy; and then he'd lived with Lou for a while when they were about seven or eight. He was at their school, probably for about a year. Then she got ill, and he had to go back to live with his mum in North London. Today was the first time she'd seen him since the aunt's funeral. Franklin's mother was a disaster. Minny had known it at age seven; she always seemed drunk or something, and usually angry when you did see her; and when she wasn't there she was talked about in hushed voices. 'Is it for good then?'

'I think they're playing it by ear. I imagine it depends on how he takes to it, being round here, and if he can keep out of trouble. I never thought he was a bad kid though.' Nita never thought anyone was a bad kid. 'He had issues. No wonder. I hope it works out.' She looked like a painting in the dark window. Chiaroscuro, that was what they called it; Minny's dad used to take them to the National Gallery and walk them up and down, talking all the time. 'Why don't you have a boyfriend?' she asked her mother.

'Why don't you?'

'Yeah, yeah. I'm serious.'

Nita peeled off her rubber gloves, ready to make Minny dance to 'Natural Woman'. 'What on earth would I want a

35

boyfriend for? I don't have time to kiss my babies at the moment. Between work and you lot and this house coming down around our ears I can't see myself contributing much to a successful romantic relationship, can you?' She seized Minny's hands from behind her back. 'Besides, my self-worth's just fine.'

'That's why people have men, is it?'

'One of the reasons. And I'm not much interested in sex right now either.'

'Oh, *Mum*.'

'Well, it's true. Maybe when you're all grown up I'll regain my libido.'

'Mum!'

'Yes?' She spun Minny around. 'I'll be a foxy – what – fifty-seven-year-old. A bit like my mama.'

'That is pure ram, Mother.'

'Prude.'

There was a patter of feet on the stairs, then a silence, and then Sel put her head sheepishly around the door. 'I'm thirsty.'

'Really?'

'I didn't like the dark up there.'

'What were you reading after I left?'

She peeped through her fringe, over the rim of the glass. 'The Book of the Apocalypse.'

Nita sighed. 'Elise was telling me at work today that her son got nightmares from Harry Potter. Some people have no idea.' She snapped the iPod dock off at the switch. 'Come on, I'll tuck you in again.'

Just as they were trooping out of the kitchen into the hall, the phone went in the back room. It was unusual for it to ring so late; it sounded like cannon fire. Selena plunged for it. 'Hello?' she shouted. Nita winced and shut the door. Minny was looking at Selena, wondering who was phoning at that time.

'Who is it?' she asked, because Sel was just listening. Sel held out the receiver. Their mother took it, then, without putting it to her ear – still holding it at arm's length – she said, 'Go upstairs now, girls. I'll be up in a minute. Go on, up.'

Minny climbed the stairs behind Selena, and followed her into Aisling's room, where Ash was lying on her stomach reading an atlas. She looked round at them.

'Dad's on the phone,' Selena said, her eyes dramatically wide, but her voice sounding surprised that it was such a strange thing to say. Dad, Dad. The last time she'd called him anything to his face, she hadn't been five yet. She'd only just started school.

Aisling didn't seem exactly amazed. Minny leaned against her radiator the way she did when it was on, in winter. Selena was looking from one of them to the other. 'Aren't you as-*ton*ished?' she demanded.

Minny shook her head.

'Why not?'

Minny shrugged.

'I spoke to him last night,' Ash said, turning back onto her stomach.

'You what?' asked Minny.

'He rang last night. You were in the bath. And Selena was in bed. And Mum was still out at work. So I picked it up.'

'And?'

'He said, "Is that Aisling?" And I said it was. And he said it was him. And he asked how I was, so I said I was fine. And then he didn't say anything else, so I put the phone down.'

'Good.'

Selena looked at her, but didn't say anything. She sat down on the end of Ash's bed and tucked her feet up. Ash carried on turning the pages of her atlas. Minny looked at the wall opposite, covered almost completely with a motley set of maps and timelines. There was only one thing framed, a huge cartoon drawing of a scene from *Wacky Races* with an extra car that had Minny and Aisling in it. Uncle Kevin had drawn it and sent it to them for Christmas the year Aisling was six. She used to love *Wacky Races*. Minny wondered again how come Aisling had got to keep it when they got separate rooms. She looked at the poster next to it instead and counted the Roman emperors on it.

It wasn't very long before they heard the light downstairs snap off and their mother coming quietly up. They waited for her to find them.

'Well. You're meant to be in bed, Selena.'

Sel bounced, once.

'So. That was your father. It's thrown me a bit. You know we haven't spoken in a while. But there's no bad news or anything like that, don't worry.'

'What then?' Minny asked, still counting emperors. Ash was lying face down.

'Listen, do you mind if we talk about it in the morning? I know, I know. But I promise, it's not anything bad – it's not that much of a big deal really, it's just that Raymond will wake up if we all stay here, and I'm suddenly very tired. Can we leave it till tomorrow? Good,' she continued without pausing. 'Into bed then now, all of you.'

'Mu-um,' Selena protested, pouting.

'Now's the time to practise some of that Christian patience you were talking about, remember, Sel? Let me get to things in my own time? Come on, to bed.'

Ash rolled over and turned off her light before they'd even left her room. Minny went into the bathroom and brushed her teeth until Nita backed out of her bedroom after re-tucking Selena in.

'What is it, Minny?' she asked in a rocky voice.

'Are you OK?'

'I'm fine.'

'Really?'

'Yes. You need to go to bed. I said we'll talk in the morning.'

Minny went into her room, changed into her pyjamas and got into bed. Her pillow felt gritty. It was rubbish being fourteen, and half being the eldest only not really. When they felt like it, and needed you to do something for them, people might tell you what was going on, but the moment they didn't, you were back to being a child.

TWO

Of course what they'd all forgotten, except possibly their mother, was that she wasn't there on Saturday mornings. She taught a drama class, which started at nine, so she was gone by eight. Minny woke up early and listened to her moving around downstairs with the baby. She could have woken Selena up and they could have gone down and ambushed her; Ash would have been awake for hours in her room. But she didn't. Which of course meant that when Selena did wake up, suddenly and with a jump like always, she was furious. Once she'd figured out what the time was. She had trouble with clocks and she wouldn't have a digital one.

'Shut up,' Minny said in the end, getting out of bed to go and see where Raymond was. 'She'll be back before lunch. You can hear all about it then.'

Saturday mornings were normally relaxed. On weekdays, it was like being in the army; they all had to sit down together to breakfast, even though it meant their mother had to be up in the middle of the night to make their lunches and have a shower. But on Saturdays she was out, and Babi always went straight back to bed when Minny got up to watch the baby; then as soon as she reappeared she was off down the road to hang out at the greengrocer's, or possibly the café next to it so that Gil could leave his long-suffering assistant in charge and slope off to meet her. The girls sat around in their pyjamas with scruffy hair and cold feet, eating their cereal wedged into corners of the settee so they could fend off the marauding baby.

Afterwards, they might have a game or two on the Wii. The baby loved it, watching was his best thing. He screamed when they finished, and sometimes, if no one turned it off, Minny would come back into the room twenty minutes later and find him still sitting patiently, hopefully, staring at the screen. They'd used to play it a lot more. But Ash got too dependent on the same games at the same time every day, even after she'd stopped enjoying them – so when Minny started refusing she threw a few tantrums but was relieved in the end. Also, it turned Selena into a raving nutbag because she hated losing so much; so now it was only on Saturdays that they could all reliably be found in front of it. It was an easy thing for them to do together.

That day they probably shouldn't even have tried, Selena was in such a mood. She always cried like a fountain unless she won pretty much all the mini-games, and when she wasn't crying she was stamping and shouting. You could hear her all over the house – they tried to ignore her, but all that meant was the same thing over and over again. 'But I did it quicker, it's not fair. I did it quicker, it's not fair.' Then there was a pause and she varied it: 'It's not fair, I did it quicker.' Today she wasn't even paying attention, just buzzing about doing headstands on the sofa right by where Minny was sitting with Raymond on her lap, then skipping round and round and round the room, counting. She didn't even try, just shouted, 'Oh, dang it,' whenever she lost and then skip, skip, skip. 'What do you think it's about?' she kept saying.

'I don't KNOW.'

And then two minutes later, 'What *could* he be calling about?'

'Guess what. I still DON'T KNOW.'

'Maybe he wants us to visit him.'

'Fat chance.'

'Do you mean of him wanting us to, or of us going? Maybe he's coming back.'

'Maybe he's dying,' Minny snapped. 'Maybe he wants a kidney. Maybe he's going to prison for life for murder.'

'Who did he murder?' Ash asked.

'I don't know. A corrupt cop.'

'Why would he murder a corrupt cop?'

'Maybe he wants to say sorry to us all,' Selena said, with her sanctimonious forgiving face on.

'Maybe he's just a big fat nothing who's done exactly what he wanted for himself his whole life and screw everyone else and I don't care about anything he does. And neither should you. He doesn't know anything about you, Sel. You think he's sitting on a sofa somewhere wondering about you now and trying to figure out what you're up to? You weren't even five when he left.'

'I know that, Minny. I remember.'

'No, you don't, because you were four.' She picked Raymond up from where she'd dumped him on the floor so she could turn around and shout at Selena. He was entranced by Wario and Waluigi.

'He's sorry about it,' Sel said.

'Who cares? How do you know?'

She was sitting on the football and bouncing. 'I emailed him.'

'What are you talking about, you can't even type.'

'I can!'

'That must have been an interestingly spelled email,' Minny said, beginning to get worked up again. 'When?' She'd known her mother heard from him sometimes, but she'd never wanted to have a conversation about it. Still, she hadn't thought other people were having conversations without her.

'On my birthday. He sent me my camera. Well, it isn't right not to talk to someone if they're sorry and they want to talk to you, and they give you something great as well.' She fell backwards off the ball and looked at Minny. 'Is it?'

Minny picked Raymond up and took him upstairs, without waiting for the scores, though Ash protested and clapped her hands. She couldn't stand Selena and her tolerant smile any more. Her finding God was one of the worst things that had ever happened. Minny wished she would lose Him again.

Being alone with Raymond was soothing. She couldn't be angry at him, he was too little. She got him dressed without him yelping too much, because she gave him their mother's alarm clock to play with. She always put his light blue silvery T-shirt on him when it was clean, because it made him even more vivid – he had goldy tufty hair and bright blue eyes and pink cheeks. He was like a little golden bull.

Her phone went before she'd brought him downstairs, so she wedged him in a corner with all Selena's stuffed toys where he couldn't do much damage. It was Penny, wailing about Jorge and the row they'd had last night. Minny supposed she should count herself lucky she hadn't got called up at midnight with all this; Penny didn't half rabbit on about Jorge. It was partly that obsessiveness that everyone seemed to get when they were going out with someone – and Penny had always been obsessive anyway – but it was also partly showing off. Minny didn't want a boyfriend. Not a particular one or a general one. But every day she continued not to have one, nor to have had one, ever, she felt as if she was giving Penny a present.

'Can I meet you?' Penny asked finally, blowing her nose into the phone by the sound of it.

'Er – you mean come round?'

'No, I can't stop crying. How about the park?'

Minny looked outside. It was warm and windless; the rose bushes, overgrown almost to her window, weren't even rippling. 'We could go swimming.'

'No!' Penny was horrified. 'If Jorge gets knocked out of his tennis early, he'll probably go to the pool. Anyway, I hate it there.' She sounded a bit more like herself – bossy. 'You're so weird, Minny. I think you're a closet exhibitionist. You just want to hang out in a swimsuit – yeuchh – and have everyone else in swimsuits too . . .'

On sunny weekends the open-air pool was always full with people from school, and from all the other schools around too, showing off in bikinis and the boys bombing each other, like a wildlife programme. It was pretty horrible, but Minny didn't see why it was so strange to want to actually swim. In summer.

She agreed to the park in the end, and they arranged to meet after lunch. Minny would agree to most things to avoid Penny coming round to the house; Penny was her oldest friend, but it was still embarrassing when Babi stood on the front doorstep smoking her menthol cigarettes, and there were Aisling's squeaks and groans and monologues, and Selena being a brat with her Twelve Tribes in the bedroom, and her mother playing the guitar and singing. Nita would probably stop doing that if Minny asked her, but she would find it so screamingly funny. Their house was like a lunatic asylum when you looked at it through someone else's eyes. Also the food was so weird: fizzy drinks weren't allowed in the door because Nita had a thing about the soft-drink industry, and then most evenings Babi was catering. Their grandmother was a wonderful cook, but it was all strange meaty or fishy things poor Penny was afraid of.

And of course the house was a bit shambolic. Many of her friends whose homes she'd visited lived in big houses with fridges that dispensed ice. Not all of them, but her own house was coming down with baby toys and hand marks on the walls; the bathmat was older than Minny and the bathroom floor was flecked with splodges of Babi's hair dye; though their mother occasionally had a cleaning fit and attacked the bedroom ceilings with bleach, mould grew black in patches around the place.

After she'd brushed her teeth she took the baby downstairs, just as her mother plunged back in through the front door, all out of breath with her huge square flat bag that always had crazy things like mop handles and shiny gold tubes sticking out of it. 'Everything all right? Where's Babi?'

'Three guesses,' Minny said, juggling the baby, who was trying to get to his mother.

'She hasn't. What time did she go?'

'About an hour ago.'

'Oh, good grief.' Babi always said she'd stay and then just went. 'One day the damned house will just blow up and then she'll learn.'

'Oh good, I'll look forward to it. Selena's been doing nothing but witter on about Dad.'

'Right. Of course.' She dumped the bag on the floor and took the baby. 'Well, let's get some lunch and then I'll tell you all about it.' At least she seemed more cheerful this morning. While Minny got a beef sandwich she wondered if her father had actually rung up to say that he was on his deathbed. She wouldn't have minded being left a stack of guilt-money.

'Right,' Nita started when they were all sitting down. By that time Minny had nearly finished, since her mother had made sandwiches for the baby, Ash and Selena as well as her own, and put a Loretta Lynn album on just loud enough to make them all feel strong. 'As you know, your dad rang last night.'

'Where's the ketchup?' Ash asked.

'Oh, for God's sake,' Selena shouted, then looked mortified and put her hands over her face. Their mother got up to get the ketchup from the kitchen. Ash needed it for most meals.

'Everything's fine,' Nita went on, as Aisling did a huge splurt of sauce onto her plate. She gave Raymond another quarter of sandwich. 'It's actually good news. I know you've all got a lot of different feelings going on for your dad, and this might feel strange at first, but do try to think of it as good news. Stop muttering, Minny. The thing is, he's back.' She coughed and took a sip of tea. 'He's back in the country. In London, actually.'

'How long for? Do we get to see him?' Selena was so like their mother when she got excited. Her hair wisped up around her face. They all had the same hair; Raymond's curls were getting a bit darker now, but still Babi and Minny were the only people in the house who weren't blonde. Nita's father was South African, but his family came from Norway originally.

'Well. He's back to live. In London,' she added quickly. 'Not right here of course. I'm not sure where they'll settle – they're staying with friends at the moment. But of course anywhere in London is reachable for us.' Raymond choked on his sandwich and threw it on the floor while he coughed.

They hadn't seen their father in going on three years. He had always gone to America quite a lot, for his job, and one time, just after Minny started secondary school, he went and didn't come back. Ever. The last time she'd heard his voice had been the big phone call, the one weeks after he should have been home and the same day their mother had finally told them he wasn't coming back. There had been times after that when she'd tried to make Minny take the phone, but Minny never would. Even Selena had stopped asking, much, if he'd ever return to England. Minny never talked about him, so she didn't know how much the others did, and now it turned out Sel had been emailing him. She wondered if Ash had too, and if she was the only one not prepared to shout, 'Daddy, my daddy,' like Bobbie in *The Railway Children*. 'Did you know about this?' she asked Aisling.

49

'Of course she didn't, Minny.' Nita sounded tired.

'Yes, I did,' Ash said.

'What?'

'I told you, he rang on Thursday,' she said to Minny.

'Was that the only time you've spoken to him? Since he left, I mean.'

'Yes.'

Then of course Aisling had to tell Nita what they were talking about, which left her looking troubled, and Selena practically choking on all her questions.

'Why is he back?' Minny got one in before Sel could start.

'He wants to be near us – I mean, you girls,' her mother said, very fast.

'Why doesn't he come here then?' Selena squeaked, bouncing.

'He hasn't wanted to see us for three years,' Minny snarled.

'That's not true, Minny,' Nita said, with her 'try not to take your angst out on your little sister's hopes and dreams' look. 'You know I think he did . . . not the right thing, leaving and going so far away, but he had things going on which help explain it a bit. We've talked about his depression. Yes, you've got every right to be angry with him . . .'

'I know.'

'But he wants to try to make amends. Some amends. He wants to get to know you—'

'No!'

50

'– and when you're ready, when you've got used to the idea – look, Minny, I just think if you don't even think about it, if you were to close yourself off completely, you might be missing out on what could, one day, be a valuable—'

'No.'

'That's not very forgiving, Minny,' Selena said.

'No, it isn't,' Minny agreed.

'Mmm – ffn,' Ash said suddenly, and pushed her chair back from the table. Then she put her hands over her mouth.

'Do you want to speak, Ash?' Nita asked. Aisling shook her head. Nita sighed, and rubbed her face. 'It sounds like it's going to be permanent, you know. He's going to be around. His job's here now—'

'Oh, well, that explains it.'

' – and I'd better tell you this now: he has a, erm, a girlfriend. A . . . partner, who's coming with him.'

'Who?'

'I don't know. A lady he met in New York.' Their mother never referred to anyone as a 'lady'. She thought it was anti-feminist. She also didn't usually talk to Sel as if she was a baby.

'He's bringing her from New York? Why would she want to come here?'

'She's English,' their mother admitted.

'Oh,' Minny said. 'Now I see.'

'Don't be so smart, Minny.'

'What's her name?'

'Her name is Harriet.' It certainly conjured up an image. Basically it came down to this – her father was back in England sleeping with someone from an Enid Blyton book and she was supposed to be pleased. 'I told him he'd have to give us time to get used to the idea. You lot, I mean.'

'How old is she?' These were unusually interesting questions for Ash to be asking – actually of course they were the same questions she asked about everyone new. Next would be Harriet's birthday and whether or not she had any brothers or sisters.

'I believe she's about twenty-six,' Nita said, pretending not to be reluctant.

'You mean you asked him how old she was and he said "about twenty-six"?'

'Minny, just calm down. I've known about her for a little while. It's not just Harriet, and it's not really about his job either – he wants to be where he can see you again, and be part of your lives.' She looked at Aisling, who was sitting looking tragic with her finger in a puddle of ketchup. 'Anyway. Listen, I've got his number – when you want to call him. Any of you. I know it's been a long time since you spoke to him, and in a lot of ways it might be like talking to a stranger at first.'

'A stranger who abandoned you when you were eleven. How can you be all right with this?' Minny demanded.

'I don't know,' Nita admitted. 'It's complicated. I spent a long time being furious with him, probably more than you realised. I've even hated him for some of it. But I'm not in love with him any more, which helps in not hating him. And I suppose I feel very sorry for him.'

'What?'

'He's missed out on an awful lot. Through his own fault. But you know that's going to make it worse,' she said. 'I've got to get a flannel for Raymond before he strangles himself trying to get out of this chair. You might not know this, girls, but guilt is the hardest thing to live with. He did what he did, but he'll have been feeling guilty ever since.' She went out to the kitchen.

'Poor Dad,' Selena said.

'My arse,' Minny said back.

Their mother said they didn't have to talk to him before they were ready, but that they should think about doing it, if only to shout and tell him how angry they were. Because talking to him might be the best way to get over it enough that they could start getting to know him. All of which made perfect sense, Minny admitted, if she had been at all interested in getting to know him. But she'd gone this long and she was fine, and she didn't think she could ever like him. Selena was acting like a child, as if all this was a game show and if she was enthusiastic enough she'd win a New Dad! who'd never done anything wrong, had no history at all in her life, but would swoop in, buy her a puppy and start teaching her to sail or something. And Aisling was just silent.

Their mother did try. 'What do you think about it, Ash?'

'I don't know.'

'Would you like to talk to your dad, on the phone?'

'No.'

'Is that because of the phone though? What about if he were to come here – not straightaway, but sometime? To see you?'

Minny couldn't imagine anything worse.

'No,' Ash said, squirming.

'Really?'

'I don't want to *talk* about it,' she said. Minny knew exactly what she meant; you didn't have to be autistic for it to be unthinkable to sit and talk about something like that. On the other hand, Minny also didn't want him coming and not talking about it because everyone was too polite, and then to suddenly turn round and find he was part of the family again.

'OK,' Nita said. 'Don't worry, Sel, I know you feel differently, and it's not surprising that you all have your own point of view about this. But there's no rush at all. We'll talk again.'

'I'm going to meet Penny,' Minny said, getting up.

'Have you had enough lunch?' Nita looked perturbed. Normally they stretched Saturday lunchtime out for ages, with doughnuts and extra sandwiches and the kind of fruit they couldn't afford for most of the week.

'I'm fine. I'm full.'

After she'd got her stuff together and was ready to leave, Nita came out of the front room and said goodbye. 'Will you talk about it with Penny, do you think?'

Minny shrugged. 'She's got a crisis, so probably not.'

'*Penny's* got a crisis?'

Minny got cross. 'Look, I know you don't take Penny very seriously, but she's upset, all right. She wants to talk to me.'

'Sorry, you're right. That wasn't fair of me. But it's OK for you to be upset about your dad and to want to talk to a friend too, you know. I'm going to be on your back about this, Minny. But I'll give you a while first.' She rubbed a blob of sun cream into Minny's forehead. 'What's wrong with her?'

'Oh, I don't know,' Minny admitted with a sigh. 'Jorge or something. The story will probably have changed by the time I get there.'

'Well, try not to let her fantasise too wildly. Or to accuse her of fantasising either. You don't want her to get into a situation where she's flat-out lying.'

'I know.'

'Because then you'd be complicit in the lie. I mean, mixed up in it.'

'I know what complicit means, Mum.'

'Right.'

Her mother had a point. Penny was a fantasist, she always had been. Ever since they were tiny, Nita said, and Minny sort of remembered. When Minny sometimes got frustrated with her, Nita told her that some people just need to embellish life, don't hold it against her, but with a distinct rider of *Don't believe a word she says*. Every now and again, because Penny did tell a story well, and after all you couldn't openly disbelieve her – you got drawn in. Sometimes they were such good stories you might find yourself telling one to someone else, and only two-thirds of the way through, when everyone was hanging on your every word, would you remember – oh, crap, this is a Penny story. Perhaps that was what her mother meant by being complicit in the lie.

Minny could have done with a few good stories that afternoon in the park, instead of the tears. She half listened to the Jorge-related wailing and looked up at the sky. The park was crowded, like you'd expect in the first real spell of summer weather, with men in flip-flops and big young dudes, not bronzed yet but with their shirts off, strutting around, and women with wooden beads and burnished skin and little kids with parents looking a bit less frazzled than usual in the sunshine. It was embarrassing sitting there with Penny sobbing the whole time. Minny kept pulling more bits of rubber off the soles of her trainers. It sounded like a serious row – she hadn't seen Penny quite this traumatised before, though she'd had to listen to a lot of philosophising and pseudo soul-searching down the phone lately, as well as at school. She wondered if they might actually break up. Apparently one of the things Jorge had shouted last night was about needing space and not feeling smothered; it was a bit rich, because from what she heard he could be a proper control freak, but Minny couldn't help having a sneaking sympathy for him. If Penny was half as obsessive over him to his face as she was being now, it must be hard to take.

Despite Penny's perpetual diet, Minny managed to convince her that an ice cream would cheer her up, so that broke the monotony for a while. They saw Juliet Langley and had to hide behind the corner of the café – they knew she wouldn't come round it, she didn't do things like eat ice cream. 'You know Juliet's going out with Henry now?' Penny said.

'Who's Henry?' Minny sat back down on the grass.

'Henry Bonnel. You know Henry. He's one of Jorge's friends.'

'Oh. Brilliant. Then you can start hanging out with Juliet and Emma, can't you?'

'Thanks very much.'

Just as Minny was chewing the wooden stick to pieces, she looked up and saw her whole family standing on the path twenty yards away, waving at her. 'Oh, bloody hell,' she said. She didn't normally see them all together like that, in a pack, outside of home.

Selena came bouncing over waving her strawberry split all over the place. Penny stopped moaning and dabbed her nose with a tissue. 'Are you all right, Penny?' Sel asked with big wide eyes.

'T'yeah – *sniffle* – I'm fine, darling.'

Babi was suddenly towering over them. 'She's probably suffering from heat exhaustion.'

'No, I'm fine.' Penny shot to upright.

'I don't understand young girls like you. There are so many of you. A hot day like this, you pick shorts out, fine, but why the black tights?'

'It's a look, Mama,' Nita said.

'It looks absurd. It looks like the way to get thrush.'

'Er –' Penny said.

'My vulva is itching just to look at you,' Babi said, turning back to the path and closing her eyes.

There was no hope, of course, that her mother would ever try to get her grandmother under control. Right now she was killing herself laughing. Penny looked horrified.

'Right,' Nita said, wiping her eyes, 'we'll leave you. Come on, Sel, you'll be late for Victoria. Ash, why don't you stay here for a bit?'

She didn't often do that, give Minny no choice about taking Aisling on away from home. But Minny knew that she was thinking it was rough on Ash that here she was hanging out in the park with Penny, and Selena was on her way to a friend's house too. Aisling had never had that sort of friend. Even at primary school where she didn't get picked on, she was never asked to people's houses, and the only parties she went to were the ones where the whole class was invited. She went to a youth group for autistic teenagers

58

and seemed to get on all right there, but not so that she would see any of them outside the group. Minny didn't mind too much on this occasion because it was only Penny, who was used enough to Ash that she was able to conduct a conversation around her and not get sucked into letting her go on and on about football, bluegrass or J. Edgar Hoover.

Anyway, Minny was pleased enough to be interrupted by a third person. She was bored of Jorge and his insufficient commitment to the relationship. Sometimes she felt that to Penny she was a handmaid, surely grateful for every detail because she didn't have this kind of stuff going on herself. A while ago – she couldn't put her finger on when – a gulf had opened up between the girls who had had at least one boyfriend, and the girls who never had. Crossing it was one of those things that just seemed to happen, randomly but permanently, to other girls, the way it had happened to Penny after Easter. It was like *Casablanca*; everyone trying to get out of Occupied Europe, knowing all they need is one opportunity and they'll be safe on the other side for good. Minny would have been perfectly happy where she was except that it was lame to be on the wrong side – and also she was afraid that at some point the situation would change again and she would be left with the girls who never *would* have a boyfriend. Because honestly she couldn't see it ever happening.

Then Penny started yet again about 'how far' to go and

all that unsavoury stuff she was always going on about, in far too much detail, while Minny and Aisling both looked a bit disgusted and in opposite directions. Minny thought she was probably lying, but it was possible it was true; plenty of people in her class seemed to be at that kind of thing. She thought she might be a bit abnormally underdeveloped about sex, herself, or maybe she was just going to be one of those people who wasn't very into it. Of course it was an interesting subject, when it wasn't being talked about by Penny anyway, but it was completely distant. It seemed so ridiculous, knowing anyone well enough to do that with them.

Aisling was getting restive and starting to tick and squeak in the background. Then, as Penny paused for breath, she broke in with, 'Did you know that Hank Williams's real name wasn't Hank, Penny?' and waited, eagerly.

Penny nailed her patient look to her face. 'No, I didn't. But Hank is normally short for something isn't it, like Henry?'

'No, it was short for Hiram, but the funny thing is, Hank Williams Junior and Hank Williams III weren't really called Hank either!' She beamed.

'Oh, right, that is weird.' There was a pause. 'I hope Jorge doesn't come here after the tournament. He might. Maybe we should move.'

Minny was fed up. Solely to change the subject, she started talking about her father. Ash stopped squealing beside her and picked up a twig to draw patterns in the patches of dust. Penny didn't say all that much, but then Minny hadn't expected her to. Ash was digging a furrow into the dry earth. 'It must be weird for you too, Aisling?' Penny suggested. 'What do you think about it?'

Ash shrugged without looking at her, but she answered. 'He shouldn't have gone in the first place. I don't want to see him either.'

'No?'

'No. He left us all behind.'

Aisling and their father used to be really connected. When one was happy, the other was; if one of them got stressed, the other did too. Things had been quite dark for Ash for a while after he left. She and Minny had both just started at their new school – Aisling had gone to a private one for a year because their father thought she would get less bullied there – another of his bright ideas. Anyway, it had been a disaster so they started at Raleigh together. And then he was gone. Ash had got all depressed and silent; Minny supposed she'd have understood him leaving even less than Minny did. She was sure Aisling wouldn't be blaming herself, because Ash didn't dwell on what was going on in other people's minds – and of course she wasn't aware how hard it was to deal with her. But sometimes Minny felt like she'd lost Ash too – all the stuff they had ever done together, the fun stuff, was with their father, like football. Every Saturday they had sat in front of the results coming in; they watched

Match of the Day every Sunday morning before church. They even went to a match once, Man United against Spurs. It was their big Christmas present that year. Ash used to make her own FA Cup draws; Minny was never allowed to make up the results or write anything down, but sometimes Ash let her pull the slips of paper out of the hat. After he left, Minny gave it up. She didn't want to like Man United any more, or football, or anything. She came back to it after a couple of weeks, it was too hard not to, but it was never the same. Like she'd abandoned Aisling.

'He's got a new girlfriend,' Minny said. She chewed a blade of grass.

'Yeah? Has she come with him?'

'Yeah.'

'Hmmm,' Penny said, slipping her bracelets back on. 'You know Jorge's parents are divorced too?'

'I don't even know if my parents are divorced,' Minny said. How strange never to have asked.

'It was really bad for him, being the oldest. He was only ten. You know he's had this really difficult childhood and everything – it's not surprising he gets depressed.'

Lying on her back, Minny shut her eyes.

'I wouldn't mind that. I mean, I want to help him. I just don't like him pushing me around.'

Minny thought that that wasn't true, really, and it was confirmed a moment later by Penny's phone ringing and transforming her into coy, radiant Penny, who went springing off to go and watch the last game of tennis, even though Jorge had been knocked out. Apparently that's what you did if you were a sporting gentleman.

Minny and Aisling gazed thoughtfully at each other. 'Sometimes,' Minny said, 'I don't know why I'm friends with Penny.'

Ash nodded. 'Why are you?'

'I think only because I always have been.'

'Not *always*.'

'Well, since we were four. I suppose she's not so bad when you don't need anything from her – except she always needs something from me – but I don't know how she ended up my *best* friend, that's all.'

'Are you going to stop being best friends with her?'

'Oh God, one day surely I will.'

'Then who will be your best friend?'

'I don't know,' Minny said. She felt miserable. 'I know you probably weren't even listening, but didn't you think it was a bit ... crass, the way I told her about Dad and everything, which is really quite major, on paper, and she ignored it and turned it round to talking about Jorge again? And then just left?'

'Crass,' Aisling murmured.

'She doesn't even pretend to be interested in my life, but she expects me to listen to her for hours every night yapping about her boyfriend, who I don't even know, because he's a complete tosser, and every thought she ever has, and be thrilled about it. I mean, the one thing she did say about it was to you. She didn't ask *me* how I felt.'

'Doesn't she know?'

'No, she doesn't know. How would she know? She never asks. And I don't like talking about it.'

'I know.'

'Well, you don't either, do you?'

'No.'

'You don't like talking about anything though, do you?' Deflating herself, Minny stared across the small piece of grass between them. Aisling was facing into the sun. She was lit up so that Minny couldn't see her properly. 'Are you really angry with him, Ash?'

'Who?'

Minny could have roared with impatience, but she swallowed it. 'With Dad.'

'Oh. Yes.'

'I am. How could we not be, right? How can Selena not be?'

'I don't know.'

'And Mum. She expects us to be pleased he's back. To want to see him.'

'Do you think she's pleased?' Ash sounded surprised.

'No, of course she's not, how could she be, but then how could we be? And he turns up bold as brass with another woman. I mean, it's not like he's been gone that long.'

'Nearly three years.'

'Right, and that's bloody ages, just to sod off without a word and not come back and see us or anything. I mean, who does that? Though men seem to do it all the time. But it's not so long he should just assume it's fine for him to bring his new woman into the country and it'll be OK by Mum. He should have waited till she had a boyfriend at least.' Minny felt hot. She groped in Ash's bag for the bottle of water she knew would be there.

'But Mum did have a man,' Aisling pointed out. 'Because she had Raymond.'

'Well, I know, but one night isn't like moving countries with someone.'

'It wasn't—'

'All *right*, Aisling, it wasn't one night, but it can't have been much more because we didn't even hear about him till just before she told us she was pregnant, and we never even met him and he hasn't been around so it can't have been that serious, can it? God, she can really pick them, when you think about it. I hope I don't take after her.'

'Poor Mum,' Aisling said, sounding soft.

'I know.' Minny dug into the ground with a piece of twig, too hard: her finger went in as well and dirt jabbed up under the quick of her nail.

'We missed him though.' Aisling pushed the top back down on the water bottle and put it back into her bag. 'All of us. Didn't we?'

'Yes. But we don't now.'

In the end they got up and straggled towards the gate. Their shadows were long behind them, and the shade from the trees around the park perimeter was reaching out. It was one of those evenings where trees looked almost furry, and Minny calmed down inside. She felt sun-soaked.

'Look,' Aisling said, 'there's Franklin.' Minny looked round with a sudden shiver, as if she'd been hot too long. He was sitting on the low corner of the wall outside the café, and he raised his hand to them. They could have just waved back, but he was on his own in what was, to him, more or less a strange park, and he'd just come to live with their granny. Minny didn't have to decide anyway; Aisling had already changed direction.

He was all elbows, he didn't look at ease in the summer. His T-shirt was dark blue with a fractured-looking logo that Minny could see had been melted with an iron; there were little yellow smudges around it. Her granny was a champion T-shirt melter. She had stayed with them once for a few days when their parents went to Paris and ruined all their wardrobes zealously. 'All right,' he said when they got up close.

'Yes,' Aisling said, hopping from foot to foot. 'Are you all right?'

'Yeah.' He looked bony, he looked dazed. Minny had seen where he lived, at least where he had lived when he was eight. This looked different, any park would have, but especially this one rammed full of people who could afford lots of sun. Franklin was winter-pale. His hair was good though. 'I just came to have a look,' he said. 'I haven't been here since I was a kid.'

'How's it going at Granny's?'

'Fine. She's OK, she's nice.' He grinned. 'Washed all my clothes already.'

'I can tell. And ironed.' They laughed. Aisling stood beside them, smiling.

'I don't mind. It's nice. No one's ironed anything of mine in years.'

'Me neither,' Minny said, looking down at her crumpled shirt. Her mother said that if you put things in the tumble dryer they didn't need ironing.

'You could iron them yourself,' Ash pointed out. Minny wasn't sure which of them she was talking to.

'Do you know anyone round here?' she asked Franklin suddenly. She wouldn't have been that blunt, only he seemed so pleased to be talking to them she felt sorry for him.

'No.'

'You know us,' Aisling said.

'True. But no, no one else, not really.'

'Not at Raleigh?'

'No.'

'Starting Monday?'

'Yeah.'

Minny couldn't imagine. Starting a new school at eleven had been bad enough, but at least Penny was there and a bunch of other people from her primary school. And even if you hadn't known anyone, there would have been others in the same boat. But to move right at the end of a school year, of Year 10 – and when you didn't even have your own home to go to afterwards – her stomach ached thinking about it. Maybe he would have to talk to her, and Aisling, to stop himself going mad.

Aisling was obviously affected as well because she started humming. In a moment it would be squeaks, probably. Of course it wasn't as if Franklin didn't know about her – that was one good thing about meeting people from your past. 'What were you listening to?' she asked. He had headphones dangling from the neck of his T-shirt, as if he might have pulled them from his ears when he saw them coming. It was blatant that she was asking to cover Ash's sound effects, but the alternative was listening to them.

He looked away, over the park. She decided it had probably been the world's most boring question. 'Guy Clark.'

Minny took a moment to make sure her brain had computed that right, so Aisling was the first to say, 'Guy Clark? Really?'

'Yeah.'

'I like Guy Clark.' Ash beamed.

'Yeah,' he said. 'I know.'

'How do you know?' Minny was amazed.

'OK, I didn't know. But I could have guessed.' A smile flashed across his face like a shooting star; you wouldn't be sure you'd seen it. 'Your mum used to like him.'

'She still does,' Ash assured him.

Minny felt her own face twitching, uncertainly but with an odd flicker of joy. 'I don't understand this conversation,' she declared. 'How on earth do you know about my mother liking Guy Clark of all people?'

'I used to come round your house, remember? Your flat,' he amended. 'And your mum always had music on.' She hadn't remembered him being there all that often, maybe three or four times, mainly with his aunt. 'I used to ask her, "What's this?" and "What's that?" And she told me a bit about them.' He shrugged. 'Guy Clark and Townes Van Zandt. And Emmylou Harris.'

Her mother would go nuts for this. Minny didn't think she'd tell her. She remembered now, remembered sitting on the black-and-white tiles of the old flat near the table, because that's where the cake was, watching Franklin through her fringe as he sat listening to Emmylou Harris. 'Boulder to Birmingham', she was sure. He had sat so still, like the fox in the headlights they'd seen that holiday they went down to Dorset. He was never normally still, back then. And of course the reason why Dad had said he wasn't to come round any more – shouted it – was because he'd broken the stereo. A different visit. She'd known at the time: he'd only been trying to put a CD on.

He was watching her, and she wondered if he'd seen the memories roll through her eyes. She laughed. 'I remember.'

'When we were having our brother,' Aisling said

informatively, 'before we knew he was a boy, Mum said if it was a girl she'd call her Emmylou.'

'What did she call him?'

'Raymond,' Minny said. Granny didn't talk about Raymond then. She'd suspected as much. Granny had been so shocked when Nita turned up pregnant. 'Jaysus, Minny, what? Well, you wouldn't read about it.' Granny never normally criticised their mother. She had lost it a bit over Dad leaving.

Now Minny wondered. 'Does Granny know about our dad coming back?' she asked Franklin. 'Has she said anything?'

He had his hand in his pocket – his jeans weren't as tight as some, but still he had to concentrate to get his hand in – and looked up, surprised. 'What?'

'We just found out our dad has come to live in London again,' Ash explained. 'We're upset.'

'I'm not upset,' Minny snapped.

'She hasn't said anything,' Franklin said.

Minny found her chin trembling. She was horrified. Franklin didn't look at her; he extracted something from his pocket and held it out, wriggling to put his other hand in his other pocket. They looked at it. It was a pack of cigarettes, brown with silvery stripes. He seemed to be pointing it at Aisling. 'When did he come back?' he asked her.

'Last Tuesday.' Ash hesitated and raised her hand. 'I'm sorry, are you offering that to me?'

'Yeah.'

'I don't smoke.'

He angled the packet towards Minny.

She might have said yes. To save him feeling awkward or something. She had tried a cigarette before, a year or more ago at a sleepover when everyone did, and she hadn't been sick or anything. But she couldn't now, not because Ash would tell at home – she could tell her not to, after – but right now she would be bound to say, 'But Minny, you never smoke cigarettes.' And then Minny would look like a perfect loser. 'No, I don't smoke.'

He lowered his arm and took one out of the packet himself. He had a lighter, from his other pocket, out now. The sun was low enough that they could see the flame flare.

'I'm surprised you do smoke,' Aisling said conversationally.

'I don't,' he said, drawing on it. Minny watched his chest contract within the smudged T-shirt.

Aisling couldn't deal with humour-by-contradiction, especially not from people she didn't know well. 'But you are smoking.'

'I know.' He grinned at her. 'I'm meant to be giving up. I can't afford it. Why are you surprised?'

'Mrs Seigel, my health studies teacher—' Aisling began.

'Mrs Seagull?'

'Seigel,' Aisling corrected, though Minny had seen her eyes flash. Later she would find that very funny, Minny knew. 'Mrs Siegel said that when a person has lived with

71

addiction, I mean lived with someone else who has an addiction, they're likely to react against addiction really strongly.'

Minny avoided looking at Franklin. Not that he was looking at her.

'So I thought because of your mum being an addict you wouldn't have smoked.'

Their eyes did meet for a split second then. She was red; she could feel it.

'Although Mrs Siegel did also say that if someone has had a tough childhood they might turn to substance abuse themselves, though I don't know if smoking—'

'Aisling. Shut up.' It wasn't subtle but she had to make her stop. 'Sorry,' she said to Franklin. 'My mum always tells Aisling she has to try to remember everything from lessons because otherwise she doesn't listen, and sometimes it comes out . . . in weird ways.' Health studies – who would have thought that Ash would actually concentrate in that?

'It's OK,' Franklin said to Aisling. 'I don't mind,' he said to Minny.

She didn't feel as if she could ask, 'How is your mother?' but it seemed so logically the next question that she couldn't think what else to say either. The conversation was rather at a close. She managed to get both herself and Aisling away quickly, since they were going to see him tomorrow at Granny's house anyway.

'You can't talk to people about their parents being addicts,' she hissed at Aisling along the way home.

'Can't you?'

'No. Maybe if they start the conversation.' Unlikely that someone would do that with Aisling. 'That was so embarrassing.'

'Oh. Sorry.' Aisling thought. 'Was he embarrassed?'

'Yes!'

'Oh.'

She looked more crushed than usual and Minny felt bad, so they stopped to get some sweets. 'Though I'm not supposed to.'

'Why not?'

'Because I want to be thinner. Maybe I'll just get something small.'

'Like a Walnut Whip?'

'No, they give me toothache.'

'Shall we get one for Mum?' Ash suggested, handing Minny her tube of Fruit Pastilles to buy. Walnut Whips were their mother's favourite.

'No, she'll think we're feeling guilty about something.'

She paid for the sweets and they left. Minny put six Maltesers into her mouth, lining them up inside her cheeks. 'Do you like Franklin?' Aisling asked, unwrapping the first pastille.

Minny nearly spat out her Maltesers, because normally she and Ash didn't go in for heart to hearts. She had never asked a question like that before. 'He's OK.'

'You think he is?'

'Yeah.'

'Do you think he likes me?'

Minny saw where she was coming from now. It had sometimes happened in the past that people had been nice to Ash and she had assumed, like a normal person, that they wanted to be friends with her and then it turned out they just wanted her to think that so they could make her do stupid things and get her into trouble. Because they thought that was funny. Or, in the case of two girls a couple of terms before, so that she would try to chat with them in front of everyone and they could laugh at her for thinking anyone would want to be friends with a freak like her.

'He seems all right,' Minny said. 'I always thought he was all right. And he's friendly to both of us.' Although it was odd that he might think she and Ash hung around together, outside home. Nice, really, that he was in Ash's year; it would be good for her to have someone she could say a few words to sometimes. 'Maybe he'll be in your form,' she said.

Aisling smiled. For a moment it felt like a real conversation, even though Minny, who was after all the younger sister, was on the wrong end of it.

When they got home Nita came out of the kitchen, carrying Raymond and looking relieved. 'Can you look after him in the front room? I've got to keep stirring the stew and Selena's on the phone in the back room and he keeps pressing the buttons.'

'Who's she on the phone to?' Ash asked immediately.

'Your father,' Nita said, looking away. 'I said she could ring him.'

'Do I have to talk to him?'

'Of course not, Aisling, not if you don't want to.'

'What's she ringing him for?' Minny burst out, so that Raymond, in her arms, looked at her in alarm and shoved a Lego block in her mouth.

'She wants to talk to him. She's only a little girl and she wants to talk to her father. I don't want you taking this out on her, Minny, is that clear? Selena's relationship with him has got nothing to do with either of you.'

'All right,' Minny muttered, spitting out Lego. 'You should have got her to ring him while we were in the park, then we wouldn't have had to think about it.'

'I couldn't. Victoria's mother only just brought her back. Anyway, your grandmother was here.'

The call didn't go on for much longer, which wasn't surprising because talking to Sel on the phone was like torture; she would recite a long list of everything she wanted to say at top speed and bat-pitched, and then dry up completely and say nothing at all for minutes on end. She came bouncing into the front room only a few moments later.

'Dad wants to talk to you!' she sang out.

'No way.'

'I don't want to,' Ash said in alarm.

'He wants to talk to you! Go on, you have to.'

'No, we don't, Selena.'

'Of course you have to talk to people if they want you to. To your father. I can't tell him you don't want to.' Her big eyes started to fill up. 'Please.'

Minny wouldn't. She wasn't going to be polited into this; she would not be bullied into pretending everything was OK and she wasn't angry. That was why she didn't want to see him: she wasn't good at being angry face to face, especially with strangers. If he actually came round she was afraid it would all end up just getting swept under the carpet. She put a Jenga piece on top of the tower she'd built, and the baby bellowed and swept the whole thing down.

'You've got to honour your father,' Selena said, bursting into proper tears.

Their mother came running. 'What's going on?'

'Selena's got Dad hanging on the phone waiting to talk to me or Ash,' Minny said. 'I'm not doing it, Mum.'

'Nor am I,' Ash said quickly.

'Right. Don't worry. Sel, what are you crying about? I'll sort Dad out. You go and run a bath. I'll be up in a minute.'

Minny hauled the baby onto her knee and tried to interest him in Jenga, but he was tired and stressed and just whimpered. Ash went up to see Sel after a while to tell her she was going to start the film – *Ponyo* that night – and there was a lot of shouting, and it turned out Sel didn't want to watch it after all, and for some reason that threw

Aisling into a meltdown and she was crying in her room and kicking the door. In the end Nita got Selena to say she would sit with Ash and read while the film was on, and she came trailing down all sulky and got the Bible down from the shelf and insisted on having the light on. Their mother went off to put the baby to bed, and since Aisling apparently didn't care whether or not Minny watched the film with her, Minny made the most of having a room to herself, and crawled into bed with her mother's old Chalet School books.

THREE

On Sunday they got dragged off to church as usual. Aisling hadn't liked it since she hit twelve and wasn't allowed to read books any more – Minny hadn't been allowed since she was nine. Selena pretended to love it, but although she jumped up extravagantly on all the standy-uppy bits, and knelt like a prayer-book angel at the right times, she found it as hard to listen as the rest of them. She was about to start training to be an altar server now that she'd made her First Communion. Minny couldn't imagine her sitting still up there and picking up her cues, but whatever. Actually the sermon this week was reasonably interesting. It was the crazy missionary priest who only appeared a couple of times a year and thundered at them about charity and Christian love; no comforting your-ticket-to-heaven's-pretty-much-bought-already from *him*. Granny wasn't there. She hadn't been lately. It wasn't her nearest Catholic church, but she used to struggle there on the bus most weeks, sit defiantly at the other end of the row from Babi and then mill around afterwards talking to the other old ladies until it was time to go and buy sweets for her grand-daughters. Babi never chatted with other women; she just stood looking disdainfully at her plastic beaker of coffee – she didn't actually seem to believe much in God either. Selena had asked her once why she went to church then. She just said, 'It's an important part of my heritage.' When Minny had pressed her, not least because some days she could feel her own heritage, all five nationalities of it, piling up and up and up, Babi said, 'This is how I honour my parents and my grandparents, and thereby myself.' Bloody hell, Minny thought.

Anyway Granny wasn't there. 'She's probably cooking,' Nita said drily. She probably was. Granny had some trouble coordinating a roast dinner.

'Maybe she didn't want to leave Franklin on his own,' Minny speculated.

'He might have come with her. I think Mr Franklin Conderer has had some fairly avid religious stuff going on himself at times.' They were back out on the street ambling home, Raymond crowing with relief to be out of the church even though he was confined to the carrier on his mother's back.

'Really?'

'I don't know the details. You'd have to ask him.'

Minny snorted.

'Who's Franklin Conjuror?' Selena asked, slurping around her fingers. They had ice lollies, it was warm, though never as warm as you thought it was going to be on the shady side of the street. Her mother was going to have to wash her hair before she went anywhere; Raymond had lost most of his lolly on her head.

It had clouded over by the time they'd eaten a sparse lunch ('You know I'll never hear the end of it from Granny if you don't eat your dinner') and negotiated Aisling's maths lesson with Nita while Minny actually finished her homework. It was quite pleasant to have got it out of the way this early on a Sunday. They took Babi's car. Gil arrived just as they were leaving; Minny saw her mother pulling a face in the car mirror.

Their Granny's house was little, on a quiet street. It hadn't gentrified as much as Babi's road had, being further out from town, but it was nice. 'We haven't been here for *ages*,' Selena said, climbing out. 'There were crocuses last time, now look at all the roses.' They didn't have to wait long after ringing the bell; Granny flung the door open and threw her arms around Ash, who happened to be at the front.

'Darling,' she said. 'Oh, come here to me, pet.' She pulled Minny in as well. 'Selena, lovey.' They all got squeezed to mush. It was dark in the corridor. She seized Nita's elbows, around the baby. 'Nita, he rang me, the fool.'

'Oh.'

'First time he's rung me in months, not a whisper of this girl the last time, though Kevin had dropped a few hints . . . Anyway, come in, come in.'

Nita shepherded them all into the sitting room, dumping

Raymond in Minny's arms, then followed Granny into the kitchen with loud comments about how delicious it all smelled and shut the door. When Minny was properly in the room she discovered Selena standing in a corner chewing her finger, and Ash sitting beside Franklin on the sofa, kicking her heels against it.

'Hi,' she said.

'Hi.'

'I don't think Mum wanted us to hear what Granny's saying about Dad,' she explained.

'What's she saying?' Selena asked instantly.

'Well, I don't know because I'm in here. Sel, this is Franklin. You won't remember him.'

'No.'

'And this is Raymond.'

'Hello,' Franklin said to Raymond.

'Are you all right?' Minny asked him politely as she plunked down in the next chair with the baby.

'Yeah. You?'

'Yeah. Well, you know. Sunday.'

'Yeah,' he agreed.

'What's wrong with Sunday?' Aisling asked.

'It's the Lord's Day,' Selena put in.

Minny ignored her. 'Well, you should know, Ash. You're the one who falls into the gloom of school straight after breakfast.'

'Oh, yeah.' Ash sank back into the sofa, though she was

still pounding her knees together. 'Don't you like school either?' she asked Franklin.

'No.'

'Makes all of us,' Minny said. She had let Raymond go and he was busy trying to turn the TV on. 'Except Selena.'

'I don't like school!'

It was easier once their mother came to get them, looking like a sea wall after a storm – she found Granny hard to deal with – and they could mill around a bit more, getting lemonade or Coke and laying the table. At dinner Nita was nice to Franklin. She was good at making people talk. She got them all to swap what GCSEs they were doing, which was lame and embarrassing but not uninteresting, and when Minny didn't feel like giving Franklin a lecture on Raleigh School Nita told him a bit about it, as if she knew anything – 'It's got a good music department. Drama, not so much. Stay away from the locker room near the gym, it's nasty.' Her mother viewed all schools, including the ones she worked in, through the lens of: where would bullies hang out? It was a good thing she didn't actually know more, Minny thought, since the answer could be: anywhere. 'Have you talked to any of the other kids yet?'

He shrugged with one shoulder. 'I met a girl who's meant to be in some of my classes. They got her to show me round. She seemed all right.'

'Who?' Aisling asked.

'She was called Veronica.'

'Veronica Sedgwick?'

'I think so.'

Minny didn't know Veronica Sedgwick at all, except that she was sort of arty and had curly hair and a nose ring. She thought about that for a while, but of course their mother couldn't keep Granny entirely off sensitive subjects, and soon the conversation became more intense. 'I just can't believe a son of mine came up this way. Ringing me, bold as . . . ! "I'm back in London, Ma." No warning.'

'But aren't you glad he's back, Granny?' Selena asked.

'Well, of course I am, pet. Of course I am. I just wish he'd seen fit to go back to his actual family, to his wife and children—'

'We don't,' Minny said.

'– that he should never have left in the first place. He's just a fool. I brought up a fool.'

'I do.' Selena glared across the table at Minny.

'Well, that's because you're an idiot.' Minny put a hand on Raymond's foot; he was sitting next to her on Nita's lap, eating only Yorkshire pudding. On the other side Aisling was putting more and more beef into her mouth.

'All *right*,' Nita said loudly. 'That's enough, girls. We really don't need to get into all of this again, especially not in front of Franklin. Judy, I know you're sad about it – we all are, or we all *have been*.' She raised her eyebrows at Minny. 'Des hasn't come back to live with us, but he is going to be around and gradually we'll all get used to the situation as we have to previous situations, and frankly I expect we'll all be glad he's so close. In the end.'

'I hope so,' Granny muttered. 'Yes, I suppose some boats were burned a good while ago, it's true.'

Minny squeezed Raymond's foot again, and he dropped a Yorkshire pudding crust on her hand.

She had felt sensitive about eating much with a virtual stranger looking at her, but she managed the apple crumble and custard. 'Mmm,' Sel said appreciatively. 'Doughy.' It stuck to the roof of your mouth, but in a good way. Then the three of them got left in the kitchen to stack the dishwasher and make tea, while Nita gave Raymond his milk and Granny found the book of paper dolls she'd bought for Selena. She always had slightly old-fashioned things for Sel, which Sel adored.

Minny was putting the ketchup away when she saw the guitar leaning against the wall, behind Franklin's chair. 'Is that yours?'

'Yeah.'

'What sort of stuff do you play?'

'Oh, you know. Guitary stuff.' They grinned at each other. 'You play?'

'Not really.'

'Yes, you do,' Ash said.

'I'm no good.'

'What about you?' he asked Aisling.

Aisling had never got close to mastering an instrument.

She didn't have a great relationship with her fingers; her trainers were always Velcro-fastening, although she'd learned good enough knots recently to tie the bathroom light cord inextricably to the string that turned on the hot water. Which was no big deal in June, but meant they'd all be showering in the dark in winter. Minny felt generous right now though. 'You sing, don't you, Ash? She used to have lessons,' she explained to Franklin.

'Yeah? What do you sing?' He dumped the meat pan by the sink.

'I don't know.'

Franklin swung his guitar out from behind the table. 'What about some Guy Clark?'

'Um. Did you know that he's a luthier, which means that he makes guitars, only here it probably would be specific to lutes but in America they say it for guitar-makers.'

'I did know that.' He was picking the guitar. Minny couldn't play like that, she only strummed. She knew the chords but couldn't have put a name to the song. Aisling came in singing just at the right moment.

'Pack up all your dishes

Make note of all good wishes

Say goodbye to the landlord for me . . .'

'Son'bitch has always bored me,' Minny and Franklin both joined in. Ash sang that line as straight as all the others.

She could really sing, Minny admitted to herself, listening.

She'd got Nita's voice. Silver. You didn't hear it very often; when you did it was something stupid and annoying she was only singing because she was stressed out. The song filled up the kitchen. Minny watched Ash singing, then she watched Franklin playing. Though she couldn't see his face much because he leaned over the guitar and his hair flopped down.

The door was ajar and at the end Nita pushed it fully open. She had Raymond in her arms. 'Wow, that was beautiful,' she said. Franklin looked shy as anything and put the guitar down. 'Ash, I didn't know you knew that song.' Ridiculous, as if she didn't play it all the time and as if Aisling didn't remember everything. 'How do you know it, Franklin?'

'I like Guy Clark.'

'Me too. That was really pretty. Minny plays too.'

'No, I don't.'

'Well, you used to. You should come round sometime,' she said to Franklin. 'And bring that when you do.'

'OK,' he mumbled.

'We've got to go now, sweetpeas. I promised Babi I'd have the car back by half six, she's going out somewhere. Good luck with school tomorrow, Franklin. I hope it goes well.'

It took them a few minutes to drag Selena out. Granny didn't look very cheerful. 'If you ever want to talk,' she whispered in Minny's ear when she was squeezing her goodbye, 'about your stupid father, I'm on the end of the phone or I'm nearly always here.'

'I'm fine, Granny.'

'Of course you are. Why wouldn't you be? Haven't you all got each other? I cannot believe it though –' she took hold of Minny's face – 'how much you look like him.'

Minny didn't say anything.

'However little he did to deserve you. Bye then, lovey.'

'You know we should get Franklin round to ours for dinner or something,' Nita said as she started the car. 'It must be terribly lonely for him, and a bit intense for them both – I mean, your granny's lived on her own for nearly ten years. And we could feed him some proper food.'

'I like Granny's cooking,' Selena protested.

'I know you do, darling. And it's certainly . . . hearty. I nearly died when you said the crumble was doughy.'

'Why? I meant it as a compliment.'

'Of course you did.' She steered out of the street onto the main road. 'The crazy thing is I think that's how she took it.'

On Mondays Minny had to pick Selena up from school. It was on the way home, although it was a pain having to show you weren't a dodgy old man at the reception desk, negotiate a sea of small overtired children and then not go nuts with Selena while she diddled around changing her shoes and trying to find her lunch box.

That particular Monday was dull. She didn't catch a glimpse of Franklin all day. Most of her friends, including

Penny, were off on a geography field trip, so Minny was even more ready than usual to leave at three fifteen. Ash was waiting by the gates. 'Can I go home with you?'

'If you want, but I've got to get Sel from school.'

'Can I come?'

They didn't talk much on the way, or rather Aisling rambled about the Louvin Brothers and Minny daydreamed – it was a sort of steamy day and she was tired – and when they got to St Francis and stepped inside it was like going back to the womb. The place was like all primary schools, apparently made out of plastic glass and by the end of the day it always smelled of Marmite. They met the deputy head, who had taught them both when they were there. She was thrilled to see Ash. Aisling had been famous at primary school. When Minny was little and had just started school, they would walk home with their mother and sometimes bump into kids from Raleigh coming the other way and they always seemed to say hi to Aisling. Of course they had been like giants at the time, though they couldn't have been more than eleven or twelve because they must have only just left primary school themselves. Nita would ask Ash who they were and she never had any idea. Everyone knew who Aisling was, teachers, kids and parents – partly because of what she couldn't do, like playing normally, but a lot because of the funny things she came out with – like saying, 'Hello, trouble,' to the headteacher in the mornings. Then there were the things she *could* do. She'd been able to read perfectly years before she started school, and in Reception to stave off boredom she used to write out little stories in the Greek alphabet. Minny had been a bit of a disappointment to the teachers. Then when she did learn to read and got quite good at stuff, no one much noticed. She'd missed her window.

It was funny, in a way, when you thought about it, that Ash had been far more of an oddball in terms of her actual behaviour at primary school than she was now – really uncontrolled tics and shrieks, and meltdowns, and inappropriate squeezing of the other kids and dreaminess and singing. And yet people hadn't minded really. No one picked on her; most people were fond of her if anything, even the kids in her own class. Minny herself had got the rough end of the stick because, unlike Ash then, she was embarrassable. She used to sit in her classroom and they'd all hear Aisling go past outside singing some made-up version of 'The Twelve Days of Christmas', and her whole class would laugh. But now, when Aisling mostly managed to sit on that kind of thing in school – she kept the odd noises for when school finished, as best she could – people treated her like poison. As far as Minny knew she didn't have any friends at all. And it started as soon as secondary did. In fact their school now wasn't even as bad as the private one they'd tried first for Ash – where no one ever spoke to her, literally, for more or less the whole year she was there. No one *spoke* to her. At their school now she got picked on a certain amount, but she'd learned to take precautions and stay with a crowd, so unless the crowd really went nuts, which of course was possible, she was safe, if not happy.

They found Selena and most of her stuff in the end, although she'd lost all her hair bobbles and her sun hat, and managed to struggle out of the back gate, which was the quickest way home. There were parents standing around gassing still, and Minny was rummaging in her pockets to see if she could find the money her mother had given her to get ice lollies on the way home, which was why she didn't notice the man who was leaning on the wall opposite the school and looking all clammy and pale.

'There's Daddy,' Selena said. It wasn't a shout or anything; it sounded more as if she might be sick.

'It's Des,' Aisling whispered. Before Minny even had a chance to look up or around, because the street was reeling, there was a man crossing the road towards them. And it was him, they were right. His hair was different – he used to have a big mop of it and now it was cut short, in a way that looked expensive as if he was playing a rich man in a soap opera. It was more silver than Minny remembered. He looked thinner too. Or something.

It was bad, because none of them knew what to do, including him – or especially him, Minny supposed – and the moment lasted so long she started *thinking* about it. Sometimes she thought she knew what it must be like to be Aisling and have no instincts about how to deal with other people, so that you had to consider every move and know you were probably going to get it wrong. They just stood in a row, looking. Which must have been difficult for him, because he couldn't look back at all three of them at once.

Luckily Selena was young enough and sappy enough just to start bawling. She said, 'Daddy!' and threw herself at him.

'Hey, hey,' he said, and swept her up. Her rucksack flew over her head and bumped him in the face. He didn't put her down. 'I can't believe it,' he said, looking at them and sounding like he was going to cry. 'You're so grown-up.'

Minny felt herself flush. If she did have to see him, she might have liked to change first, and not have her sweaty hair all jumping up around her face the way it was. She'd already been worrying about meeting Franklin, or anyone, on the way home looking like she did and this was miles worse. She hadn't seen her dad since she was eleven. She felt like asking him what he expected – English time to freeze just because he sodded off to a different continent? He was still holding Selena but he put one arm out towards Minny and Aisling – they both cringed away. Eventually he put Sel down but kept hold of her hand, and kissed them both on the cheek. Minny's head was burning. Ash was white except for her ears, which always went fluorescent when she was under stress.

'I've missed you so much,' he said, still in his teary voice. Minny supposed he had to lead with that. She scuffed her

91

toes on the gravel and noticed that there was a woman on the other side of the road, where he had been, watching. 'I suppose you're wondering what I'm doing here. I know you weren't all dying to see me, but I couldn't keep away any longer – I mean, not when I was actually here – I was at my mother's house for lunch, and then I just had to call round . . .'

'Does Mum know you're here?' Minny asked.

'No. Well, she may do by now. She wasn't at home.' He smiled. 'Your babička shut the door in my face. But I thought Nita would be picking up Selena from school, and when I didn't see her going in I couldn't bear not to wait around on the chance of seeing you.' He ruffled Sel's hair. 'I didn't realise I'd get all three of you at once.'

'Right,' Minny said, and gazed over his shoulder at the woman across the street.

'Of course,' he said, in a fake bumbling-Irish way, 'I haven't introduced you. Girls, my darlings, this is Harriet.' She crossed the road like she'd been poised on a spring. 'She's dying to meet you.'

'I've heard so much about you both,' she said, with a big wide gappy grin. 'About you all. You look so much more grown-up than your photographs.' She wasn't exactly jolly hockey sticks like Minny had been picturing, but she wasn't exactly not; and she was bigger than Nita, for instance, though not fat. She looked strong, and had a lot of wild curly dark hair. She could have been a sixth-former.

'You weren't meant to be here today,' Aisling said. It was the first time she had spoken. Her father looked crushed.

'I know. Your mother said you weren't ready to see me yet. But I was in London!' He laughed, as if he knew they couldn't resist his charm. 'Obviously there are things we need to talk about, that you probably want to say. You must be . . . furious with me.'

'I'm not,' said Selena, who was still clinging to his hand.

'Well, you've got every right to be. And confused, and hurt, and anything else too. But for you to be able to say it, I need to be here, you know. You wouldn't even talk to me on the phone.'

'Are you coming back to the house with us?' Minny asked.

'Yes. If that's OK with you.'

'Can I still watch *Pointless*?' Aisling was looking down at the ground.

'*Pointless*, eh? What's that – a game show? I bet you're brilliant at that.'

'No, Minny's better than me.'

'She just likes watching it,' Minny said.

'I see. Of course you can watch it, if that's what you normally do.'

'Let's go then.' Minny led the way around the corner to the main road, hoping they wouldn't see *anyone*. As if it wasn't enough for him to ambush them when their mother wasn't even there, or Babi either, he had felt the need to bring his bimbo with him, to make her a witness to the first time they had seen him in almost three years. She could have spat on the pavement.

The walk home seemed longer than it normally did; it was less than a mile but it felt like ages. Minny found herself wanting to keep Aisling and Selena right beside her, almost hold their arms, which was weird since it wasn't as if she was afraid her father would actually leap into a moving car and vanish with them. She couldn't anyway. They couldn't walk five abreast down the street, and Selena was sticking with her father; she hadn't let go of his hand, though she seemed keen to keep him between her and the woman. Minny tried to walk beside Aisling, but she couldn't keep running round the others when they got mixed up crossing roads. Luckily Ash kept stopping dead and waiting for Minny to catch her up.

Their father was trying really hard. The thing about him was that he was very funny, sometimes. He always had been. He had them laughing after five minutes. He was spoilt. Aisling didn't laugh, not that that meant anything; you never knew which way she'd jump when something unusual happened. Sometimes she woke up a bit; this time she was more in her own world than usual, not even muttering. She only started talking when they got to the newsagents, because she wanted her ice lolly. The last thing Minny wanted was to prolong this walk, but she could tell there wasn't any way she was getting Aisling past that shop so she asked the others to stop and started fishing for cash.

'Oh, I'll get them,' her father said straightaway. 'What a good idea, in fact why don't we . . . ?' He waved towards the café next door, which sold fancy Italian ice cream in beautiful flavours.

'Mmmm,' said Selena, drooling over the window.

'Aisling's dairy-intolerant,' Minny said.

'Of course she is, how stupid of me.' He looked uncomfortable. 'I had remembered, honestly. I've even brought dark chocolate. I just forgot for a second.'

'I don't mind,' Aisling said. 'I can just get a lolly. Minny, will you get it for me?' She didn't like buying things in shops; she got flustered. Minny went in with her. It was dark after the glare on the street, and tropically hot till she opened the freezer and leaned in.

They had to queue behind a bunch of loud sweary boys, who were really cool except that they all had to count pennies into the guy's hand to pay for their sweeties. So by the time Ash and Minny came out, their father and his woman and Selena were standing on the curb licking ice creams. He held a cone out to Minny as she came up. 'Selena said you still like chocolate.'

It took them ages to trail up the hill. Her father kept looking round and telling Harriet and Selena stories from the past, as if he was returning to where he spent his wartime childhood or something. Minny ate her ice cream and said nothing. She was wondering whether Babi would have got hold of her mother by now.

'I thought you were English,' Aisling said to Harriet. She was holding her sticky lolly stick awkwardly in front of her and stumping along looking at the ground.

'I am,' Harriet said. She didn't sound it. 'I spent some time in the States growing up, but I'm English, honest to God.'

'Oh,' said Ash, who still hadn't looked up.

Babi was waiting by the front-room window, sucking her beautiful fingernails. When she saw them she stayed where she was, so Minny had to use her key, but she came into the hall as they filed through the door.

'Hello again, Milena,' their father said in a steely voice like James Bond.

'I don't know what you're doing here, Desmond,' she said. 'Nita isn't home from work. This is inappropriate at best.'

'I can see your point of view. However, we walked home with the girls from school and I'm sure it's best if, having come, and having seen my daughters, I wait and see their mother too.'

Babi nodded and went towards the kitchen, but turned back to say, 'If this was still only my home, you would not be allowed over the threshold.' He rolled his eyes, but Harriet, who was taking off her shoes because everyone else had, shook her head at him and he didn't say anything.

'I'll put the kettle on,' Minny said, since she didn't think Babi would be serving tea and she wanted to get away from them for a minute.

'Look at this.' Her father was standing transfixed in the hall. 'I'd forgotten about this.'

He'd only been gone less than three years. Minny wasn't sure how he could have forgotten it when it had hung on her mother's wall since university. It was a blackboard topped by an enamelled green steam train, with enamel letters that said 'Life is like a train so hop aboard!' Her mother had had a party the last night of university or something, and all her friends had scribbled stupid things underneath, which Minny had been looking at her whole life – pretentious things mostly, like: 'Life is like a train, you better make sure you know where you want to be going'; and 'Life is like a train, it rushes past you if you're not on board'. Some of them didn't even make any sense, like 'Life is like a train so mind the gap'. A couple were silly – 'Life is like a train: mucky' and 'Life is like a train, covered in f***ing graffiti'. Her dad was squinting at the bottom; he gave a roar of laughter and turned to Minny, grinning. She blushed. When she was in a bad mood after her mother had told her she was pregnant, she had scribbled at the end: 'Life is like a train, and mine is overcrowded'.

'What about *Pointless*?' Ash said. The others had gone into the back room, their father still laughing, but she was standing against the hall wall, looking at the floor.

'It's not on for more than an hour,' Minny pointed out. With any luck they would be gone by then. Babi was in the kitchen, leaning against the sink and sucking her nails again. Minny switched the kettle on and they looked at each other.

'Do you know that's the first time I have said a single word to your father in three years? Since before I knew what he was going to do?'

'Do you want tea?' Minny asked.

'For God's sake,' Babi muttered, sweeping the mugs out of Minny's hands. 'Get in there and look after your sisters, will you, and I will make the damn tea.'

Minny went reluctantly out and into the back room, where the only free chair was the one at the desk. She wished she could just turn on the computer and escape into it. For a minute she thought of Uncle Kevin, sat at his laptop in a room she'd never seen above a bar in a tiny town in Ireland, and wished she was there. Not that she would have been safe from her father there either; obviously he had nothing against popping up without warning in places he'd once lived.

Selena was sitting on the yellow sofa, squashed between her father and Harriet and looking uncomfortable. It looked as though she'd wanted to sit on his lap and then decided she was too old. Ash was in the big white chair with her feet tucked up.

'When's your mother back?' Des asked.

'Soon,' Minny said.

'She doesn't work late then?'

'She does a lot at home in the evenings.'

'She goes out in the evenings too,' Selena piped up.

Minny liked the idea of him imagining a really hot social life for her mother, but she clarified it. 'That's just for now. She's putting on a play with her drama group.'

He looked interested. 'What drama group? Is it at the school?'

'No, not exactly. It's through the school but it's open to other disabled kids too.' Nita taught part-time at a special school for kids with behavioural and social difficulties, visited other schools to do drama and music therapy and for the last two years had also run a drama group. 'She's got a lot of rehearsals because the performance is in a couple of weeks.'

'How interesting,' Harriet said.

'Right up Nita's street, that,' Des told her. He was looking round the room. 'I'm sorry we're making you miss your programme, Ash.'

'That's all right, Des.' Aisling had always called their father Des. Minny had never really known why. She had tried it herself once when she was a kid, but it didn't catch on. 'It's not on till quarter past five.'

'Hey, are you still as good at capitals as you were?' he asked. 'Listen to this, Harriet: what's the capital of Kyrgyzstan?'

'Bishkek,' said Selena eagerly, looking up at his face and waiting for the next question.

He looked astonished and laughed. His laugh was a

gurgle; if you leaned against him you could feel it at the top of his stomach. Minny could see his thoughts swirling. Selena was an oddball; people sometimes assumed, if they knew about Aisling, that Sel was on the autistic spectrum too, but she wasn't, she was just a bit weird. The Bishkek answer came from living with Aisling; they all knew every world capital. And the '-stans' were a gimme anyway, because there were only a few of them. Watching her father try to show off Ash, without knowing what was showy about her these days, was a strange feeling. They used to be really tight. And he'd always been the one who'd make her perform. Nita would look unconvinced, but he would say, 'What better way to boost her self-esteem than people telling her how clever she is?' They had a video of her at a cocktail party, reciting capitals and then singing 'The Periodic Table Song', when she couldn't have been more than six or seven. So capitals were really old hat.

It was weird, having them in the house. No one Harriet's age was ever there because why would they be, none of them knew anyone who was twenty-six. And her father, with Selena squashed up against him, as if one of the photos Nita insisted on leaving on the wall had come to life, only with Sel no longer a toddler. Or as if it was a photo of Des with Ash aged seven. They were both just like their mother. Minny wondered if she looked like he expected.

'What about the old football, do you still follow it?' He leaned back on the sofa, looking more at home.

'Yes.'

'Of course.' She didn't want him thinking he owned football. They were Manchester United fans in their own right, just as much as he was. It made her angry because she could remember the day she considered giving it up – as if it would get at him somehow.

'And play it on the Wii?'

'No.'

'No?'

'We never finished the season we were on when you left,' Ash said.

He put his hand over his eyes and cleared his throat. Minny prayed he wouldn't break down and drag them into some real emotional scene before her mother even got back, but he didn't. 'You won't believe it,' he said, 'but this woman is a Liverpool fan.' He smacked Harriet on the back. She groaned and beamed at them, obviously expecting someone to provide the punchline. But they were all silent. Minny didn't spend much time predicting stuff about her dad, but she would never have expected him to hook up with a Liverpool fan.

Before any of them had stopped goggling, Babi brought in mugs of black tea and plonked them down on the table, with the old stainless steel jug of milk. It was probably off. 'Thank you,' Harriet said quietly, and looked at Des.

'Harriet doesn't actually drink tea,' he said. 'But I expect I'll get around to drinking hers.'

Babi was bored by the situation now, Minny could tell. She didn't have a great attention span. 'You make her some coffee,' she said to Minny. 'I have to go upstairs.'

He laughed again, probably before she was out of earshot. 'Your babička is just the same,' he said. 'I knew I could rely on her not to have changed.'

'Well,' Harriet said, 'she's probably angry with you. Not exactly surprising. Isn't she beautiful though. Does she look after you a lot?'

'She lives here,' Sel said cautiously.

'Would you like some coffee?' Minny asked, standing up.

'No, honestly, I'm fine. It's too warm for me. I've got my flavoured water.' She pulled it out of her squashy leather handbag, the kind with beads on it, and smiled at Minny. 'Babička, is that right? Is that Polish?'

'Czech,' Aisling said. She hummed and squeaked. 'CZECH! Yeah.' He obviously hadn't told Harriet anything at all about them if he'd missed out their mother's mother being Czech, or her father having been South African and Norwegian for that matter. People's families and where they come from, that's important – that's what everyone had always told them, including him. Even though they only went to Ireland that once, and even then hardly met any relatives as far as Minny could remember – they didn't even stay with Granny and Grandpop, who was still alive then. They only visited their house once and that was the only time they met their grandfather; he was very big with silver hair and he didn't say anything at all to Minny or Ash. Granny gave them lots of cake in the kitchen; they heard their father shouting, and Grandpop too, and then Des came out and said they had to leave, and they both cried because they weren't allowed to finish their cake. But Granny came running out after them and gave them milk-flavoured ice lollies through the car window as they were driving off. Still – he was always talking about being Irish.

'There's so much you've got to tell me,' he said, looking round at all of them. 'It's kind of like meeting three entirely new people – three completely fascinating people. I don't know who your friends are any more, or what you like at school, or what you want to be.'

'Selena wants to be the Pope,' Minny said.

'Wow.' Selena's face lit up at the idea.

'Well, now, that's something I want to hear about. I must say I'd picked up a few hints in your emails, Selena, that you might be into that kind of thing. But listen, before I can expect you to feel OK about us talking, I've got to say sorry, for being so far away for so long.' Minny thought he caught the glint in her eye. 'And I know that won't really do, but I want you to know I mean it and I'm going to try to make it up to you from now on, though I might need some help figuring out the right way to do that. I want you to know you can trust me. Harriet and I have got a flat now; we're moving in this week.'

'Where is it?' Selena asked, looking excited.

'Ladbroke Grove, very handy for work and not too bad for here either. It's quite nice and big, with three bedrooms so plenty of room if you all come and stay, which I hope you will. And the best news is it's near the station, so when you're used to it you'll be able to hop on the Tube and come over any time you feel like it!'

Just then, before any of them had time to say what they thought of that idea, they heard the kind of loud grizzle from upstairs that meant Babi must have been changing the baby's nappy. He didn't like having his poppers done up again afterwards, and he was always grumpy when he'd just woken up.

'Ah,' their father said, twisting round and staring at the door, 'the famous baby. Interested to meet him.'

Minny got up to go and get him. He liked to see her after she'd been out at school all day, especially when he'd been at nursery and Babi had picked him up. She stopped because her father said, 'What's his name again now?'

'Raymond,' Aisling and Selena said together.

Minny clenched her fists, literally. Because her father had that tone of voice on that meant he was gearing up to be sarcastic about her brother's name.

Babi came clumping down the stairs and into the room. The baby was all damp sticky-up tufts of hair and rosiness after his nap and started squirming to be put down as soon as he saw Minny. Babi stalked over and he did his sideways fall into Minny's arms.

Des was staring. The sly look on his face had vanished and he'd shifted around on the sofa so that he was practically sitting on Selena's lap. He looked astounded. 'Aahh,' said Harriet, like a matter-of-fact, hard-headed woman who can't resist a coo at a particularly nice baby. Minny glared back at her father, her chin raised high over Raymond's head. At precisely that moment they all heard Nita's key in the door and she walked in looking flattened with tiredness.

She wasn't at her very best, she never was after work, when her long hair had been fluffing itself up all day, and she was wearing a long skirt she'd had since she was married and a cheap red T-shirt Minny had bought by accident for herself before she realised it made her look like a balloon. She went cloud-coloured when she saw her husband, or ex-husband; still, Minny enjoyed the effect she had on Harriet. Her mother was very good-looking.

'Des,' she said, in a small voice. Raymond hadn't stopped struggling, because he wanted her now, but she stayed put in the doorway. 'What's going on?'

'Dad came to meet us outside school,' Minny said. She had been waiting for the proper authorities to turn up so that she could get angry.

Her father had stood up. 'Nita,' he said, for all the world as if he had a reason to be annoyed with her, 'can we have a word, please?'

'Certainly,' she said, and they went off into the other room. The baby wailed. The rest of them were left looking at each other; everyone was mortified except Aisling, who was just staring into space. Obviously Babi was determined not to be the one to break the silence, despite being the only actual grown-up present. She was bloody-minded. Selena thought up some small talk before anyone else.

'So, Harriet,' she said, edging away to a more polite distance before crossing her legs and folding her hands on her knee, 'what is it that you do?'

To give her credit, Harriet giggled. 'I work in advertising, like your dad.' Selena nodded intelligently, and Minny found herself copying her. They were all copying her. 'That's where we met.'

'In New York,' Babi said in a harsh voice, and then coughed. 'So, why now? What made you both come back now?'

'Well,' Harriet said, 'it's not a bad time for a change for us, work-wise; Dessie got a promotion that meant he could ask to move back here. But I think he's been gearing up to this for a good while, getting ready for it. He's been missing you terribly, you girls. Ever since I've known him.'

None of them made a sceptical noise. They wouldn't be impolite to a stranger. Raymond started banging on the French window, so Minny got up to open it for him. It was after four so he wasn't going to get sunburnt. Nita came back in then, looking pink and pushing back wisps of her hair, as if she'd walked out on him. Des followed. He had nailed the genial expression back on his face to introduce his new woman to his old one. 'Well, well, this is all really fascinating. Seeing you all here . . . and a new little man. Change! Change is good, of course.'

'And to be expected over a period of three years,' Babi said to the ceiling.

'He's a bonny little fella, I must say.' Des stood looking through the open doors at the baby, who was throwing sand over the side of his sand table. 'Very cute. Nita, though, I've got to ask – Raymond?'

Minny couldn't bear it. 'What's wrong with Raymond?'

'Nothing's wrong with it, nothing at all. It's just a bit . . . fruity. I don't remember it coming up when we were talking about possible boys' names. I'm pretty sure what I'd have said if you had suggested it though, Nita.' He sat down there on the little yellow sofa where men never sat, criticising her mother and making fun of her baby brother. He laughed and said, 'Still, they say bullying is good for the soul.'

Bullying wasn't something you laughed about in their family. He must have forgotten that. No one said anything.

'Anyway,' he charged on, 'with the house so full – can't imagine where you're putting everyone – you'll be glad to get rid of the girls every now and again, and I'm sure they'd like a change of scene. We were just telling them we've got us a flat, in Ladbroke Grove so not too far away, and we're dying to have them come and stay.'

'No,' Nita said in a rush.

'What?'

'Of course I don't mean no. I mean, it's up to them.' She looked down at her lap. Selena was bouncing about on the edge of the sofa. Ash was banging her knuckles against the wall behind her chair and humming again.

'I don't want to,' Minny said; the words sort of fell out of her, after all, without her having to psych herself up.

'Ah, don't say no, Minny,' he coaxed. 'You don't have to say yes either, but say you'll think about it.'

Nita coughed. 'Look, Des, I think this is something you're going to have to give them time to get used to. I did actually tell you that on the phone. You can't just ring up, or turn up for that matter, and expect to take up exactly where you left off.'

His eyebrows were drawn down the way they always were when he was simmering; it used to be all he needed to do to get them pussyfooting around him, except Ash, who wouldn't notice or at least wouldn't know how to pussyfoot, which is why it was usually her who kicked off his big strops. 'You don't have to talk to me as if I'm a child, Nita. I would have thought you had enough actual children to fulfil your maternal needs. Harriet and I have settled here now and the girls can have all the time they need, and everything else they need from me too.'

'So, what is it you think?' Minny asked. 'That we've managed nicely without you for three years but you expect us to be thrilled you're back? Just because you've decided you're ready to play daddy again?' Her chest hurt.

She wasn't expecting him to laugh. 'Well, now that you mention it . . .'

'Dessie,' said Harriet.

'There is some news we weren't sure whether to pass on today or not. Harriet thought not, but since I've seen your, er, brother, and how much, er, things have moved on around here – yes, we're having a baby too. Harriet's pregnant.'

No one said anything, though Selena sort of squeaked. There was dust dancing in the sunlight, and Minny could hear Raymond talking to the pebbles he liked to dig out of the side of the decking and suck. Aisling had her elbows on her lap and her hands over her ears.

Her mother stood up. 'You point-scoring piss-wipe.'

He looked astonished. 'Steady, Nita.'

'How dare you come here, to their own house, and tell them something like that just because you're still offended that I dared to have a baby of my own? How dare you just turn up after all this time and then treat them like this? You should be prostrate with shame for what you've done, not bragging about impregnating . . .'

Harriet shifted on the sofa. Even her neck and chest were flushed.

'There's no reason for anyone to be upset by this. I meant it as good news. I don't see why it shouldn't be.'

Babi snorted. 'Not even for the child?'

'There's no need for that.' He looked upset suddenly.

'I was a good father for most of their lives, and I'm going to be again.'

'That's the point, Des,' Nita shouted. 'You can't take a break and still have been a good father. It's all or nothing. And you – you gunged it up when you took off and didn't see them for the best part of three years. Selena had only just started school, for God's sake; she was a little child. You weren't there for everything that's happened at school, or when they got their periods or Selena lost her first tooth or the time Minny got suspended for pushing someone down the stairs . . .' Oh good, Minny thought, lovely.

'I know I wasn't there.' He looked plain angry. 'I can't apologise enough for that. I want to do what I can to make up for it.'

'It's a long road back, Des, and there aren't any shortcuts.'

'I know that. But I hope you won't try to prejudice them against me, Nita. For a start I don't know why this was sparked off by the idea of me having another child. You had one.'

'Oh yes.' She flung her arms in the air. 'That's what this is all about.'

'Not really,' he said, raising his voice. 'Not much comparison between our situations. After all, I'm in a relationship, a stable relationship. While you—'

'Watch yourself,' Babi hissed.

'– while you were already a single mother of three, one on the autistic spectrum and needing a lot of attention – all of them needing, and deserving, a lot of attention. Well, it was your right to decide you could cope with another one, a fatherless one.' Nita was looking at him, aghast. 'I just hope the girls haven't been the ones to pay for that.'

'We were ALL fatherless,' Minny shouted. It seemed she'd been wrong to worry he would be such a stranger that she would feel forced to be polite and un-angry with him. 'You sodded off to bloody America without even telling us you were going and never came back; *you* made Mum a single mother, and now you're criticising the job she's done. You're unbelievable. I never want to stay in your horrible flat. Get lost.'

'I don't want to stay in your flat either,' Aisling said quickly. Selena slid out from between him and Harriet and went to stand in the corner, near her mother, who put her hand on Sel's back.

'I think you'd better go, Des.'

'Don't make it a choice between us, Nita,' he said, deflated. 'I know I can't win that way. I just want to see my girls.'

'I know. And you've made a start. Not an especially good one. We can talk about it another time.'

Harriet got up in a hurry, riffling through her bag and not looking at anyone. Des looked at them all. 'I'll call you,' he said. 'OK, Selena? I'll call you soon.'

When they heard the front door shut they all breathed out at the same time, except Selena who ran upstairs howling. Nita sat down flat on the arm of the sofa as if she needed to brace herself for a minute before she went after her. Babi had sat down too, sinking together with elbows and knees sticking out like a bayou witch. 'The girlfriend is different anyway. Obviously he thinks he needs a lot more woman than you, Nita.'

Nita looked cross, as much as she ever did. 'Mama, is it too much to ask for you not to criticise women, not to speak of pregnant women for their build or appearance in front of my daughters?'

'Surely these are exceptional circumstances.'

Nita definitely laughed on her way up the stairs.

FOUR

Minny was left alone for the rest of the evening. Nita and Selena got into a pretty heavy chat upstairs, and Minny suspected her mother would have had a crack at getting Aisling to talk about it too – it was so hard to tell when Ash needed to bury something and when it might be the kind of thing to send her into a crashing meltdown any minute. Her mother probably thought that Minny needed to think about it for a while before she was ready to talk. As a matter of fact, what she needed was not to think about it at all, so after she'd sort of done her homework and they'd had dinner she went and sat in the bath for an hour and a half and read *Harry Potter*.

It was funny next morning, it felt like something major had happened and things were all new, but it was just a Tuesday morning. Minny didn't have to worry about dodging any conversations because there was never time to have one before school; it was all banging on bathroom doors and shouting because someone had left the jam out and someone else had wasted five minutes searching the fridge for it; stuff like that. Aisling wanted to walk to school with Minny and she said, 'Fine.'

As it turned out, once Penny had arrived and they'd all three set off, most of the journey was spent being questioned about Franklin. Penny had gabbed compulsively for five minutes without drawing breath about how she and Jorge had made up their row and were fathoms-deep again, and Minny brought up Franklin in desperation.

Penny listened in silence to Minny's brief rundown on why he was around, and then she exploded. 'I can't believe you're hanging out with Franklin Conderer. He was *always* awful.'

'We're not exactly hanging out,' Minny protested. 'I mean, he's moved in with my grandmother. What are we supposed to do?'

'Yeah, now he's been ASBO'd out of North London. God. He's probably planning to run off with her pension book or something. And trying to get you to smoke!'

'He didn't,' Aisling said.

'That is so like him. You didn't, did you? Minny?'

'No, I didn't, Penny, but I don't see what the big deal is. It was a cigarette, not a crackpipe.'

She shook her head. 'It's gross and filthy and I don't like hearing you say it's not.'

'I didn't say it's not.'

'I bet he smokes other stuff too.'

'Oh, *Penny*. You're such a square.'

'I am not, I just think . . . I just don't like him.'

'You haven't even seen him since you were seven.'

114

Just then Aisling started chuckling uncontrollably. Minny and Penny glared off in opposite directions, until Ash was actually bent double laughing, and saying, 'Mrs Seagull.'

Things were a bit uncomfortable, so after school Minny agreed to go round to Penny's house for a while. It was ages since she'd been there. She'd always loved it; it was everything her own home never was – empty and peaceful, with big clean bright cushions and a gracious white staircase. Penny's bedroom had a double bed in it and a white lacy duvet cover. There was a piano downstairs, and a big tiled kitchen, and the bathroom was always clean. Penny's mother wasn't usually there after school; she was a bit remote but seemed well disposed towards Minny.

Unfortunately today her mother's girlfriend was working at home, which Penny only told Minny when they were on the front doorstep. Alison was the opposite of Penny's mother, Cora – she never left you alone. She always wanted to talk about what you were *into* at the moment. Minny felt her flesh crawl when they came into the kitchen to get something to eat and Alison was sitting on one of the high stools absorbed in *Twilight*. Hideous. She looked up at them with a start. 'There you are! Wow, Minny, I haven't seen you in ages! How are you? How's your sister? Is she? Did you have a good day at school, Pen? Cora's not home yet. I thought we'd get a takeaway later, do you want to join us, Minny?'

'Er –'

'You said you've got to get home for dinner,' Penny reminded her. 'Do you want a biscuit?'

So they had to sit around the marble-surfaced island in the kitchen on high chairs and drink tea and eat biscuits. It was more or less what they always did, and always had done, at least since they grew out of watching *The Princess and the Frog* on repeat, only Alison was there so it was challenging. Normally they had the place to themselves. If Penny's mother was in they would be in Penny's bedroom, watching nonsense TV and talking over the top of it. Before Jorge, even considering Penny's massive tendency to bang on about herself, that had been OK. Hardly anyone could make Minny laugh as hard as Penny could sometimes, and no one ever laughed as much at Minny as Penny did. Minny had been half thinking that, if they could get some time together when Penny didn't happen to be in crisis mode, that might happen again, but now it was scuppered because Alison was there and she hadn't been living there that long and Penny was completely fine about her moving in and really, everything was fine; which all apparently meant that they couldn't leave Alison downstairs on her own. Penny didn't actually get on all that well with her mother, but she never talked much about it. Minny respected that. She wondered if she opened up about it all to Jorge.

She went home for dinner, salivating because they'd had the Chinese menu out at Penny's house before she left. It was unnaturally quiet as she opened the front door, although

116

Raymond's face appeared around the corner and he came crawling to greet her as she was taking off her shoes. Minny picked him up and poked her head round the door of the back room. Selena was sitting huddled on the sofa, watching a very brightly coloured cartoon about ugly animals with the sound turned low. 'Where is everyone?'

'Babi's in the kitchen cooking. Mum's upstairs.'

'Where's Ash?' She should have been gearing up for *Pointless* by now, nagging Selena about switching channels in time.

Sel sniffed. 'She's in the front room,' she said, turning the volume up.

Minny had put Raymond down and he was banging on the front-room door. She opened it for him. Ash was sitting in there with her elbows on the table, watching Franklin, who was beside her tuning Nita's guitar.

'Hello,' Minny said.

'Hi.'

'I didn't know you were here.'

'I met Ash on the way home,' he said, not stopping what he was doing. 'That's better, I think.'

'Yes,' Aisling agreed. 'Are you going to play another one?'

'No, I've got to go.'

Her mother was tripping down the stairs behind her. 'Oh, really?' she said, overhearing. 'You won't stay for dinner? Hi, Minny.'

'I can't,' he explained, laying the guitar on the table. 'Judy said she's making tea for half five so I'd better get back.'

'All right then, fair enough. Come round another time though.'

Minny stood quietly while they were all saying goodbye. She thought there might be some further explanation once he'd gone but there wasn't; Ash just went off to watch her programme, causing screaming hysterics from Selena, who'd ever-hopefully started watching something else. Nita took the baby upstairs to change him. Minny went out into the garden and found Guts the cat, who was more than happy to have his head stroked as he lay with his paws tucked neatly under in a fall of sunlight.

Dinner was fairly quiet; no one seemed in a chatty mood, not even their mother who could usually be relied upon to keep a conversation going, even if it was with herself. 'How come Franklin was round?' Minny asked in the end, forking up the last meatball.

'*I* don't know,' Selena muttered.

'I met him,' Ash said, when no one else answered, 'on the way home. He said did I want to sing some more, and I said yes, so he came round.'

Minny wiped her chin. 'You didn't . . . make him come round, did you, Ash?'

'Of course she didn't,' her mother snapped.

'I only meant . . . he might have not felt able to say no, or whatever. It's just we don't know him very well or anything, he might have been embarrassed.'

'It was his idea. He obviously enjoys Aisling's company.'

118

'Bit weird,' Minny said, under her breath.

Aisling squeezed out more ketchup into the sea of it on her plate. 'I didn't make him come round.'

Selena went to bed early, even before Babi had left for her evening with Gil. Ash had some documentary to re-watch on her computer. After the baby had settled for the night things were very quiet and Minny started watching a sitcom. Then Nita came in, shut the door, turned the TV off without asking and sat down on the coffee table.

'Minny,' she said, 'I got a call this afternoon from Ms Lynley at your school.' Ms Lynley, the deputy head, was actually Mrs Lynley, but Nita converted everyone to Ms. 'She said she found Aisling eating her lunch in the toilets.'

Minny was surprised. She thought she had Ash convinced to avoid the toilets except when strictly necessary.

'Can you see that that's really bad, Minny?'

'Yes,' Minny said, and moved to the other corner of the sofa, a little further away from her mother.

'Quite apart from hygiene, and even apart from safety – look what happened the last time – what does it say about how lonely she is, and intimidated. It's heartbreaking. And I can't get my head around how alone she is at that school when you go there too. I know you're in a different year and you can't do anything about lesson time, but couldn't you sit with her at lunch or something, spend some breaks with her?'

Minny wished her mother would stop looking at her.

119

She could see Nita was upset, and that fobbing her off wasn't going to work – her mother had a fairly reasonable grasp of the way things were, normally, so she tried to explain. 'No. Not really. I'm not in charge of everything that happens at school, and I'm not – you know – an island. I can't just . . . inflict Aisling on my friends all the time. I couldn't really do that even if she wasn't the way she is, it would be weird.'

Nita put her face in her hands. 'Look, Minny,' she said through them, to the floor, 'I don't ask you to be my eyes and ears at school. That's quite difficult for me.' She sounded all rational. 'Because I can't rely on getting any information at all from Ash, however vital it is. But I respect that you have your life and that school has rules, so I try on the whole to leave you alone. But you've got to understand a bit more what's going on here. I spend my whole life trying to build up your sister's self-esteem, because I'm afraid of what will happen to her. Sometimes I just need you to reach your hand out to her and help make things a little bit easier.'

Sometimes Minny got sick of it all at once, her life. Besides, she hated being told off. 'No one else has to look after their sister, their *older* sister,' she burst out. 'It's not fair.'

Nita stood up and started dusting the top of the ridiculous aquarium-like gas heater with her fingers. 'Oh yes, because you're the one getting the raw deal,' she said. 'I suppose you think Ash did something to deserve it—'

'No.'

'– and that you're paying the penalty for that. Listen, her autism affects us all – that's just the way it is. I know we're all struggling with stuff at the moment, and if I could do anything about that I would. Things could be a lot worse, maybe they could be better – they could certainly be easier – but this is our life.'

'I know.'

'I get tired and curse things too, you know, especially your bloody father who left me to pick up the slack on my own and is adding to my problems today. I've got a seven-year-old girl upstairs who cried herself to sleep because her dad didn't call her to say goodnight.'

Minny wiped her nose. 'Selena's all right, she's just a drama queen. At least it gives her something to offer up to God.'

Her mother didn't laugh; she didn't say anything for a minute but just looked at her thoughtfully. 'You're very hard sometimes. Your grandmother says it's your age, but I wonder.'

She never got this, these kind of stern and disappointed looks, not from her mother. She found she couldn't shut up. 'At least you've always got Babi and her homespun wisdom to help you out; things could be worse.'

'That's the other thing I've got tired of lately.' Nita was on her way out of the door. 'Stop all the snarky digs about your grandmother. She may not spoil you, but she's vital to our lives and she saved us by letting us come to live here. So show her some respect, and stop groaning every time she has a friend round. I won't have you making her feel uncomfortable in what is still her home.'

Minny didn't sleep very well. Raymond was normally pretty good at night, but something must have woken him up because she heard him yowling at about two. With Babi not having come home, she thought it was quite likely that everyone in the house cried that night.

Wednesday was all subdued. Minny's face felt as if she'd washed it with soap and not rinsed it, and no one was talking much. She didn't say anything about it to her mother, but she asked Aisling if she would wait a few minutes so they could walk to school together again.

Penny was a bit weird that day. She asked them on the walk in if they'd seen Franklin again, which considering that Minny had been at her house till dinner time the previous evening, Minny considered little short of psychic. Aisling happily told her about bumping into him, and him coming round to sing.

'To *sing*? Sing what?'

'Some country songs,' Ash said.

'*Country*?'

'*Yes*,' Minny said, imitating the tone of her voice. 'I told you you were missing out.'

'What does he know about country?'

'Quite a lot.'

'He heard it round at our house,' Ash explained. 'When we were little.'

Penny immediately pulled an extreme face. 'That's a bit creepy.'

'Oh, shut up, Penny.'

'Well, it is. I didn't know you liked singing,' she said to Aisling.

'Oh.'

'*We* should do more music,' she added to Minny. Once they'd had a plan that they would form a band when they were a bit older and knew some more people who played the right kinds of instruments. They used to practise sometimes. But Minny got tired of it because all it meant was her strumming in the background, badly, while Penny sang awful songs over and over again with one hand to her ear as if she was in a recording studio, so she was happy enough when it tailed off.

'Well,' she said now, 'let me know when you've got five minutes off from Jorge.'

'What's that supposed to mean?'

'Oh, nothing.'

'You've got a bit of a problem with Jorge, haven't you?'

'I don't even know him, Pen.'

'Yes, you do, Minny. You've met him loads of times.'

'Well, I suppose I mean we haven't bared our souls to each other in big sweaty bonding sessions then.' He hadn't

123

said more than three words to her, or looked at her with even the slightest glimmer of interest.

'At least he's . . .'

'What?' Minny said. Penny flushed, and she wondered what she could possibly have been about to say. 'At least he's what, Penny?'

'At least he knows how to behave.'

'Who?' Aisling asked with interest.

'As opposed to me?' Minny asked.

'As opposed to your new . . . friend.'

'What, Franklin? What are you on about? Are you still harking back to when we were little kids?'

'We're going to be late,' Aisling said with sudden panic. She was used to getting in early, before the rush began.

'We're fine.'

'No, no. Life is like a train,' she buzzed. 'You need to make sure you get to the station on time.' That was another one off that daft blackboard; her mother had used it for years as a way to get Ash to understand similes, and now they popped out of her at odd times.

'Come on then,' Penny said, 'let's run. I need to finish my French anyway.'

She was peculiar all the rest of the week. School was stressful enough at the moment since not even English was fun any more, and Minny could have done without Penny's odd vibes; she found herself trying to avoid anything that could possibly lead to the mention of Franklin's name. Annoying, and impossible when Ash was around. And Minny tried to keep her around. She had little rambles around the school at break times, till she'd located Aisling, and even passed half an hour in the library with her at lunch. She didn't explain it to Penny, who kept wondering, aloud, where she was hiding herself. On Thursday at break she grabbed Minny and ordered her to come and eat with her and Jorge at lunchtime. 'Fine,' Minny said, 'but I'll have to bring Aisling. I said I'd meet her.'

Penny looked at her oddly. 'Where are you off to now? The bell's about to go.'

'I'm just making sure Ash is OK. You don't have to come.'

'I'm just asking, why today?'

'My mum asked me to.'

'Yeah? Is she guilting you out a bit?'

'Not really.'

'She can't expect you to give up your own life or whatever to look after other people.'

'Look, I'm just . . . keeping an eye on her at the moment, that's all.' They rounded a corner and saw Ash in the corridor, talking to Franklin. 'Oh. Well. She looks OK right now.'

'No, no,' Penny said, marching on, 'let's check.'

They were talking about maths. In some ways school should have been the perfect place for Ash, Minny thought, since it was actually meant to be about learning and everything, but not even the teachers seemed to have the imagination to get on her wavelength enough to teach her properly, let alone have a conversation. Instead she was just a target. Minny felt a wave of really violent liking for Franklin; she didn't know if he was even into maths himself – it seemed unlikely somehow – but he cared about Aisling enough to drop into her world for a minute. She was looking all bright-eyed and intelligent, till Penny walked up to them and started being breezy.

'So, that's so interesting,' Penny said as Aisling finished a sentence about proofs and infinite numbers of primes. 'And you haven't told me anything about American politics in ages, Aisling, I feel really uninformed.'

The bell went over her last word. Ash stood on her toes, poised and paralysed between her inner timetable and the temptation to talk about the House of Representatives. 'I've got to get my book before English.'

'Well, go on then,' Minny said irritably. 'Else you'll be late.'

She took off down the corridor.

'Come on, Minny,' Penny said, taking her arm. 'We'll be late for physics.'

'I've got to get my books too,' Minny said, taking it back. 'I'll see you there.'

'Your friend's strange,' Franklin said, watching her flounce up the stairs.

'Yes, she is. It's nice that you can talk to Ash about maths. No one else does except my mum.'

He shrugged. 'I didn't understand a word of it. She's clever.'

'Yeah, she is. At maths.' Minny turned to go to her locker. 'See you later.'

He was still there, holding out a memory stick. 'I thought you might like these. It's just a Steve Earle album you don't have – I looked on your shelves – it's one of the best, so – and this Ray Stinnett album. And some Bobbie Gentry – seems like your kind of thing maybe.'

'Oh.' She took it. 'Thanks very much.'

'Play them to Aisling too.'

Minny listened to the music he'd given her a lot at home over the next few days. Her mother was out in the evenings, gearing up for her play, so there was no one to notice and say anything sly. Everyone seemed busy; Selena was immersed in her Bible almost all the time. Minny caught her saying the rosary when she leaned over the side of her bed in the morning. She duly mocked her the first time but then let her get on with it; it was too odd for her to want to deal with it. Sel was also strangely affectionate – she kept kissing them all goodnight before she went to bed, and goodbye in the morning, and coming into rooms just to say something before she left again. Ash trailed around after Minny a lot, and on Friday evening came into her room where she was listening to 'Goodbye' again, carrying the guitar. 'I thought you might feel like playing it.'

'Er – why?'

'I don't know. I'd like to sing more, I thought you'd like to play the guitar.' She propped it up in the corner and left again. Minny eyed it for a while. When the album finished she turned off the iPod, ready to go downstairs, but instead she picked up the guitar. The thing was, she really hated tuning it. But Franklin had done quite a good job of that.

They all had plenty to think about anyway because Nita had announced that she'd invited their father and Harriet round for tea on Sunday. So that they could talk in a civilised way about things. She said Minny wasn't allowed to skip it, though Minny couldn't see how they wouldn't be better off without her if they really wanted things patched up.

'If I'm doing this because I think my daughters need a father, it pertains to all my daughters,' Nita said when she argued.

'But I don't want one, Mum, not like Selena does. I don't care about him.'

'Right,' she said, in an un-Mum-like way, like she couldn't be bothered being discreet and tactful any more. 'That's why you've had Kate Bush and David Bowie plastered to your bedroom walls since you were ten years old.'

That was below the belt. Minny liked Kate Bush. It wasn't anything to do with the fact that her father used to be obsessed with her. David Bowie, either. She spent all that evening thinking about what if they had to show him their rooms when he came and he thought she had them up there because of him? On the other hand she couldn't take them down, because then her mother would think whatever she would think. She cut up a bunch of magazines that night and stuck more pictures up so that none of them would stand out so much. It took absolutely ages. It was a shame none of them were of her mother's favourite singers, but it was hard to find disposable pictures of progressive country artists who'd had their pomp around 1978. Sel lay and watched her. She'd probably tell him they were all new anyway.

She hadn't emailed Uncle Kevin since the drama of her father coming back and then appearing outside Selena's school. Her relationship with Kevin had nothing to do with her father; it never had really, certainly not since he left. She didn't even know how close they were. It was possible Kevin might not know about his brother being back, and about Harriet and the baby and everything, although she was pretty sure he'd have heard by now from Granny. So late on Friday she tried to send a nice normal email about books and so on, and just mentioned in passing that they were coming for tea. Kevin was always nagging her for gossip about friends and especially about boys, and she never had anything to tell him, so this time, just for fun, she mentioned that she'd been hanging out a bit with someone who was a bit more interesting than usual. She didn't say it was the boy who was living with Kevin's mother. When she checked her emails about an hour later she already had a reply. He answered what she'd said but without his usual vim, and then got stuck into things about her father. Apparently she needed to have a more open mind. '*He may not have been the greatest father for the last few years, Minny, but he is your dad. I'm not saying this for his sake, you know. I think he needs to hear what you have to say, and I think all you girls might be better off having a dad, even if he's not the most reliable one.*'

Since they were coming on Sunday, of course her mother went nuts cleaning the house as soon as she got home on Saturday morning. As if Des didn't used to live with them; more to the point as if he hadn't seen it only a few days ago. 'Only the downstairs,' Nita said, polishing the bathroom door handle.

'What are you trying to impress them for?'

'Because I want him to think I've done an adequate job as a mother despite not being good enough to be his wife,' she said. Which took the wind out of Minny's sails. Her mother didn't usually say things like that. 'What are your plans this afternoon?'

'I'm going to the cinema with Penny.'

'OK. Just do me a favour and change your sheets first.'

Minny hated changing her sheets because, having the top bunk, it was virtually impossible. She had to perch at the top of the ladder and stretch all the way across without resting any weight on the mattress, or she couldn't get the fitted sheet around the top corners. The phone went downstairs while she was doing it, and she hoped it might be her father ringing up to cancel.

'Change your T-shirt,' she heard her mother saying as she padded downstairs with her bundle of dirty bedclothes five minutes later. 'And give your hair a brush.'

Aisling looked down doubtfully. 'What T-shirt shall I put on?'

'The blue one,' Nita suggested. 'It brings out your eyes.'

'Why does Ash need her eyes bringing out?' Minny asked, dumping the sheets.

'I'm going round to Granny's house to see Franklin.'

'What?'

'Franklin rang up,' Nita said, looking flushed and pleased, 'and asked Ash to go round this afternoon.'

Minny bent down to put the sheets in the washing machine. 'Will you come, Minny?' Aisling said.

'Was I asked?' Minny didn't get up or look round.

'I asked if you should come and he said sure.'

'I can't.' She stood up. 'I'm going to the cinema.'

'Oh.'

'Anyway, I'm not like you,' she said, since her mother had left the kitchen, hoover attachment in hand. 'I don't go places I haven't been invited.'

Minny and Penny went to see films all the time. It had tradition attached to it. They met in the shop on the corner opposite the cinema and bought a big bag of Minstrels or sometimes a box of Maltesers, and then they ate nearly all of them during the trailers. Which film it was didn't matter very much. Sometimes they didn't even pick until they got there. As it happened, the previous day they'd decided on a cheesy-looking semi-romantic comedy. Minny was just coming up to the shop, sweating from walking so fast over the bridge, when she heard Penny calling her and looked up to see her at the doors of the cinema. With Jorge. She was gussied up, with make-up on and heeled shoes. Minny hadn't even brushed her hair that day.

'Hello,' she said warily after crossing the road.

'Hi,' Jorge said, looking at her hair.

'Jorge wanted to see the film,' Penny explained, beaming. 'He likes Katherine Heigl.' Which seemed like a strange thing to make her happy.

'OK. Have you got the tickets?'

'Not yet.'

'Have you got the chocolate though?'

'Oh. We thought we'd get popcorn today.'

Popcorn. And not even salted popcorn. Overpriced, tongue-irritating butter popcorn. Minny slouched in her seat and tried to ignore the fact that she was blatantly playing gooseberry on someone else's pervy early-afternoon date rather than playing gooseberry with her mad sister and her new friend – or, she supposed, cleaning the house with her mother and little sister, which had been the other choice.

'I thought you might bring Aisling,' Penny said to her, coming up for air in the break before the film started.

'I never bring Aisling.' Minny took another handful of popcorn.

'You've been hanging out with her a lot lately though, haven't you?'

'Well, she's my sister, Penny.'

'I know.'

Minny tucked one foot under her. 'She doesn't like the cinema.'

'Oh.'

'Anyway,' Minny added suddenly, 'she's singing with Franklin today.'

'What do you mean?'

'Franklin Conderer?' Jorge asked from the gloom beyond Penny.

'Yes.'

'He's an idiot.'

'No, he isn't,' Minny said loudly.

Jorge stuck his hand into the popcorn. He didn't look away from the screen. 'He's a chav.'

Minny had unacceptable words boiling up sticky in her throat, but she could also feel Penny shrink a little beside her. The music started just then. She stared at the screen without seeing any of the credits.

It was a good film, but she couldn't laugh at any of it. She didn't take any more popcorn either. There was no one between her and the end of the row, and as soon as the film finished she stood up abruptly without waiting for the lights to come on. 'I've got to go.'

'OK,' Penny said, blinking up at her. 'I'll call you later.'

'Great.'

She thought about staying on the bus and going round to Granny's house, but decided she was too cross and would just get frustrated, since she could hardly tell Franklin the story. She might go home and tell her mother instead.

As it happened, when she got in Aisling had just got home anyway. She got nervous in other people's houses; not so much in Granny's usually, but none of them had been with her today. 'Did you have a good time though?' Minny asked her.

'Yes. We sang "We'll Sweep Out the Ashes in the Morning".'

Minny wanted to ask if she'd been mentioned at all. She also half wanted to apologise for having been mean, but they didn't do that kind of apology much in their house, and Ash probably hadn't even noticed it in the first place.

'And Granny liked it. She said we should make a record.'

'Nice.'

'Franklin taught me a new song. It's called "Clay Pigeons". He wrote the words down for me.'

She extended a grimy halved piece of paper, covered in red biro. Minny looked at it; the handwriting was jerky. The one good thing about Aisling was that you could ask her certain questions without having to worry about looking like a chump like you would with anyone else, because she didn't read into stuff. You weren't guaranteed to get an answer of course. 'Did you talk about me at all?'

'Yes. Franklin said he'd teach you to play the song if you wanted and why didn't you come round. I said you didn't want to.'

'You said I didn't want to?'

'Yes.'

'Did you say I was at the cinema?'

'Yes. Was the film good?'

'It was OK. What did he say?'

'He said, "Oh".'

Penny did ring her, just before dinner that evening. 'You rushed off.'

'Yeah, I had to get back. We had a lot of stuff to do.'

'Like what?'

'Cleaning.'

'Cleaning? You didn't mind me bringing Jorge, did you?'

'No.' Which wasn't exactly true, but it hadn't been the problem.

'I thought you might have done. You weren't very friendly, Minny.'

Minny thought for a moment about reassuring her. Ignoring her outrageous front in saying such a thing, and appeasing her, because it was just Penny and the way she was, and Penny was her friend. But her mother was calling her from downstairs anyway to wash her hands for dinner. 'No. He wasn't very friendly to me either. And I didn't like what he said about Franklin at all.'

'Oh, Minny. So he doesn't like Franklin, so what? Franklin's suddenly your best friend and we can't say a word against him?'

'Not a word like *chav*, no,' Minny said. 'It's a really terrible word. Look, I've got to go, it's dinner time.'

FIVE

All the cleaning must have disturbed the wildlife. At three o'clock next day, just when the guests were due to arrive, they were all in the kitchen bunched up around the kettle and the mug tree and Minny saw a fist-sized spider on the edge of the sink. It was one of the butch ones with thick black legs. She screamed and Babi spilled boiling water over half the ginger buns. Then there was a panic battle when they all got in each other's way, except Raymond who was trying to put the football into the washing machine, and suddenly they were all outside the front door.

'That was the biggest spider in the world.' Selena had gone as far as the street; she was white.

'What are we going to do now?'

'I hope someone has got keys,' Babi said. She was already smoothing her hair. She hated being undignified, but she was terrified of spiders.

'We left the baby behind,' Minny said.

'Oh God. I can't go back in there.' Nita breathed hard. 'What sort of mother abandons her own child in a moment of fear?'

'It's only a spider,' Ash said in a sensible voice. 'It can't hurt him.' Then they all started laughing, and next thing a car drew up behind them.

Their father was wearing his strategy like a suit of clothes. He was all friendly with Nita, polite and unhostile with Babi. He put his arm round Selena, but only kissed Aisling on the cheek as she stood looking awkward and didn't try even that with Minny – he just touched her arm for a second. Which was fine. Then they had to explain why they couldn't go in.

'I've got to though,' Nita said, suddenly alarmed, 'because Raymond can get the cupboards open and there are things in there – there's bleach under the sink.'

'Can't you go and put it outside, Dad?' Selena asked. 'Far outside?'

'Like over the road?' Minny suggested.

'Er –'

Nita grinned. Lines came on her face when she smiled, but they didn't make her look any older. 'Your dad's as bad as the rest of us, don't you remember? He'd run a thousand miles from a spider like that.'

Des rubbed his hands on his legs, looking uneasy. Harriet was laughing. She took the key Aisling was holding out – 'I'll do it.' When she'd gone inside no one looked at anyone. Des leaned forward and pulled the door shut again as if the spider might come stampeding out towards them.

'Hellooo.' There was a bit of a thin quaver and they turned to see Granny stumping across the road from her little car.

Selena ran to meet her, and Aisling shuffled that way too. Minny looked in surprise at her mother.

'Oh yes, I didn't say. Judy rang me this morning and I invited her. I hope that's OK, Des, and not uncomfortable?' Nita said rapidly.

He rolled his eyes.

Harriet had only been gone half a minute; Selena was still looking sick, though she'd started gabbling about the school play she was in, her head turning between her father and his mother, when Harriet opened the door again, holding Raymond.

The ice had to be re-broken then. Harriet looked dismayed when she saw the most recent arrival. Babi seemed amused; Minny supposed the more people there were there, the less risk Babi ran of actually having to talk to anyone. Granny kept patting all the girls whenever she got near them.

'Why did you invite Granny?' Minny hissed while she and her mother were waiting for the kettle to re-boil. 'I thought you wanted this to be as civilised as possible.'

Nita looked unhappy. 'She rang up, and she was saying she felt wretched because they just had a row, I think, when your father and Harriet were round there on Monday – not a good day for them; no one was very pleased to see them. I said I felt terrible about Harriet because we were so unfriendly – we didn't even ask her when the baby was due or anything like that—'

'You're unbelievable.'

'– and somehow I ended up saying, "Why don't you come along too?" Oh well, we all have to be able to be polite to each other.'

'Well,' Minny said, pouring boiling water into seven mugs – no one quite got a full one – 'we'll see, I suppose.'

Everyone was still milling around, except Aisling, as if no one wanted to be the first to sit down. Ash, who already had her fingers to her ears to block out all the strands of chat, had picked the corner of the sofa nearest the door, so that Minny had to keep squeezing past her with the tea. 'It's ginger and lemon,' she told Harriet, shoving it at her. Her mother had bought it especially. Her mother was too soft for her own good.

'Oh, gorgeous.'

When everyone had their tea, Minny had to find somewhere to sit – Nita had tried to dot the dining chairs around the room, but it didn't make it feel much less formal because the table was still there. Harriet was sitting on the sofa, next to Aisling, who had curled up as tight as she could in the corner. They were much lower down than everyone else. Minny heard hissing in the corridor, which was obviously her mother telling Sel to go and sit between them. The buns were nice.

Anyway it got a bit less awkward for a minute when the cat wandered in, then caught sight of the baby and immediately left again. Des looked incredulous. 'Was that really Guts?'

'"Guts"?' Harriet said, as if it was the most outrageous name in the world.

'I thought for sure he'd be dead years ago.'

'It's really Vonnegut,' Aisling explained to Harriet.

'Pretentious, much?' Dad said.

'But it got shortened to Guts.'

'Guts,' Harriet said, and began to giggle.

'I can't believe he's still alive.'

'He's not that old, Des,' Aisling said. 'He's only eight.'

'No, he must be older than that.'

He wasn't, Aisling was right – of course. Minny remembered perfectly well when they got him, three days after their grandfather died, to cheer them up. Of course it had the effect of making them want to skip the funeral to look after him: Ash screamed all the way there. When Penny's mother split up with her other mother not long afterwards, Penny's consolation prize was going to Disneyland in Florida. Parents did that sort of thing. In fact when her own mother had turned up pregnant with Raymond, Minny had half wondered if she'd done it to distract them from Dad being gone.

'Poor old Guts, he's no spring chicken anyway,' Nita said with a sigh. 'Raymond's doing his best to chase him into his grave, aren't you? He spends most of his time hiding under Aisling's bed.'

'Reds under the bed,' Ash intoned. Harriet looked at her. 'Reds under the bed, under the bed,' she whispered to herself.

'Aisling,' Babi said, 'not the reds again, please.' Babi had a thing about that particular phrase because she said none of them had enough awareness of their Czech heritage, and what the Communists did there and all that. But it was just sounds to Ash.

'So, Maude,' their father said, sipping his tea at Granny, 'where's Harold today?'

Nita and Harriet both looked at him.

'If that's a reference to Franklin, Desmond, then it's over my head, but he's visiting his mother this afternoon.'

'Oh yes? Dropping off your TV, is he?'

'Franklin's become a good friend of the girls, all over again,' Nita said loudly.

'What?' He looked at her, and them. 'What do you mean? He's only been with Ma a week, hasn't he?'

'Yes, but he's been round, and they've been round there.'

'You are kidding me. After all the effort we went to, finding somewhere with a good school full of reputable families, and you start setting our daughters up with the Boy from Borstal?'

Nita only half laughed. 'Des, you are the most insufferable snob. And you shouldn't talk like that in front of the kids.' Ash was staring into space, but Selena was listening and frowning thoughtfully.

'Sorry, sorry. You're right. I need to get back into practice, don't I, Sel?'

'You should never have got out of practice,' Granny said

over Sel's reply. 'It's disgraceful, talking about children like that. And Franklin's a lovely boy.'

Sel humphed a bit, but no one except Minny seemed to notice.

'You should hear him, playing the guitar, and Aisling singing like an angel.'

'All right, Ma,' he said, giving Minny and Ash both a quizzical look under his eyebrows, 'I'm sure he's a saint. It's just the idea of him living with you takes a bit of getting used to, that's all.'

'I don't see why. We're two lonely individuals: I had an empty room, he needed a home.'

'Yeah. Though if you're that lonely, I don't understand why you didn't just pack up and go back to Donegal a long time ago. Plenty of people there, and Tommy Feeney might rook you over the house repairs, but at least you wouldn't have to worry that he was actually going to run off with the silver every time you left him alone.'

'Oh, go home, is it, and abandon these children, the way you did?'

'Stop it,' Nita said. 'Des, that's enough about Franklin now. While he's living with Judy, not to mention friends with Aisling and Minny, he's part of the family, OK? You know, like you want to be.'

The doorbell went. 'Oh good,' Babi said. 'That will be Gil.'

Minny gathered from her mother's face that not even she had known Gil was coming round. Excellent. Still, why not.

He came in and had to be introduced – by Nita; Babi wouldn't lower herself to explain anything to Des. Or Harriet, or Granny. He bumbled around trying to find somewhere to sit; he did glance at the sofa as if he was thinking of squeezing on, but Ash looked horrified and Selena somehow managed to thicken herself instantaneously so that she was touching both Aisling and Harriet. Minny stood up in the end and gave him her chair so she could go and put the kettle on again. She didn't linger in the kitchen; she didn't want to miss anything. Her father was being quite good actually; he was polite to Gil and didn't try to wind anyone up. Granny looked hilarious, studying him through narrow eyes. Then she caught Minny's eye across the room and grinned.

'We brought presents,' Des said suddenly. 'Nothing big, only chocolates. Real presents a bit later on when I've caught up with what you like now. Here you go – Thorntons all round. Milks for Selena and Minny, darks for Ash and Milena – I looked all round for a box of Black Magic for you, Milena, but I couldn't find one anywhere—'

'Dessie,' Harriet said. Minny saw her mother glance at her and thought how strange it must be for her to hear someone else scolding Des.

'And for you, Nita, something special . . .' He handed her a gift box of Walnut Whips.

'Oh,' Nita said, taking them. Her cheeks, which were nearly always the colour of milk, flushed bright red.

'They're still your favourites?'

'You haven't been gone that long, Des,' she said, trying to laugh, and then looked even more embarrassed.

'Do you remember,' Aisling said, and Minny knew it was going to be one of those devastating moments, 'when you said Mum would do absolutely anything for a Walnut Whip, Dad?'

It was horrifically embarrassing, one of those times when it could have been nothing, but actually it was like her words were a huge church bell echoing around between everyone's heads. Just for a second of course. And the worst thing was that instead of being frozen by it like she normally would have been, Minny couldn't stop herself laughing. She tried so hard not to, she got hiccups.

'What about me?' Granny said after a moment.

'Well, now, Ma, I didn't know you'd be here, or I'd have sourced some Raspberry Ruffles,' Des said. 'And I brought you that bottle of Jameson's the other day.'

Granny sniffed.

'Anyway,' he went on, as they all got tied up in cellophane, 'there's so many of us here now, I hope no one minds but I want to hear all about my girls. What you love these days, friends and all that. Selena!'

Selena had no problem talking about herself in front of a roomful of people. Minny had sat down on the floor with her back against her mother's chair; Nita pinched her between the shoulder blades because she was still laughing and hiccupping through a mouthful of chocolate. By the time she got herself under control, Sel was telling her father all about how she got into feeling so religious – 'because once I could read *A Bear Called Paddington*, I just read them all, and then the next book on the shelf was the *Children's Bible* so I picked that up. And I really liked it, you know, the stories were really exciting, but it was, you know, a bit childishly written . . .' On the sofa next to her Harriet was riveted, but Des suddenly looked up at Minny and smiled. And she smiled back before she could stop herself.

'Of course some of it's a bit scary – there are whole books where it's all about people being terrible and horrible and God being angry and smiting them, so Mum makes me read a nice soft bit before I go to sleep every night. And then of course I say my prayers so that puts me back in touch with Jesus anyway.' She took a swallow of her juice and looked over the rim of the beaker.

'Well. Wow,' Harriet said.

'What a lucky thing the Bible was next to *Paddington Bear*,' Des said. 'Things could have been so different.'

'I know.' Sel nodded.

'I've never known such a bright little girl,' Gil piped up, managing to annoy both Minny and Selena at once, 'or such a serious one.'

Des looked at him. 'Oh, there's a joyful side to the Bible, isn't there, Selena?'

'There certainly is,' Granny said, glaring at the heathen.

Not many laughs though, Minny thought; she had to give that to Gil. Raymond had finished his milk on Nita's knee and got down to crawl over to the fireplace where his jigsaws and things were kept. Granny pushed her chair back out of his way. They all watched him.

'He's gorgeous,' Harriet said. 'How old is he?'

'Fourteen months,' Ash said. She had just been humming in the corner of the sofa while Selena banged on.

'Does he walk, and all that?' Des asked. He had leaned back on his chair and crossed his legs.

'No,' Nita said. 'Only crawling so far.'

'He crawls really fast,' Minny said. Her father looked at her and smiled suddenly again.

'You like him, Minny?'

'Yes,' she said, looking away.

'What about you, Aisling?' he asked her. 'Do you like having a baby around?'

'It's fine,' she said, shrugging. She did like Raymond, now he was older; she'd ignored him for most of the first year, just like she'd done with Selena, but now she was used to him. She read to him sometimes.

The doorbell went again. Des looked up to heaven. For once Selena stayed where she was, so Minny scrambled up and went to answer it – it was Franklin.

'Hi,' she said.

'Hi. Sorry. I forgot my keys,' he mumbled. 'I knew Judy was here.'

'It's OK. Come in.'

'I don't have to, if I can just get the keys.'

'Come in. Do you want some tea or something?'

He stood transfixed in the doorway; they'd all heard the bell and had gone silent, waiting to see who it was. Now they were all looking at him. 'He was locked out,' Minny explained.

'Oh, Franklin, sorry, love.' Granny started heaving herself to her feet.

'I'll make you some tea,' Minny offered again, and left him, but he followed her into the kitchen.

'God,' he said. He looked unnerved.

'I know. It's a bit of a pile-up. That's what our family apparently looks like these days.' Then she wished she hadn't said it, but she added bravely, putting a teabag into their very last mug, which was a Kit-Kat one Selena had got with an Easter egg, 'How's your mum?'

'Oh. All right.' He leaned against the cupboard and stared out of the window as she poured the boiling water. 'I didn't really go to see her. I mean, I just went in for two minutes to make sure she wasn't dead or anything.'

'Oh.'

'I just said that to Judy because she's a bit iffy about me going back to the estate. I think she thinks I'll disappear back to my criminal past.'

'Like Oliver Twist?'

'Probably. But I had to see my mate.'

'Oh.'

'Just had to make sure she was OK.'

'Oh, right,' Minny said brightly. 'Biscuit?'

'Thanks.'

'Girlfriend?'

'What? Oh. No. Nothing like that. She just used to live next door to me, that's all.'

Minny couldn't think of much to say. 'You tuned the guitar really well.'

'Really?' He grinned at her over the biscuit. 'Yeah, that's a talent. Have you been playing it?'

'Yeah, a bit.'

'When are you going to come round so we can play the two together?'

She cringed. 'I'm really not very good. You should bring yours round here. Then I won't be so embarrassed.'

Her mother came hurrying in carrying all the chocolate boxes. 'We need more biscuits; if Ash eats any more of this she'll puke, and that would just be the icing on the cake this afternoon, wouldn't it? Franklin, darling, have you got some tea? Well, both of you, come in then, please. If Aisling has to answer any more questions she'll run away for ever and your father's getting frustrated.'

'And how's school?' he was asking as they all filed back in. His eyes combed Franklin down before he smiled at Minny. 'How do you both like Raleigh?' He'd left only about a month after they'd started there, Minny in Year 7 and Ash in Year 8.

'I hate it.' Aisling had stopped trying to avoid his questions, though she looked like she was on the verge of running out of the room.

'Really?'

'Oh, Ash,' Nita said. Of course she knew school wasn't heaven for Aisling, but they didn't ask that kind of flat-out question very often in their house, because no one could deal with the answers. After all, you had to go to school.

'What about friends?'

'I don't have any friends.' He'd obviously forgotten what not to ask Ash.

'You have me,' Franklin said. Aisling smiled.

Her father shifted in his chair. 'Are you two in the same class?'

'Yes.'

'And you like some of the kids, don't you?' Nita encouraged her.

'A couple.'

'Well, that's friends, in a way, isn't it?' God, Minny thought, he was really clunky. He used to know Ash so well. 'What about the lessons? You were always so good – you must still like some of them?'

'What about you, Minny?' Harriet asked, which was a huge relief to everyone. 'What do you like at school?'

She shrugged.

'English?' Harriet hazarded. 'Your dad says you're a big reader.'

'No, I don't like it. I don't like my teacher this year.'

'Who have you got?' Franklin asked. They were both standing just inside the door.

'Mrs Lemon.'

'Oh yeah. Me too. She's rubbish.'

'I know.'

'My last school was rough, but the teachers were better. I don't even think she can read.'

Minny laughed. Ash, who also had Mrs Lemon for English, looked confused.

'What I'm dying to know,' Des said loudly. 'Well, one of the things, is how brilliant you all are these days. How you *do* at school.'

'They're all extremely bright,' Nita said.

'I thought so.'

'Now you can attend their parents' evenings,' Babi said from the back of the room.

It was bearable. It was awful, and not something anyone should ever have to go through, but it wasn't killing anyone; even Ash had managed to stay in the room, and it was civilised. Minny was just hoping no one would mention visiting Dad's flat, as if that was something they were going to be doing now. Babi, looking long-suffering, had taken the baby up to have his nappy changed, which allowed Nita to muster up the courage to talk to Harriet about her pregnancy. Minny heard her say the baby was due in September, which made everyone's heads shoot up because it was sooner than any of them had been expecting.

'Gosh,' Nita said, a bit lamely. 'You're tiny, considering.'

'Well, it seems to have spread all across me rather than just being a bump,' Harriet said. 'But apparently it's normal not to show till late the first time. Everyone I know has been threatening me, saying the second one makes you pop out straightaway.'

'You should try the fourth,' Nita said sadly.

'Anyway, I actually can't wait. I'm on tenterhooks.'

'And we've got some more news!' Des announced, rubbing his hands. '

'Oh God,' Minny said, 'it's not twins, is it?'

They all laughed, and she got embarrassed, but he said, 'No, but it is about our family –' he circled his arm energetically to show he meant him and Harriet – 'the new branch, if it's not too weird to call it that . . .'

'It is *quite* weird,' Aisling said.

Their granny rolled her eyes.

'But Harriet and I are getting married.'

There was a silence.

'Oh!' Nita said.

Selena squealed, in a non-verbal way.

'Mother of God,' said Granny.

'Oh, thanks, Ma.'

'Well, now, you're going to have to give me some time to get used to the idea.'

'Of course,' Harriet put in hastily.

Des waited a moment. 'And we would love it if you guys would be part of it. More specifically, we hope you three will be bridesmaids.'

This time it was Nita who got the giggles, and Minny who felt like pinching her. Things had been so polite she felt she couldn't just say, 'I don't want to be a bridesmaid.'

'I don't want to be a bridesmaid,' Aisling said. Thank God for that.

'Me neither.'

'Now, don't say that straight off.'

'I'm not going to put you in puffy pink dresses,' Harriet said. 'Unless you want me to.' She smiled at Selena, who looked troubled as usual.

'That's not really the point, Harriet.' Nita had got rid of her giggles quicker than Minny had. 'I'm sorry, but I don't think you can really put the girls in this position quite yet, Des.'

'Well, maybe I shouldn't have brought it up then. The wedding's not till next year anyway, so there's plenty of time to think about it.'

'I don't want to,' Aisling said.

Her mother glanced at her. 'I think I'm going to say right now that Ash doesn't have to.'

'Well, of course she doesn't *have* to—'

Nita cut him off. 'You might have forgotten, Des, that Aisling can feel very stressed out and pressured by things she thinks she's going to have to do, even if they're a long way ahead. And I can't see her changing her mind on this one. It's not the kind of thing she's going to like.'

'How do you know?'

'Excuse me?'

'Well, she's never been in this situation before, has she? It might be good for you, Ash.'

'How exactly might it be good for her?'

'Dessie,' Harriet murmured, 'we don't need to push this now.'

'And this is her father's wedding we're talking about; it's being a bridesmaid; it's the kind of thing most little girls dream about.'

'What, bridesmaiding when their father marries a woman who's not their mother?' Minny asked. 'That's some weird fantasy for all little girls to have, Dad.'

'I'm not a little girl,' Aisling said.

'That's right, Des, she's nearly sixteen. It's been quite a time since she was a little girl, but that's the time you missed. You can't come in here and suggest that your daughters owe you anything, or that one of them is strange or abnormal for not wanting to wear a ludicrous dress in front of a lot of people and be part of your wedding to a woman – excuse me, Harriet – she hardly knows.'

'Two,' Minny said. 'Two daughters. I'm not doing it either.'

'Now hang on a moment.' Her father was sitting in his annoyed-bear position. 'You can back off, Nita. If the girls truly don't want to once they've had a chance to think about it, then that's up to them. I'm just saying, this would be a chance to do something nice, not just for me, or for their new brother or sister, but for themselves. Get all done up, wear a pretty dress – it looks to me as if they might not often get the chance just to do that—'

'What?' Nita said loudly.

'Well, they're three gorgeous girls, Nita, growing up, and I just wonder, have your own personal opinions, and your feminist spirit – which you know I've always admired—'

'Oh, get to the point, Des.'

'If you let them wear what they might like to wear, and make the most of being beautiful girls.'

There was a pause. Most people in the room were rigid with embarrassment. 'What the hell are you talking about, Dad?' Minny asked.

'Do you get to buy many new clothes, Minny, that's what I'm asking.'

'Well, we don't have that much money.' She was surprised to find herself shouting.

'Now, I think everyone should just calm down,' Judy said.

Des ignored her. 'Mmm. And, Nita, how has the baby affected your finances, if you don't mind my asking?'

'I mind you asking.' That was Gil, of all people, suddenly standing up.

But Minny was already yelling over him, before she knew she was going to. 'Probably not as much as your new FAMILY.'

She was aware of Aisling and Sel sitting together on the sofa looking scared. And Franklin, though he was so close she could only see him out of the corner of her eye.

'It's all right, Minny,' Nita said. 'Des, you have to stop crossing lines like that. If you've got questions to ask me that are rude and intrusive, please don't do it in front of the girls.'

'Don't do it at all,' Gil said. He was tall, probably taller than their father.

Des stood up too. Only a little shorter actually. 'If it's not my business, Gil, it's certainly not yours.'

'I don't want to see anyone bullying Anita.'

'That's all right, Gil,' Nita said. 'I can stand up for myself.'

Everyone just wanted to hide by now, but thankfully Des and Harriet left quite quickly. Babi came downstairs with the baby and Gil swept her off, probably so he could give her the lowdown on what had happened. Judy and Franklin stayed to finish their tea, which was good because it kept Selena distracted and not actually crying. Nita wasn't in a frame of mind to comfort her, nor to talk to guests; she stomped all over the house and curses came whistling out from odd places every few minutes. Aisling had gone into her room. Minny read some books to Raymond and then left him piling up Jenga blocks with Franklin for a minute and went upstairs. Nita was pretending to tidy her room.

'He was always like that,' Minny said.

'Arrogant, egotistical, control-freaking insensitive arsehole.'

'Yeah, like that.'

'I shouldn't have lost my temper. Not in front of you three anyway. I shouldn't have let him lose his temper; he'll be sorry by now. But honestly . . .'

'Do you know she's a Liverpool fan?'

'What?'

'Harriet, she's a Liverpool fan.' Her mother had her mouth open, like a toddler when you distract it from screaming with something shiny. Then she started giggling, and they both giggled for a bit until Selena heard them and came upstairs with brimming eyes to ask just what was so funny.

SIX

They didn't talk about it much after that, except when Nita calmed down she and Babi did have a conversation that began at Gil. 'I'm not saying anything against him, Mama, I was honestly touched that he was defending me, but it was unnecessary.'

'You say that, Nita, but you always end up bowing down to Des and what you think he needs.'

'Not any more.'

'Oh, please. It didn't take long for him to be sitting in my front room with his . . . girl, his unborn child and his mother, did it?'

'I know it's your front room, Mama . . .'

'That's not the point.'

'But I really didn't need anyone to stand up for me. I already had to calm down Minny. Also, it ratcheted up the tension even more, which was not what I wanted. I want things to be easier for the girls.'

'You need to remind him of that.'

'I did, and I will.'

'It wasn't Gil's business,' Minny said, to no one in particular, gathering up dishes to lay the table.

'Look, Mama, the bottom line is that Des is the children's father.'

'Yeah,' Selena said, glaring at Babi. 'He is.'

'He is,' Aisling confirmed.

It got hot and sunny that week. On Tuesday Franklin came back from school with Minny and Aisling and they sat outside in the garden, taking it in turns to play the guitar and sing, while Raymond splashed in the paddling pool. Of course they'd had to laugh about the Sunday tea before anything else. Franklin was fairly careful not to mock their father too much, so they spent more time on Gil. 'He was pretty tough,' Minny said.

'Yeah, it was sexy,' Franklin agreed.

'Almost felt sorry for my dad there.'

Selena came out in her swimming costume and sat beside them for a while. She wanted to sing 'Midnight Special', and Franklin obligingly strummed along for a bit, but then she had more and more ideas, until Minny had to tell her to go away.

Penny was around more than usual all week because Jorge had some deadline for a module in geography. He finished on Friday and Penny had to go off to meet him. 'Do you want to go to the park later?' she asked Minny at lunchtime.

'Sure, maybe.'

'Good. Well, Jorge and I might be there too. See you if we are.'

Left alone, Minny sighed. Actually she was glad Penny wasn't going home with her, because she had to pick up Selena from school again and had already told Ash she could walk with her. She'd been sensitive all week about Penny *watching* her watch out for Aisling. Besides, she wasn't feeling very sociable by the time school finished because of PE being last thing. Back to tennis today; she only hit the ball once during the whole lesson, and sent it out.

As it happened, Franklin joined them as they were leaving school. 'We've got to get Selena from her after-school club,' Minny explained.

'I don't mind.'

'OK, but we'd better hurry up. If we're a minute later than half three they charge Mum more. I wish we were rich. Then we could just leave her there all night. In fact we'd never have to see her.'

'Poor Selena,' he said. 'We could go to the park after we've picked her up.'

'OK. If we go home now Gil'll just be there, and we're not allowed to make him feel uncomfortable so let's just stay out.'

'What about *Pointless*?' Ash asked from a few metres behind.

'Oh, watch it on the internet later. Or you can go back home if you like.'

'No, I don't want to.'

They were a few minutes late. Sel was standing in the

corridor outside her classroom waiting, tears leaking down her cheeks. 'What's wrong with you?' Minny asked.

'Nothing.' She was clutching her lunch box and water bottle and a sweaty handful of the stupid little animal toys she insisted on taking to school every day. 'I couldn't find my bag.'

'Did you look properly?'

'Yes.'

'Well, you'll find it on Monday.'

'But I can't carry all this stuff.'

'Here, gimme that. Ash, you take the lunch box.' But she couldn't get it into her bag.

'I'll take it,' Franklin offered.

'No,' Selena snapped. 'Then I'll forget it and I won't have it next week.'

'Give it here.' Minny emptied all the litter in it into the big bin which was supposed to be for paper. Used lunch boxes smelled terrible. 'Put your stupid toys in it and Franklin can put it in his bag for now, unless you want to carry it yourself.' Selena wiped her face and looked sulky.

The park was nice when they got there. Hot and green but with a breeze blowing up the paths off the river. They wandered down one, taking the longer, cooler way to the playground.

A man was fishing off the towpath, from one of those green folding chairs. He looked almost asleep. The river was fat and flat and oily. The water nearly always looked filthy, but it was still pretty at the park because there were so many trees, and green space on the other side, and ducks and swans swimming all around the moored boats. Minny always wondered who those boats belonged to. She'd lived around there all her life but never known anyone who owned a boat.

'And I will make you fishers of men,' Selena said absently.

'And they straightway left their nets, and followed him,' Franklin murmured on the other side of Minny.

They all looked at him, Selena sticking her head past her sister and squinting. 'It's "*at once* they left their nets and followed him."'

'OK.' He shrugged.

'There are different translations,' Minny pointed out.

Selena looked furious. 'No, there aren't.'

'There are, Selena.'

'No.' She ran off ahead. By the time they got to the playground she seemed to have stopped being sulky and was dangling from the monkey bars like a normal seven-year-old. Aisling could never resist swings. Minny found herself sitting on the metal fence with Franklin.

'How come you know Bibley things?' she asked after a while.

'I used to be into that stuff. Last year.' He shrugged. 'I stayed with some people for a while that were like a community – a religious community, you know?'

'Yeah?'

162

'They were OK; they were nice. I always sort of liked going to church anyway; it's chilled out. But it was a bit weird staying there, sort of too much. They didn't really have room anyway.'

'So you went home?'

'Yeah. Not really, that's when I came here.' He seemed fairly comfortable perched on a narrow metal cuboid.

Minny shifted a little. 'So how's it really, being at Granny's?'

'It's OK, honestly. There's plenty of space and everything, and it's quite nice having someone checking if I've done my homework or had breakfast before I leave.'

'I bet she fusses around you like anything.'

He looked thoughtful. 'She's not too bad really; she leaves me alone as well. I think she's afraid I might run off if I get annoyed.'

'Would you?'

'No. I haven't got anywhere else to go.'

'You couldn't go home?'

'Not for now. My social worker set up a deal to keep me out of trouble. I'm not meant to live with my mum again.' They watched Selena on the obstacle course. 'Course, I'll be sixteen this time next year, so I can do what I want then. But I won't want to go back to my mum's.'

'You don't miss it?'

'No.'

'How about school, is it OK?'

He shrugged. 'You tell me. No, it's good. It's different here – I don't know – you don't get the feeling that you're just stuck here. For life. There's loads of morons, but that's just like all over. And I'm the new kid, so I'd get nonsense anywhere.'

'What, are they picking on you?'

'Nah. Do you think if I get Selena an ice lolly she'll like me better?'

'I think if you get Selena an ice lolly she'll follow you home.'

They got down from the fence and strolled towards the café. It wasn't as festive as the ice-cream van by the river but it was cheaper. 'It's not bad for me, really,' Franklin said. 'I reckon if Aisling can put up with it there, I've got nothing to complain about.'

Minny stopped to look at the menu on the wall outside. 'Is it bad in class?'

'For Aisling? Yeah.'

'Like what?'

'Oh, I don't know, they groan whenever she says anything. And laugh and stuff. There's some name-calling. And no one ever speaks to her unless they're taking the piss, you know?'

'Yeah.' Minny's heart was heavy.

'The teachers just kind of ignore her, it's like they don't want to have to think about it. Not all of them, but some.'

'And what's she like, is she . . . is she distracting, or what?'

'No, not really, that's the thing. It's like they only pick on her because they know she won't deal with it, not because she's done anything to annoy them. She just sits there quiet most of the time. She ticks a bit sometimes, but that's pretty much it.'

Minny ordered two strawberry splits and a lager-and-lime lolly for Aisling. 'And – what do you want?'

'I'll get a strawberry one too, but I'm paying.' They wrangled for a bit and split it, so that Franklin could tell Selena he'd bought hers.

'Does anyone . . . touch her or anything?' Minny asked as they left the café. 'Get physical?'

'I've seen a bit of pushing and shoving. You know, some people will do it to any girl they can, only most girls know to stay clear, you know?'

'Yes.'

'She doesn't know when it's coming, that's all. It's not the end of the world, Minny. She might be miserable now, but you know, people are going to grow out of this crap eventually.'

'Not all of them.'

'No, but it'll get easier to avoid.'

He wouldn't come back to the house with them; he said he had a lot of work to do because he was going off back to North London tomorrow. Minny thought she might as well break the habit of a lifetime and do some homework too, even though it was Friday, not that she had any plans for the weekend. She looked over at Aisling, trudging beside her. Selena had run ahead. 'Franklin says people pick on you in class,' she said. 'And the teachers don't do much about it.'

'Yes, sort of.' Ash sort of wriggled, as if she was trying to shake off the question.

'You know that shouldn't happen, right? You know you're not doing anything wrong?'

'Yes.'

'Why don't you ever tell Mum about it?'

'I'm not good at saying things.' It's what Ash always said when you asked her that. She had learned to say it years ago; she had a set of stock phrases that she had learned placated people.

'You don't deserve that kind of crap.'

'Mum says this stuff happens. And I just have to put up with it for a while longer and it will get better.'

'It doesn't mean you have to put up with absolutely everything. Without saying anything. You can . . . not let them away with everything.'

'I'm not good at talking about it.' She struggled. 'I don't want to think about it when I'm at home.'

'Oi, you two,' Nita called from the doorway. 'Are you coming in? Because Raymond is mounting a bid for freedom here.' The baby was three-quarters hanging out of the front door. Selena's head appeared underneath her mother's arm.

'Did you get my lunch box off Franklin?'

166

Minny looked at her impatiently.

'Did you get my—'

'*Yes*, Selena, I've got your lunch box. Jesus.'

Minny couldn't get her head out of worrying about Aisling. In the middle of the night she woke up and found herself still doing it. Not only could she not forget about how miserable things must be for her almost all the time at school, she suddenly found herself considering what was going to happen to Ash afterwards. She couldn't see her in a job, or living on her own, or with anyone else. It was all very depressing. It also meant she didn't protest when Nita said that she was taking Ash shopping for 'a few bits and bobs'. Even though Minny's own trainers had holes in the bottom and she hadn't had any new clothes in ages. Her mother looked a bit startled when Selena didn't complain either. She'd been quiet for a few days, but she cheered up when Nita reminded her she had a birthday party to go to that afternoon. 'And what are you going to do, Minny?'

'Don't know.'

'Not meeting Penny?'

'No.' Her mother looked over at her, eyebrows raised. 'I might go to the park. Some people from school said they were.' Now that she was almost avoiding Penny, she found herself hanging out a lot more with girls from her form who also did not have boyfriends.

'What about Franklin?'

167

'He's seeing his . . . mother today.'

'You know,' Nita said, still sorting washing, 'you ought to invite him round for dinner. He hasn't eaten here yet. I think maybe he feels shy about staying. And it would probably be good for him to feel he has somewhere to go – you know, a nice, normal family like us. You should invite him properly.' She saw Minny's face. 'What's wrong with that?'

'Nothing. Only the food we eat isn't nice and normal. I mean, it's nice, but . . .'

'OK, I see what you mean.'

'Babi would be bound to cook brains, or something.'

'Well, how about we choose an evening when I'm doing the cooking, and I'll promise not to serve brains? Or offal of any kind?'

'. . .'

'You can choose what we have, how's that? Within reason.'

'All right.'

'So what will you choose?'

'I don't know.' Minny shuffled her feet. 'I don't know what he'd like.' You'd want to choose something sophisticated enough that you didn't look like a hillbilly, but on the other hand you wanted him to be able to eat it. He might not like fancy stuff; he might not have been exposed to it or whatever. Oh God, she sounded like such a snob even to herself.

Her mother gathered up the bundles of clothes. 'Oh, come on, Minny, he's probably not that fussy. He's been living with Judy and he hasn't starved to death.'

Minny had always known that her mother didn't have a great deal of respect for Granny's cuisine. Her father hadn't either. She hadn't particularly understood it as a child, when a meal that wasn't actually smoking or black didn't seem overcooked and when Granny served up stuff they never had at their house – roast dinners at weekends, and thick heavy puddings with custard or ice cream, or during the week pale chips glistening with fat from an actual chip pan and delicious 'Southern Fried Chicken' that came out of a packet wearing the brown coating. They weren't allowed it at home because their chicken had to be free-range. They hardly ate meat at all in those days, funny to look back on. Her father was a vegetarian. After he left there had been this evening when Nita was cooking veggie sausages and the pan caught on fire. Minny didn't suppose veggie sausages were particularly more flammable than meat ones; it had probably been an old disgusting pan that hadn't been cleaned properly because her mother was a bit crazy at the time, or else she had the heat up too high. The smoke alarm had gone off and Nita had literally thrown the pan into the sink with a cloth over it and then whacked it with the wooden spatula until the spatula broke. By then they were all crying and she gathered Selena, who was only four, into her arms and swept Minny and Aisling in front of her up to the shop on the corner and bought three packets of pork sausages and cooked them. They were eating cold sausages all the next day. After that she started cooking completely different sorts of things –

Czech food like Babi's, and other things she said her dad had taught her: big meaty curries and stews and dumplings. They even had meatloaf, and one kind of meat stuffed with another sometimes – it was usually delicious but really wrong at the same time. She said quite often that they should cut down again, that it was environmentally irresponsible and they were all going to die of bowel cancer.

'You could ask him what he likes,' Nita suggested.

'No, I don't think I can. That would just be weird.'

'Well, give him a choice. How about, the next time you're talking to him, you say, "My mother says why don't you come round to tea on Monday?" And if he says yes, say, "Would you rather have spaghetti and meatballs or chicken satay and noodles?"'

'Hmmm,' said Minny.

She went to the park in the end, because she was bored in the house on her own after Babi had taken the baby out, and she knew that people from school were gathering there, friends other than Penny, from her maths set, whom she didn't normally see outside school. It was still so hot that she wore a dress. The park was full of adults sunbathing, some of them even in bikinis, as if the word had gone out that this was the sunniest park in England today and busloads had been driven in from Margate or Blackpool. One woman was topless.

They were all sitting in a big clump at the edge of what was the rugby pitch in winter, and the muddiest bit of the whole park, but it was nice and verdant now. There were at least twenty people, all watching a handful of boys kick a ball over the rugby posts. Minny shuddered, particularly when she realised that one of the boys, all well-built and tanned, was Jorge. Penny was sitting with Emma Daly, who was there because Juliet was going out with one of Jorge's even more Jorge-like friends. Sophie and Marta, whom she'd been planning to meet, were about a metre away from them. Minny considered just going home before they saw her. On the other hand, she and Penny had been on the verge of a row all week; only serious defensive manoeuvres had prevented endless conversation about Jorge, his issues and his qualities versus Franklin's; and if Penny saw her before she got out of sight, it wouldn't be good.

'What are you sighing about?' She turned and Franklin had sauntered up behind her, his hands in his jeans pockets.

'What are you doing here? I thought you were going home.'

'Yeah, I didn't. I bumped into your mum and Aisling near the station and they said you were in the park.'

'Oh.'

'Meeting that lot?'

'Sort of.'

'Mind if I come too?'

'Sure.' They went up the path rather than cutting across the pitch, because the rugby ball was still flying about. 'I hate rugby.'

'Yeah, I can see that.'

'I hate anything to do with *balls*.'

'Right.' He raised his eyebrows. 'I'll remember that.'

Minny saw Emma look at them and say something to Penny while they were still a way off; Penny turned round and watched them coming. They'd been joined by Linnea Jessop, who was the most womanly looking girl in their year and had very long thick straight hair. In Year 7 Minny had accidentally set it on fire in chemistry.

'Penny doesn't like me,' Franklin said.

'Oh, pay no attention. She doesn't like anyone except Jorge at the moment.'

'Hello,' Penny said as they came up. 'I didn't know you were coming.'

'Well, here we are.' She sat down. 'Do you know Emma and Linnea?' she asked Franklin. He was still standing up, and she had to shade her eyes to look at him.

'No.'

'Why don't you sit down? This is Franklin,' Penny announced, to everyone within a few metres. 'He's just started at Raleigh.'

'Do you like it?' Linnea asked, looking at him.

'Yeah, it's OK.'

'Are you in our year?'

'No, he's Year 10.'

'Where's Aisling?' Penny asked.

'Out shopping. Why?'

'I just haven't seen you without her for a while, that's all.'

Jorge had stopped messing about with his ball and now threw himself down beside Penny. 'And she's hard to miss, isn't she?'

Minny looked at him frozenly.

'I mean . . . she's got a big personality.'

'How come you've moved school now?' Emma asked Franklin, her nose twitching the way it did.

Jorge rolled over against Penny, grinning. 'Oh, you got expelled, didn't you, Franklin?'

'Really?' Linnea breathed.

'Well, that's what he told us. Drugs, wasn't it?'

'Remind me, Jorge,' Minny said, pulling up grass, 'didn't you get asked to leave your last school because your marks weren't up to scratch?'

Penny glared at her. 'No, that wasn't the situation, actually, Minny.'

'Yeah, I got kicked out for having marijuana on me,' Franklin said, much more loudly than he usually spoke, 'but that was a while ago. I've just moved here – that's why I started Raleigh now.'

'Well, I think that's brave,' Linnea said.

'Oh, shut up, Linnea,' Penny snapped, echoing Minny's thoughts.

'I'm going for a smoke,' Franklin said, getting up abruptly.

'You can smoke here.' Linnea pressed her elbows together

and patted the ground next to her thigh, but he was already walking off. They watched him go.

Penny said, 'I guess he feels he can't.'

'Maybe it's what he's smoking,' Jorge said, getting up again to get the ball.

Minny wished she had gone with Franklin, but he hadn't even looked at her. She couldn't go and join a different group now. She lay on her back with her eyes shut instead. Emma started talking to Penny.

'You've been going out for a while now, haven't you?'

'Three months.'

'And is it . . . serious, would you say?'

Jesus, Minny thought, not again.

There was a lot of mumbling and giggling. 'I did actually go round to his house for dinner last night,' Penny admitted. 'His mum's so nice. She's really pretty as well. And she'd made this lush meal, it was the best salad I've ever tasted.'

'I suppose it had gold in it,' Minny said, without opening her eyes. Not very mature, admittedly.

There was a pause. 'What's that, Minny?'

'God, Penny, you're becoming a parody of yourself. The best *salad* you've ever eaten? What are you talking about?'

'What's your problem, Minny?' Penny looked ready to stamp. 'This is all Franklin.'

'No, it's really not. If anything it's Jorge – you don't like Franklin because he doesn't.'

'That's not true.'

174

'You don't even know him, Penny. You don't like him because Jorge doesn't, and Jorge doesn't like him because he's poor.'

'Oh, that's a good one. As if you don't only like him *because* he's poor.'

'Just like you like Jorge because he's rich.'

Emma and Linnea were trying to shuffle away without actually getting up.

'I can't believe you're saying this,' Penny said.

'Well, I am, so.' She jumped up. 'And now I'm going. I need a smoke as well.'

She found Franklin standing in the shade of the park-keeper's shed with his face against the wall. 'I'm going home,' she said, making him jump. 'I hate my best friend.'

'I'll walk you back then,' he said.

'I'm sorry about that moron Jorge.'

'Not your fault.'

'I know, but . . .' Minny shoved her hands in her pockets bravely. 'Are you OK? I mean, is your mum OK and everything?'

'As far as I know.' They trudged along the path side by side.

'I mean, last time you said you were going to check she wasn't dead. I know you were joking, only . . .'

'No, she's not that bad.'

'And I know that . . . the reason you moved here – you said you were in some trouble.'

'Yeah, only little stuff. Not only . . . you know what I mean. I just kept getting caught tagging stuff, and I was in a couple of fights, and then I was with a mate when he nicked a car . . . well, it added up. But I wasn't, like, dealing drugs or anything.'

'I know that, I wasn't saying that. It's just . . . I'm not being nosy, only if you ever want to talk about it. You've probably got loads of people to talk to about it, I mean.'

'Not really.' He jumped to catch hold of a branch for a second. 'Thanks.'

'S'OK.'

It was going on evening. By the time she got home she felt better, though a bit drained. Raymond came barrelling out to meet her in the hall, so she picked him up and carried him into the back room. There were bags all over the place. Her mother was lying on the sofa looking shattered and Sel was watching *Spirited Away*.

'Look,' she said, pausing it, 'look at my shorts!' They were pink with strawberries on. 'And this is for you!' She lobbed a bag towards Minny.

It had a Snoopy T-shirt in it and a yellow square scarf to tie over her hair. 'Wow,' she said. 'Thanks. What's all the rest of this stuff?'

'Most of it's Ash's,' Nita said. Minny dumped Raymond onto her middle and bent to pick up a bag she'd accidentally trodden on. A bra slithered out of it. It was beautiful, pink with spots and ribbons, and also clearly push-up. Her mother looked up at her. 'I thought she was old enough for some real underwear now. Your turn next.'

Minny didn't mind Ash getting a new bra. She was only a bit surprised because Nita used to harp on about how awful it was that shops sold these things for young girls. But then Ash would be sixteen in two months.

'And they went to the hairdresser,' Selena piped up, pausing her film again. 'Ash got a haircut.' Aisling never went to the hairdresser, since she had had a meltdown there when she was five. Nita cut her hair.

'Well, I was sick of her looking exactly like me,' their mother said, shrugging. 'I'll take you next time, Minny. Just because my hair just hangs off my head, there's no reason why you lot shouldn't have actual hairstyles.'

Minny heard Ash coming in and turned round. It was amazing. She couldn't say anything for a moment. Ash's hair had got longer and longer over the years since she'd stopped minding washing it, and it did a pretty good job of hiding her face. Now whoever had cut it had really taken a lot off so that it was just down to her shoulders, and they'd also cut a fringe, a really thick one. There she was with this blonde bob, all chic and everything. It was weird. 'You look different,' Minny said.

'I know.'

People noticed at church next morning. Lots of old people telling her how grown-up she looked. She looked worriedly back at them and dipped her shoulders at first; by the time they got to their normal row of seats – near enough the door to get out if someone had a meltdown, and near the kiddy books for Raymond and Selena – she was just ignoring them.

'You should say thank you when people give you compliments,' Nita whispered as they sat down.

'I don't want to.'

'Well, all right then, but try to smile if you can. It's nice of them really.'

'I would smile,' Selena said.

'We know you would,' Minny assured her.

Granny, in the row in front, turned round just then, saw Ash, put her hand to her face and nearly started crying. Franklin just nodded.

'Ask him round for dinner,' her mother hissed later as they came back from Communion.

'No, it's too weird.'

'Then I will.'

Granny was full-on chatting with one of her Irish pals when they met in the crush leaving the church. 'Did you see my granddaughter here with the hair? Isn't it terrible the way they grow up?'

'Oh, it is, Judy, it is.'

'Aisling, you are a beauty, child.'

Nita reached out over Selena's head and seized Franklin's elbow. 'Good to see you, Franklin. Surviving school so far? Would you like to come round for tea this week – say on Thursday?'

178

'Er – yes,' he said. 'OK.'

'That's great.'

'What do you want to be asking the boy over for,' Granny said, turning round. 'Won't your mother be cooking? And Franklin's not used to that kind of thing.' Minny and Nita were both taken aback. 'You know. What are you having, some old thing with pickles in it or something?'

'No,' Nita said. 'I was going to ask what you'd both like. You'll come too, won't you, Judy? I was going to ask if you would like spaghetti and meatballs better or –' Minny could tell she was rethinking the satay – 'or lamb? Or chicken?'

'You gave them three options,' Minny said to her as they left the building together, Selena dragging her feet and Ash skipping ahead.

'I had a sudden vision of all three of you – and me too – sitting looking at Franklin with spaghetti all over our faces.'

Once she was out of church, Minny noticed that Aisling seemed quite pleased with her hairstyle; she caught her looking at herself in the front-room mirror that afternoon. Still, walking into school with her on Monday, she wondered if it was really a good idea, giving a makeover to someone who would probably choose to be invisible if she could. Not that anyone said anything, except Andrew Fogarty, who bumped into them outside Minny's form room and told Aisling she looked like Goldie Hawn. Which was strange

179

on a lot of levels. But she heard people muttering, and one boy in her year, Matei Gonzalez, who was disgusting, said to her at lunch, 'Your sister, Minny, eh? Getting herself a nice little figure,' and nodded in a terrible way. Minny could have understood if he'd said something about her hair, but the fact that he noticed the very first *day* she was wearing a new bra – it was repellent.

'It's not as if she's suddenly a page-three girl, for God's sake,' she said to Franklin.

That evening she was watching TV on her own because the others were in bed when Nita came in. She thought she was in trouble again, but Nita asked her very nicely if she'd mind turning it off so they could talk.

'What about?' Minny asked, pressing the off button. She hadn't really been watching it anyway. She was thinking, depressedly, about English, and the fact that they were meant to read *Jane Eyre* over the summer. She'd tried it before, and it had been too hard.

'Well, I've been speaking to your dad a bit on the phone lately.'

'Oh.'

'Now don't shut down. Let me tell you what about.' Nita was putting on music as she spoke, Aoife O'Donovan, which was what she listened to when she was melancholy but didn't want to be. 'He's really anxious to start . . . building bridges with you girls. You know what I mean. He's dying for you to come round and see his flat, for instance. And

I've been thinking that it might be easier for all of you to really talk to him if you did go round there. And if I wasn't there, I mean, or your babička either.'

Minny didn't like the way this was going. 'Why?'

'Oh. Because I don't want you having to deal with any sort of misplaced sense of loyalty to me, I suppose, as well as all your other feelings. You know that I would like it if you could have a relationship with your father, don't you, Minny?'

'Yes,' Minny said, because she didn't want to listen to her mother denying that her father being around made her sad.

'And it's not as if we're talking about going to see him somewhere far away, is it? I mean, I wouldn't have shipped you off to New York, for instance. But it's London. If you were hating every second, or if something happened, well, you could just come home.'

'When are we talking about here, Mother?' Minny interrupted.

'You know I have to go up to Edinburgh in August, don't you?'

'Is that definitely happening?'

'Yes. Someone came to watch the rehearsal and talk to me and they think they definitely want it.'

'Wow. That's good.'

'Yes. But I've been worrying about what to do with you kids. Because you know yourself that Babi's attention span isn't the best for these things. Now, leaving her with Raymond alone I think would be safe . . .'

'In August?' Minny wailed.

'Yes. But the thing is, I don't want to just pack the three of you off there without – I don't know – making sure it won't be a complete nightmare. For you, or for Ash, or for Selena either.'

'What are you suggesting?'

'I'd love it if you would go and stay there for a couple of days sometime soon.'

'What, on my *own*?'

'Yes.'

'That's a terrible idea. Why can't one of them go?'

'Now, Minny, you know I couldn't possibly send either of them anywhere on their own. They need either you or me with them when they go to new places. And Aisling – especially right now—'

'But Sel's the one who wants to go. I don't want to.'

'Let me tell you why I think it would be a good thing.'

'You already did.'

'No, I mean for you. You would get a couple of days away from us here, which I think you might enjoy – in itself, I mean. You could do with a break. And you're the one who's really in control of how this goes with your dad. Yes, Selena is dying to see more of him. And when she knows him better, she can do that, independently of you and Ash if that's the way it works out. But, for now, she needs you to smooth the path.'

'How is that about what's good for me?'

'I got sidetracked. No, I didn't. Listen, you know you would like a relationship with your father. It's OK to admit that.'

After a struggle Minny shrugged. 'Maybe if I could design my own father. But I can't. The only one on offer is crap.'

'I grant you he's been a bad dad so far, all in. But he's not a bad *man*, so he's not going to screw you over on purpose. And he's desperate to rebuild this relationship, which means you're in a position of power. You call the shots. So take what you want. By which I do not mean money – before the dollar signs light up in your eyes, or else you get shocked with me – I'm not sure which is more likely with you. But figure out what you might like in your life that you don't have, and maybe you can get it from him.'

'But Mum – look how things got left,' Minny protested. 'I can't go round there on my own, after shouting at him the last time I saw him – and her.'

'No, OK, I can see that. But he's already apologised to me for what he said and, as a way of easing you in, he wants to take all three of you out for a nice afternoon.'

If she had led with that there was no way Minny would have agreed. Now she felt she couldn't not. 'Mnnn,' she moaned.

'Look, at the moment you've got no relationship at all with him, so what have you got to lose?'

Minny didn't have anything to say. The only real reason she had left for not agreeing to a weekend staying with them was that it was scary. The idea of going to stay, on her own, somewhere she'd never been was scary; the idea of having to hang out with two adults that, truly, she didn't know was scary; the idea of having to tell one of them why she was really, really angry with him was terrifying. But that sounded too pathetic, and anyway, it was more reason than ever to agree to this afternoon out, where at least she'd have Aisling and Selena to protect her.

SEVEN

It was a hard week at school. It was all getting a bit too much, between avoiding Penny all day, watching out for Aisling, and at home keeping an eye on Selena, who was very highly strung lately and kept bursting into tears, plus all the normal family stuff and Gil coming round all the time – and dreading going out with her father. They weren't told what he had planned, only to be home from school smartly on Thursday. 'But that's when Franklin's coming for dinner,' Minny said.

'And Granny.' Selena was doing a handstand, which was forbidden in the kitchen.

'Oh, that's right. Well –' Nita looked frazzled – 'do you think Franklin would mind if we asked him to come on Saturday instead?'

Minny sighed. 'I don't know. He's probably busy.'

'Go ring your granny and ask?' her mother begged. She was trying to wash up with Raymond balanced on her hip; he was teething and needy.

'Oh God, do I have to? It's a bit embarrassing. "You can't come round after all because we're going out on a picnic with our daddy".'

'Is it a picnic?' Selena asked, resurfacing with pink cheeks.

'I don't know yet, sweetheart. But your father's taken the afternoon off work especially so I think . . . oh, I'll ring them in a minute.'

'No,' Minny said, 'I'll do it.' She got Franklin of course. Typical. He listened without comment while she explained. 'Mum says can you both come round on Saturday instead,' she finished.

'Sure, probably.'

'You're not busy?'

'I don't think so. I'll get Judy to ring you.'

'OK.' She waited. 'I'm really sorry. None of us actually want to go. But . . .'

'You have to. Yeah. It's your dad and everything.' He didn't have a dad of course. Minny wished it was Penny; she'd never much minded putting Penny off, whatever was happening. 'I'll see you at school,' he said.

'OK.' Actually he probably wouldn't. At least she never seemed to see him there much.

On Thursday Minny was poised to leave school sharply at ten past three. She had even grabbed Aisling on her way to the cloakroom to get her things, and pinned her in a corner so they couldn't lose each other; she'd promised Nita, and Selena, they'd both be home by half past. Only Penny came belting up to her just as she was slamming her locker shut. 'Minny – can I talk to you?'

'Um – I have to go.' She gestured at Aisling, who was gazing into space.

'Please. Can we talk?' She looked upset.

'I can't, really, Penny. Unless you come with us right now. We promised we'd be home by half three.'

'Why?' Penny demanded.

Minny sighed. 'We're going out with my dad.'

'With your *dad*?' Of course, she didn't know any of the ins and outs of this.

'Yeah. Sorry, can't be late, we said—'

'Fine.' She flung off without even saying goodbye.

When they got home Nita was belting around finding sun hats and enough sun cream for everyone, and before they got any questions answered they had to go upstairs and get changed into clean clothes. Their dad turned up before they were done and shouted, 'Hurry up, the light's going,' up the stairs, which was ridiculous considering it was twenty to four on a midsummer afternoon and absolutely blazing sunshine outside. Then, just as Minny was about to run down the stairs, he yelled, 'Bring the guitar.'

'What?' she demanded, hesitating at the top. 'Why?'

'To add to the romance of the evening.'

'You're not putting us up on some stage, are you?'

It turned out that what he had planned was an evening going up the river in a boat – or down the river – Minny had never grasped which way was which, but anyway it was a turn-up because they'd never done that sort of thing before. The girls all looked at each other, unsure, but their mother said it was a great idea. 'What will you do?' Minny asked, getting sun cream rubbed energetically into her shoulders.

Nita laughed. 'Oh, Raymond and I have got big plans about dinner and the park. He'll be walking when you get back, all he ever needed was a little one-on-one attention.' She picked the baby up as they were going out and held him like a teddy bear.

It was the worst-looking boat ever. Des had clearly not seen it beforehand because he looked very doubtful as they all clambered in; it looked most like a tin bath. It did have a motor; at least they didn't all have to learn to row. There were life jackets, but only for Selena, because she was under eight, and Aisling, who couldn't swim. Minny was pleased she didn't have to try to carry one off. It was scorchingly sunny on the river at first but after a while it got a lot softer and the breeze was cooler. It was all very strange – they didn't go further into London – 'too much traffic,' he said, looking slightly anxious – and so everything got greener and greener, with willows dipping their fingers in the water like Selena did (till Aisling mentioned the rats), and gold-and-green meadows, and old grey houses all in rows looking like something out of Charles Dickens, only cleaner. The horse chestnut trees were lit with pink-and-white candles. They saw horses a couple of times. Their father insisted that they all try driving the boat; Minny nearly put them into the bank, but Aisling was surprisingly good, and Selena, with her legs dangling down like Kermit the Frog, kept it straightest of all. Her father took the guitar and reminded them of the old songs that had been in the house a lot when they were small. Aisling naturally remembered all the words. He couldn't concentrate though, for watching where the boat was going, so he passed the guitar over to Minny. When they'd finished singing 'I Shall Be Released', with Minny strumming, hotch-potchily, behind the voices, he leaned back and stretched.

'Beautiful,' he remarked. 'You sing just like your mother, Aisling.'

'I know.'

'And you, with the guitar,' he said to Minny. 'Did you ever hear the story of how your mother and I met in the first place?'

'Yes,' they said together.

'*I* haven't.' That was Selena, still concentrating on the steering.

'Oh, Selena,' Minny said impatiently, 'you must have.'

'I haven't.' It wasn't much of a story really, more of an atmosphere, and they knew it backwards. Their father had heard of a band, when he was at university, who were looking for a second guitarist – 'I thought it would help me meet girls' (their mother would say he'd worked his way already through all the girls on his course) – and then he turned up to a practice to meet them and the singer, and guitarist, *was* a girl, Anita Andersen, their mother. And even though the kind of folky, country music they were playing was not

189

at all his kind of thing, he immediately turned hippy and gave up rock. It was so familiar, listening to it, even though they were in a boat and everything was different, that Minny almost found herself wishing that the last few years hadn't gone the way they had, and that her mother was the love of her father's life, the way she'd been meant to be. For all the good it did.

The sky was turning pale blue behind them when he started looking out for the stopping place – a beautiful old pub with outdoor tables where they bought chips and burgers that seemed to have half a chicken each in them. He had deep-fried halloumi in his, but he didn't get to eat much of it once Selena found out it squeaked in her mouth. Minny watched Sel throwing bits of her bun at the ducks, and Ash talking to Des about football transfer rumours, and reminded herself that the weather, and the river, and the English landscape were all on her father's side today and giving him a distinct advantage. But she couldn't help feeling mellow.

'You know, Ash,' her father said, pinching chips off Selena's neglected plate, 'the last time we talked about this kind of stuff, most of the time you were on about made-up players and your own version of the leagues.'

'Hmm. I know,' Aisling said, going a little pink. 'But do you think that Man United will buy him?'

'I don't know. It's interesting. Do you never make up people now? You used to love it.'

'Not really, Des.'

'Why not? Did you grow out of it?'

'Hm, maybe.'

'The one I really missed,' he said, draining his pint, 'was Roger Ram.'

'Oh, Roger Ram, yes.'

'We still hear about Roger Ram sometimes,' Minny put in.

'Roger Ram was never one of the people I made up,' Ash said seriously. 'I just sang the song about him.'

'Yes. To annoy everyone.'

'Well, I missed him,' Des said. 'In crowded New York subways and in Central Park and up the Empire State Building and – especially – going round the Guggenheim, I missed him.'

Then it was all pile back into the bath because they suddenly realised it did get dark even in July, in the end, and they didn't know what to do about lights or anything. But they made it back safely, going rather faster and straighter, and seeing the houses and trees start to loom on the banks as the shadows got deeper. 'Shall we have the old guitar out again?' Des asked as they passed the horses, standing peacefully in the dusk.

'No,' Minny said. She was too settled to want to move. 'I think I've exhausted my repertoire anyway.'

'Do you remember when you were going to be in a band, with your friend Penny?' he said. 'What happened with that?'

'She just wanted to sing awful songs and wear lipstick

and cropped T-shirts,' Minny said. She leaned back against the side of the boat. It was tempting to trail a hand in the water, now that it was reflecting the lights from along the banks like rippled green glass. 'How do you know about that anyway? That was after you left.'

'No, it wasn't.'

'I'm sure it was.'

'I distinctly remember the pair of you in cropped T-shirts creating a lot of noise.'

'Disgusting pop songs,' Sel said with relish. 'Raunchy.'

'They were not raunchy, Selena,' Minny said, while their father roared with laughter. 'We weren't doing anything raunchy AT ALL.'

'Well, would you have sung them to Father Hilary?'

They quietened down after that, and Sel was asleep when they moored. 'I hope she didn't get too much sun,' Des said, lifting her up. Minny was thinking about her mother – she'd felt oddly guilty leaving her behind earlier.

'So you had a good time?' Nita asked, after Des had left and she'd got Selena into bed. Babi was still out, and she'd been drinking wine and listening to Townes Van Zandt.

'We did.'

'I don't know why we've never done that before. It seems crazy when you think about it, living on the river like we do.'

'Yeah.'

'So . . . you're all right about going to stay at the flat?'

Minny wouldn't have said she was all right. She was dreading it. One afternoon with her father and sisters was not the same as a whole weekend at his unknown flat on her own with him and his pregnant girlfriend. Still. It was more than a week away. This weekend all she had to do was entertain Franklin Conderer at dinner.

'I'm sorry we had to go off on Thursday,' she said to Franklin, while they were laying the table on Saturday evening.

'It's OK. It worked out quite well, I went up North London instead. To see the guys at Wellspring. You know – where I was staying before I came here.'

'Oh, right.' She hauled the table around so that Babi's place would be straddling the table leg. 'Actually, no, I don't really know. You haven't said much about it.'

He moved the pepper closer to the salt. 'It was just a place, with people living in it who were, you know. Into God and stuff. Spreading the Word. Some of them were really good guys.'

'How did you end up there?'

'It was my mate, who lived next door – she knew them from her church. And I couldn't stay at home because my mum was going a bit nuts and taking loads of drugs and stuff at the time. I'd been getting into trouble, but they still said I could go and stay there, if I behaved.'

Minny straightened the chairs. 'Could you have stayed on for ever?'

'Not really. My hearing came up in the end. The thing was, they didn't really do things like taking on full-on parental responsibility, and I couldn't ask them to do it for me. And my mum didn't want me living there.' He grinned. 'She thought it was a cult.'

'So did she want you to come home?'

'That wasn't going to happen. But she thought of Judy in the end and got the social worker to ring her.' He shrugged. 'I'm glad really. It was all right there, but it was a bit intense for long-term.'

'You're very calm about it all,' Minny said. She felt shy. 'I mean, your mum and everything. You were pretty mental when we were little, the way I remember it.'

'I don't know. You can be all angry. But there isn't much point really. I mean, this guy Christopher, at Wellspring, he said something to me when I was a bit cut up once about my mum being so useless. He said that you can't change the past, you can only change the future.'

'Right.'

'And that's all anyone can do. So it's best not to be one of the people who get all hung up on the past.'

Pondering, Minny went to get drinks while her mother served up the chicken diablo. When she came back Selena was capering around wearing Gil's hat, which he'd left behind the previous evening. Franklin and Ash were laughing.

'I'm Gil,' Sel said, thrusting out her hips. 'I've got a big tummy.' It wasn't exactly biting satire, but it made Minny giggle. Unfortunately Babi was just coming in with the rice.

'I just find it a little offensive.' She was still going on about it after hands had been washed and grace said. It wasn't like Babi not to play it cool, especially in front of Granny, who seemed to think the whole thing was hilarious. 'When Gil is here with us he is my guest. He is also a gentleman of a certain age who is entitled to a little respect.'

Granny speared a piece of chicken and muttered something about being a certain age herself and beyond being told who to respect.

'Anyway,' said Minny, 'I don't see why we should respect him just because he's old.'

Babi glared at her. 'It's not just because he's – it's not just because of his age.'

'Well, what then? Because he was in the army?'

'Yes, maybe.'

Minny put her knife and fork down, ready for an argument.

Nita sighed. 'Look, let's not talk about it any more. It's a bit difficult to cope with the parameters of this family sometimes, that's all. Girls, leave Gil's hat alone in future, all right?'

EIGHT

Trying to keep her eye on Aisling at school turned out to be a giant fail the following week. Minny was in the chemistry lab one afternoon doing some unbelievably tedious experiment badly when the door opened – they were very thick heavy doors, but still it nearly slammed back against the wall, and Franklin busted in. Penny, who was on the next bench, dropped her test tube and then immediately cut her finger on the fragments.

'Franklin Conderer!' Mr Gilliam barked. 'Have you never been taught how to enter a room? We're conducting an experiment here. What do you want?'

Franklin didn't say anything at all to the teacher, just kept on looking around the lab till he saw Minny. He was panting. 'Er –' he said, coughing hackingly. 'I think you'd better come. It's Aisling.'

'What is?' Minny asked, starting across the room still holding her boiling tube.

'We had PE – I don't know, I was playing basketball, but we just came back in to get changed and someone's ruined her clothes. She's upset.'

Minny was at the bench nearest the door before she

thought to put down the boiling tube, which also broke.

'Minny!' Mr Gilliam shouted.

'I'll be back in a minute,' she shouted back. Then she was galloping down the stairs with Franklin wheezing beside her. She started undoing the string of her lab coat.

'I said, should I get you, and the teacher said no.'

'They don't normally.' She nearly tripped as they rounded the corner of the second-floor landing. 'After I got suspended that time, they said to remember my school experience has its own integrity or something.'

'Yeah,' Franklin panted, 'but that's bollocks, isn't it?'

'What happened?' She didn't know why she was so panicked; she didn't normally feel responsible for Ash when she had a meltdown. Franklin having fled across the courtyard and up three floors to get her probably had something to do with it.

'Bitches in my year. Stuffed her clothes in the toilet while we were outside.'

Minny could hear Ash screaming as they went in the door of the main building. She wished her mother was there, and that she was fitter.

They were all standing around; the teacher hadn't even thought to tell them to sod off so that Ash could have a chance to calm down. Mrs Lynley was walking around her helplessly in a circle trying to be heard, and the SENCO teacher was just turning up. No one had even got the clothes out of the toilet, though Minny could see why. They weren't just stuffed in there, they were soiled. She went up to Ash and put her arms around her tightly. Sometimes that worked when their mother did it. Ash was bright red, every part of her skin that could be seen.

'It's OK,' Minny soothed through the shrieks. Aisling took a huge breath that made her choke. 'It's only clothes.'

'It's my favourite j-jeans and my . . . new underwear.'

Minny could see the pink strap of the bra, trailing out of the toilet bowl. She let go of Ash, who banged her head against the nearest metal locker. 'Who did it?' Minny said, only it came out as a shout.

'That's not the point right now, Minny,' Mrs Lynley said. She started trying to get near Ash again.

'Aisling needs to get a grip on herself and calm down,' Miss Lloyd the PE teacher sounded actually angry. With Ash. Minny noticed she had her arm around Maria Hoyle, who was holding onto her own face and apparently crying.

'Was it her?' she demanded.

'Shush now, Minny. Shouldn't you be in class?' Mrs Lynley had got between Minny and Aisling.

'Was it you, Maria?'

'Leave Maria alone.'

'Leave her alone?'

'Yes!' Mrs Lynley lowered her voice. 'Aisling hit her in the face. I know she's distressed but – we need to get her to calm down. She's not doing herself any good.'

Minny looked around at them all. There was half a classful of them standing there, watching; no one was sniggering now, like they must have been ten minutes before when Ash came into the locker room; they all looked shocked because she'd lashed out in total despair at one of the people being cruel to her. Now she'd probably be the one in trouble. Mrs Lynley, and Miss Lloyd, and Miss Terry, who was supposed to be the teacher with special responsibility to protect Ash, were all just standing there, with the people who'd been in her class since she was twelve and Maria Hoyle with her slightly marked face.

'Right,' Minny said. She went around Mrs Lynley and over to Aisling's locker. She knew there would be a plastic bag in her school bag 'for emergencies'. She found it and started putting the clothes into it, which was icky. They were all watching as if they were in a trance. Then she put her arm around Ash and guided her towards the door.

'Thank you,' she said to Franklin, who was almost breathing normally again.

'You can't just walk out of here,' Mrs Lynley called. 'This is school.'

'Yeah, OK,' Minny called back, steering towards the main door.

She managed to get Ash right out the gate and down the street; it took all her strength, not that Aisling was resisting exactly, but she didn't know what to do with herself. 'We're going home,' Minny kept saying. She could never drag her all the way there. Thankfully she had her mobile in her skirt pocket. Her bag with her keys was still up in the chemistry lab though. When they got to the corner with the main road and she could see there was no one coming after them, she stopped where Aisling could lean against a wall and called her mother. Of course Nita didn't answer, she never heard her mobile when she was teaching, but Minny left a message. Then she tried the house in case Babi was already there, but no one picked up.

'What are we going to do now?' Aisling asked, wiping tears and snot back to her hairline.

'Shhh,' Minny said, 'don't worry.' She dialled her father's number.

He answered immediately. That was working in an office for you. He listened, and was decisive. 'Call your babička,' he said.

'She's not at home. I think she's in one of her meetings.'

'Call her on her mobile. If you can't get her, go straight home. Straight home, but let me know and I'll get my mother round. I'm on my way, you hear me?'

'Yes.'

'I'm getting a taxi.'

'But we'll be all right once we're home. Mum will be back soon anyway.'

'I don't care, I'm on my way. Just get your sister home.'

She didn't know why she'd called him really, except she sort of wanted him to come steaming across London with three lawyers and scare the bejesus out of everyone at the school. She called Babi, who sounded guardedly surprised as she answered her mobile but who said she'd be right there.

They waited. They were on a good stretch for the car to stop. When Babi pulled up they both got in the back.

'Your mother is picking up the baby. They'll be home in a few minutes,' she said. 'I didn't try to call her because I was afraid she'd want to go to the school straightaway.'

'We're not going near the school,' Minny said.

'No,' Babi agreed, and did a screeching U-turn right in the middle of the road.

It took all afternoon for Nita to calm Aisling down in stages and be on the phone to the school in between. Their father spent most of it looking after Selena, who was upset, partly because no one had remembered to pick her up on time, but he did have one short conversation with the headteacher, Mr Boyne, which almost blasted their eardrums in the next room before Nita hurriedly shut the door. Eventually the clock ticked round to takeaway-time and Babi took Selena and the baby out to pick up a Chinese. Nita called Minny into the back room, where Aisling was huddled on the sofa and their father was waiting. 'We don't need to make major policy decisions right now,' she said, 'we're all upset, but I just want to reassure you, Ash, that this was a big deal and that we're not going to try to forget about it or anything. Also to tell you both that you are not in any trouble.'

'No, you are not,' Des said.

'I can't say that we're on precisely the same page with the school on that at the moment, but that will absolutely be sorted out.'

'Yes,' said their father, 'because otherwise I will sue them through the courts and they won't like that.'

It seemed to Minny that her sister needed to hear something more definite about her future, however upset they all were. 'Aisling can't go there any more, Mum.'

Ash looked up at her and wiped her nose on the cushion. Nita put her tea down and rubbed her eyes with the heels of her hands, so that the remainder of her mascara and eyeliner smeared all around her eye sockets. 'What do you say about that, Ash?'

Ash didn't say anything.

'It's not fair to make her go back. She's had enough.'

Nita looked at Des. 'I think Minny's right.'

'Yes.'

'Would it make you feel better, Aisling, if we said you don't have to go back to Raleigh?'

Aisling removed the cushion from in front of her face. 'Never?'

'Well. It's nearly the summer holidays, which will give

us a bit of time to explore options to get you through till sixth form—'

'Never, if you don't want to, Ash,' their father interrupted. 'Look, Nita, I'm sure you know a lot more than me about what's available, and I know you've been teaching her maths for ages anyway, but I have a bit of spare cash now – we could look at tutoring. We'll figure it out.'

Nita looked at him, and then at the girls, wearily. 'Yes. We will figure it out. Aisling, if you don't want to go back to that school you don't have to. Ever. Tomorrow we'll figure out a plan so you can do some work here, till term ends. I'll have to jig my hours a bit so you're not on your own too much, and we can worry about next year later. OK?'

'OK.'

'Come and help me lay the table – they'll be back with the dinner soon. I bet you're starving.'

Des leaned back and rubbed his hands together. 'Great. We'll get this sorted, Minny, you'll see. Now I almost hope the school does push it and try to take us on, so I can really bring them down.'

'Great,' said Minny. 'Thanks very much.'

'Oh yeah, I forgot you'll still be there.'

'So what's the plan now?' Minny heard Babi ask as she was taking the cardboard lids off the containers and Nita was tying the baby's bib on.

'There isn't one yet. We'll have to think, but we've got

time before September. Tutoring maybe, if I can find the right—'

'Who's going to pay for it?'

'Well, Des is talking about—'

Babi snorted.

NINE

Going into school the next day was intense. Minny kept telling herself it was pathetic to feel nervous, because nervous of what? None of the teachers were going to get in her face after the pasting they'd been promised by her father, and she wasn't going to get bullied. She wasn't Aisling. Still, on top of the oddness of things with Penny, who'd been ignoring her even more vigorously since the afternoon they'd had to leave early to go on the boat, the strange feeling of pride about yesterday and the contempt for almost everyone in Aisling's year – she was adrenalised.

Franklin was hanging around outside her form room. 'Is Aisling all right?' he said, straightening up when he saw her.

'Yeah, I think she will be. She was really upset all yesterday, but my parents calmed her down. My dad put a rocket up Mr Boyne about it.'

'Good.'

'Yeah. So. But I don't know what it will actually achieve, like if anyone's going to get punished.'

'I heard they might get suspended.'

'Really?'

'Yeah, if only they can sort out exactly who it was. But for a bit yesterday I thought Aisling was going to be in trouble for hitting that girl, she's not, right?'

'No.' Minny leaned on the door. 'That was partly what Dad was screaming about on the phone to Mr Boyne.'

'Screaming? Was he really?'

'Yeah, it was loud. But anyway it wouldn't have mattered, probably, because Ash isn't coming back.'

'What do you mean, she's not coming back?'

'Mum's going to try and make other arrangements – I suppose like a college or internet tutoring or whatever. Home-schooling. For next year.'

'You mean she's finished here?'

'Yep.'

'God. Well, that's good. For her, I mean. Isn't it?'

'Yeah, it is,' Minny said. 'I mean, no one can say we didn't give it a good go.'

People in Minny's class asked her about it, but she tried not to say too much because her parents had advised her it wouldn't be helpful. She saw Penny looking at her in biology, not that she said anything.

Then, at break, when she was walking across the courtyard on her way back from the science block, Maria Hoyle came stalking up to her. Minny stopped.

'Where's your sister?' she demanded.

'She's not here.'

'She's trying to get me expelled.'

'I really don't think she is,' Minny said, looking to see who was around them.

'It wasn't even me, you know. I had hardly anything to do with it.'

'Well then,' Minny said cheerfully, 'be sure to tell Mr Boyne who did do it, and I'm sure you'll be fine. Pip pip.'

Veronica Sedgwick, Franklin's pal, was standing near the outside door, watching. She had patchwork shorts on that showed the bird tattoo on her thigh and a smock top that literally had paint on it. 'Are you all right?' she asked as Minny went past.

'I'm fine.'

'She wasn't trying . . . ? Minny, how's Aisling?'

Minny stopped to look at her. She didn't know her very well. 'She's traumatised.'

'Yeah. Will you tell her I said hi?'

'Sure.'

She did tell Ash. They went for a walk that evening because Nita said Aisling had to get out of the house, she'd been in all day. Franklin was there too, and with three of them, Minny felt quite safe taking Ash to the park, where people from school might be. 'Veronica Sedgwick said to say hi.'

'Oh.'

They walked past the huge weeping willow near the tennis courts, and Aisling pointed it out to Franklin.

'That's the church.'

'What?'

'When we were little,' Minny explained, 'we used to call that tree the church.'

'Why?'

'Well. Come in and see.' She held back some of the drooping branches and ducked underneath. In summer you could hardly see out, or hear much from outside either, and the branches arched far over your head like a tiny cathedral. The light was all yellowy green in there, and the ground bare and dusty. Aisling sat down, as a matter of course, so the others did too. Franklin lit a cigarette.

'I thought you were giving up,' Minny said.

'I am. First today.'

'I like the smell,' Ash said absently.

They didn't stay long. They were giggling as they crawled out because they'd been talking about Gil. 'Your gran's pretty sexy in her way.'

'EW.'

'So what does she see in him, do you reckon?'

'I don't know. I said that to Mum once and she'd asked Babi – well, not in those words – and Babi just said something about him having been in the army. Which is really weird because she's always telling horror stories about soldiers – you know, back in the day in Czechoslovakia, and she hates England anyway. But Babi just told her he was more interesting than he looked.'

Clear of the willow, she straightened up. Typically, Penny

was just walking past with Emma and Andrew. She stopped and stared, really more than was necessary; Minny muttered 'hi' and was prepared to walk past, but Penny said, 'Minny, can I talk to you?'

'OK.'

'We'll wait by the gate,' Franklin said. 'Come on, Aisling.'

They walked onto the tennis court, away from the curious eyes of Emma Daly. Penny turned with a loud scrunch of gravel. 'What are you doing?'

'What do you mean?' Minny asked, nonplussed.

'I mean you're acting really weird. I'm quite worried about you.'

'Oh. No need to be.'

'It's not just how you've been with me, although that does fit in, now that you're all lying under trees smoking – stuff – with Franklin Conderer . . .'

Minny laughed. 'I wasn't smoking anything actually.'

'And hanging around with Veronica Sedgwick.'

'I haven't been.'

'Veronica "I'm so cool, with my nose ring and junkie-looking boyfriends" Sedgwick. I saw you with her at school.'

'She said two words to me . . . Why are you being like this, Penny? It's really strange, it's like you're trying to control me.'

'I'm *concerned*.'

'Well, you don't have any need to be. You can't possibly

think that what you're saying is rational, so I don't know why you're saying it and . . . leave me alone.'

'Fine, I will then.'

'Go back to Emma and Andrew and play croquet or something.'

'Oh, get stuffed, Minny.'

Minny walked swiftly to the gate, smiling as she rejoined Franklin and Aisling.

'OK?'

'Yeah. She's flipped out, but it doesn't matter. Bit strange though.'

She had to find a new pattern for the mornings, leaving on her own instead of with Aisling or Penny – and her mother was usually frantic first thing because she was so busy with work and she had to worry about Ash being in the house on her own for too long; and also Babi wasn't there half the time; she was spending more and more nights round at Gil's house, which was only in the next street, but if she appeared at all in the mornings it was to lock herself in the bathroom for reparations to her face. It was too gross to think about and, while Minny appreciated a little time off from her, it meant there were fewer hands to do things like make breakfast, wash up and sort Raymond out. Aisling was normally still in her pyjamas when Minny left. She wasn't exactly cheery, but it always took her a while to get used to new situations; anyway it was the holidays soon.

The other thing that made mornings even more fraught was that since their day on the boat, and more especially since he'd come over to sort out the school, her father had taken to ringing up. By the end of that week they all rolled their eyes when the phone went.

'How's it going at school?'

'Yeah, fine.'

'What have you got today?'

'Er, French, history, maths, drama.'

'Sounds OK. Go on, tell me about them.'

Minny tried to talk to him, but honestly, at that time of the morning she had very little to say to anyone and she had to get *out*. So she'd pass the phone to Aisling, who might manage one sentence before giving it to Selena, who would jabber for thirty seconds before realising she'd be late if she didn't get ready right now, so he'd end up talking to their mother, who was trying to dress the baby at the same time. 'No, Des, they're not being unfriendly or sulky, they're just in a hurry. Honestly, if they spoke to me that nicely I'd be overjoyed. Des, I've got to go I'm afraid, it's mad here –' and then, the third time, when he clearly hadn't said goodbye or stopped talking, she'd asked in exasperation, 'Why are you calling *now*, Des? How come you've got the time?' And it turned out he was just walking up Westbourne Grove on his way to work and had absolutely nothing else to do. So it looked as if he'd be calling every day.

* * *

Franklin came round a lot after school. Minny hadn't mentioned that Aisling might be feeling a bit lost and isolated, but perhaps he'd thought of it by himself. She would have been mortified if she thought her granny was making him. Granny had been absolutely incandescent when Nita summoned up the courage to ring her – she was all for finding out the names of the bullies and crushing them in individual and violent ways. 'And are they at least going to be expelled?'

'I don't think so, Judy, but the school has suspended two of them.'

'Suspended them? What good will that do?'

'I don't know.'

'Sure, they suspended Minny that time for nothing.'

'Well, Ash is out of there now.'

'Thank God for that anyway. That school was never the right place for her, the poor child.'

Nita came off the phone exhausted. 'You would think,' she said to Minny, 'from the way some people are reacting to this, that I have been nothing but selfish, neglectful and irresponsible where Aisling is concerned. All for sending her to school. What was I supposed to do?' She drifted off into the kitchen, muttering.

'Your poor mum,' Franklin said. He was sitting on the patio, strumming. Minny handed him an ice lolly and sat down beside him to peel another open for the baby. 'No one treats her right.'

'We do,' Minny protested. Raymond lunged for the guitar and she distracted him just in time with the green lolly.

'I don't mean you lot. I mean your dad, and Judy, and her mother and everyone. And whoever the baby's dad is – I mean, he's not around much, is he?'

Minny didn't want to talk about that.

'Women like her always get stuck with tools.' He waved his lolly. It was unusual for him to make gestures. 'I mean, women who just do things for everyone and no one admits it, no one says thank you. That's the kind of person she is, isn't she?'

'I suppose she is.' Minny had supposed that was just what mothers were like, although of course his wasn't. And frankly, when she thought about it, she wasn't sure she could ever see herself being like that.

'My aunt was, a bit,' Franklin said. Minny held Raymond's lolly vertical for him and listened. 'She threw me a birthday party one time in a church hall and made all the lunch herself, and it was sort of a disaster. But only because all the kids were so stuck-up.'

'I was there,' Minny said, startled. She remembered it as if it was last week: the big light empty church hall and all the kids standing around looking unsure; none of them much liked Franklin anyway – he was the weird aggressive boy who hadn't been around long. And then the food was polystyrene cups full of tomato soup, and sandwiches made out of cheese spread and the kind of pâté that comes in a fat tube you have to cut the end off. The kids all ran around making sick noises and hid in gangs outside. Someone dropped their soup and it made a hideous mess on the paving. All Minny's friends were calling to her to come out. She'd gone to stand beside Franklin at the table, and eaten her way through an entire plate of pâté sandwiches. She'd stayed there even when everyone else was reluctantly dancing and playing Port and Starboard. And then she'd gone home and puked.

'I know,' he said.

She had a strange conversation with Babi that week. Her stay in Ladbroke Grove was coming up and she'd been on the phone to her father making arrangements for where he should meet her – he'd wanted to come and pick her up, but she'd dissuaded him. Then she had to give Raymond a bath, because her mother was out at a rehearsal again. Babi came and helped, which meant watched.

'So, you're going to stay with your father.'

'Mmm.' Minny splashed water around the baby's shoulders. He threw an orange boat at her.

'I can't help remembering what you said about that idea at first. Not long ago.'

Minny frowned. 'Yeah, well, so what? It's what everyone wants, so I'm doing it.'

'That's not why you're doing it, little liar,' Babi said with a laugh. 'You're going because you want to; that's the only thing that's changed. He has charmed you again. It's fascinating to watch.'

'He hasn't charmed me.' Minny was crouched on the floor with her head turned backwards to have this conversation, and it was painful. Besides, the baby was splashing up a fountain around her.

'Of course he has. It's what he does.'

'So you're saying I shouldn't go? Why don't you tell Mum that?' She tried to stop the baby from hugging her head, since she'd just blowdried her hair.

'I'm not saying that. God knows it's time he started to put some hours in. I'm just saying that I still have my doubts, for what it's worth, and I think that you forgive too easily. You get that from your mother. You forget too easily too. Your father is a man who, when he thinks he can get away with something . . .'

'Yeah? What?'

'Then he will do that thing.' She dropped a green towel on the floor beside Minny. Raymond had just poured a jug of water over the side of the bath. 'But I hope you have a nice time. He certainly owes everyone a nice time.'

She spent ages thinking about what to take; she needed books because she didn't know what they'd be doing and there might be a lot of nothing time when it would be awkward not to have a book. And her homework. Which didn't leave much room for clothes anyway.

Selena was gutted that Minny was going and she wasn't. She didn't make any fuss about it; her mother had explained it all to her, how it was just the first step and next time she could go too, but she looked like an abandoned dog when Minny said goodbye. Ash just looked a bit sad. Minny herself almost got choked up hugging Raymond, which was ridiculous because she'd only be away for two nights.

'Now, you do know where to change.' Nita stood in the hall watching her put her shoes on.

'Yes, Mum.'

'And you've got your phone.'

'Yes.'

'Although it doesn't work on the Underground.'

She rolled her eyes. 'I've been on the Tube before, Mum.'

'I know. But don't talk to any men, all right, and make sure you don't sit too far from other people.' Nita grabbed her into a hug. 'Are you nervous?'

'Yes,' she admitted.

'There's no need to be.'

'I just don't know . . . how it's going to be.'

'Don't think about it. Pretend it's happening to someone else.'

Minny loved being on the Tube on her own. She loved London, she loved walking around the stations on a swelling tide of people. There were so many interesting and devastatingly boring people to look at, talking impenetrable languages or having the most personal conversations on

216

their mobiles as if no one around could hear, with weird haircuts or outrageous clothes, like this Chinese girl at Shepherd's Bush market who was with a flock of other Chinese girls in very traditional English-looking tartan school uniform, but in her case teamed with huge boot-shaped bubblegum-pink trainers. Her mother said they were lucky to be able to walk or take the bus to school, but Minny wouldn't have minded getting the Tube every day – she would have liked the reinforcement of her identity as one of the great gang of London schoolchildren.

She'd never been to Ladbroke Grove tube station before, but she just went up the steps and looked for the WHSmith, because Des had said he would be in there standing by the girlie mags – actually he was by the free newspaper rack, getting in the way of everyone who wanted a free paper. She had no time to step away from the hug. He was talking like a brick wall. 'It's not far to the flat. I thought we'd drop your stuff off and you can have a look, then go out for a pizza or a Chinese or something. What kind of food do you like?'

'I'm not fussy.'

'Because we've got all kinds of restaurants round here. There's a nice Moroccan, and an Italian that looks OK, and a Thai . . . Well, we'll see how we feel. Harriet is out tonight with some people from work. She said she'd give us this evening just the two of us, and we're all going to do something together tomorrow.' Minny walked beside him, looking round at the colourful scruff.

The flat was in a tall thin Victorian house with deep bay windows, in a street full of them. They lived up on the first floor. Her father held the door open and she walked through it straight into the big light sitting room. There was a smell of paint and incense and a massive empty fireplace with a huge mirror above it.

'It's a bit sparse at the moment,' Des said, watching her. 'And a bit studenty. We drove up to Harriet's mum and dad's last weekend to get some furniture. They've got one of those huge houses people have when they live in the countryside, up on the Wirral, so I thought we were going to come back loaded with chintzy sofas and antique lamps, but actually Harriet just raided her old bedroom. Which was as she left it when she left home at twenty-one.' There were great piles of CDs on the floor in the corner, and books against another wall as well as stuffing the one bookcase, and even posters pinned up with famous landscapes on them. Minny peered at the nearest one. 'We're going to get frames,' he said. 'Next time you come it'll be a bit more in order.'

The mantelpiece was covered in photographs: some of Harriet looking even younger and wearing silly clothes with other girls the same age, but mostly of Aisling and Minny and Sel. There was a copy of the one they had at home of the day of Aisling's First Communion. Ash had such a beautiful dress; Minny remembered the biting envy, even though Nita had sneakily bought her a new dress too – pink, although she pretended to hate pink. On the actual morning it was cold for June and Nita had made her wear a cardigan over the top. Ash's hair was pulled back just a little bit so you could see the roses in the circlet on her head. She looked very serene. Minny was squinting because the sun was behind whoever was taking the picture, and her face was all screwed up. The next year of course it was her turn to wear the white dress, but she'd known it wouldn't look the same. Nita had toyed with the idea of getting her a new one, but Des had said that was ridiculous – he'd paid this extraordinary amount last year for an absurd flouncy white dress for a seven-year-old on the understanding that at least it would do for both of them.

There was one of herself she didn't even recognise, grinning on the front step of the flat the day she'd started secondary school, and a baby picture of Selena sitting on the old blanket of knitted squares that Raymond had had in his pram till this spring, and several others. Minny wondered if her mother had sent him more recent pictures, or if he'd kept up on Facebook, and if so what he'd thought.

She was sleeping in what was going to be the baby's room, he told her, because the one they'd designated as hers for the future – and Ash and Selena's – was all primed for painting. 'We thought you could have a look at the colour charts and pick a colour. Then we can start. If you're swift and decisive, we could get the paint tomorrow and you might give us a hand.'

Minny couldn't help but melt that weekend. She knew she was being spoiled, but it was working. She kept remembering things she hadn't thought of for years, because the time after he left had come on top of the time before he left, when he was miserable and he and Nita did nothing but argue, and the world was rocky. But now memories of before, and of when he had been just with her and Aisling, came creeping back.

He took her for dinner in a Lebanese restaurant that evening, accompanied by a bottle of wine, which made him even more talkative, and he told her a lot about his time in New York and what had made him not come back. Minny listened and ate her way through more unbelievably tasty dishes than the waiter could easily squeeze onto the table top. He said they needn't do more than scratch the surface unless she wanted to just then, but the thing about depression was that it could make you feel that you were poisoning everyone's life and that you should get yourself out of the way. He said it had taken him months and months to shake it off in America because it got worse, missing them all so much and knowing, deep down, he'd done a terrible thing leaving them. He said he'd felt so guilty that even when he started being able to think properly he couldn't bring himself to disrupt their lives again by coming back. 'Harriet got me there in the end,' he said, mopping up the baba ganoush with a strip of pitta. 'Harriet listened to me for months, Minny. I was constantly full of self-pity and self-loathing and maundering on about how much I missed you all, but how afraid I was to come home and see you; she was so patient. Until one night a few months ago she lost it and told me I was the only one who could change things and I needed to before it was too late. It was the kick up the arse I needed to get me out of that spiral.'

Minny nibbled another golden chicken wing. 'So it wasn't just that she wanted to have the baby in England?'

He looked shocked. 'No. No, Minny, no.'

'All right then.'

'Is that what you've been thinking? I'm sorry, Minny, I'm so sorry. It's the worst thing I've ever done in my life and I have been sick with it ever since I left. How you can eat that, I will never know. That is the worst thing about coming back, finding you such a rabid carnivore. It's a change I wasn't expecting.'

'What were you expecting?'

'I don't know, to be honest. Luckily you're still recognisable.'

'Oh yeah?'

'The reading, the mouth on you. You always had a fierce sense of justice. The guitar. How protective you are of your sisters.'

Minny let that pass.

They went back to the flat then and Des told her to have a look through the DVDs and pick one to watch. She got the giggles, lying under the desk where they were piled, because they were all so super-girly. 'I'm getting the feeling that either you or Harriet has a thing for Leonardo DiCaprio.'

'I don't know what you're talking about,' he said, putting down the two mugs of tea he'd just brought in and peering under the desk. 'Oh God, you're right. God, this is terrible.'

Minny crawled out to make more room, and slurped the tea. 'It could be worse.'

'Minny, Leonardo DiCaprio is five.'

'He is not, he's like your age.'

'I don't believe you.'

'What don't you believe?' Harriet asked, bursting through the door with a big paper bag in her arms.

'Your secret passion for Leo,' Des said, climbing up from the floor. 'I'll never feel secure again.'

'You'll have to deal with it,' she said. 'I loved him from age ten to age twenty at least, so that is my longest ever romantic relationship. I've got ice cream.'

She had proper ice cream from a special ice-cream café, three tubs of it: chocolate, banana and pistachio. They watched *Point Break* and ate it all. 'It's brilliant being pregnant,' Harriet said, scraping out the banana pot with her fingers. 'You can be really disgusting.'

'Bed,' Dad said when the FBI badge hit the tide at the end. 'No staying up all night reading just because your mother isn't here to check on you. What are you reading at the moment anyway?'

'I'm just starting *The Grapes of Wrath*.' It was Kevin's recommendation, pretty slow getting going but she could see it was heading somewhere. No need to mention that she was rereading *What Katy Did Next* alongside it.

'Is that for school?' Harriet had ice cream round her mouth.

'No, but I've got to read *Jane Eyre* for next term.'

Her father looked up, his hands full of spoons and empty tubs. 'But you've already read it, haven't you?'

'Yeah, but ages ago.'

'Yeah, I remember. She was only ten,' he told Harriet, tipped his head and went out carrying cushions.

'Ten?' Harriet said to her. 'Hanging out with your family kind of makes me feel stupid.'

Minny went to bed feeling quite good about herself, except she wondered with some guilt whether Aisling and Selena would be there with her now if she hadn't kicked up so much fuss to begin with. On the other hand it was luxurious sleeping in a room on her own. She couldn't think of when that had ever happened before, not for a whole night. It wasn't a real bed, of course, but it was squashy and it had three pillows. 'Well, I use three pillows,' Harriet had said. Minny lay in her Cookie Monster pyjamas under the duvet, which had no cover but was brand new so it wasn't ratty or grey, and looked up at the blank ceiling. She wondered sleepily if it was OK to be happy, if her mother, and Selena, and Aisling would be pleased or sorry.

The next morning there was no one talking to her or telling her to get up and watch the baby; the only pressure was a full bladder which wouldn't let her relax. When she did get up her father was already in the kitchen, slugging coffee and wearing a suit and a furious expression. It turned out he had to nip into work for a couple of hours but would be back for lunch. Minny had only seconds to feel awkward after he left before Harriet swept in in a silky lilac dressing gown with her hair piled up on top of her head, and went straight to the kettle. 'Right, better get your clothes on Minny. You can have a piece of toast or a crumpet or something, and then we've got to get down to work.'

There was sourdough, too beautiful to be toasted and too beautiful not to be, so she had a slice each way. Harriet was already poring over a paint colour chart. 'Hurry up and decide,' she said, sliding a cup of tea across the counter, 'because we've got to run out and buy it so that we can make a start before Des gets back. Otherwise he won't let me up the ladder, and he hasn't got a clue how to paint a room, so if you want it to look decent HURRY UP.'

Minny had never chosen colours for a room before. When they first moved into Babi's the bedrooms needed doing up, but Selena was only five and threw an immense strop anytime it was suggested it might not be pink. Minny had been so desperate to avoid it – especially because the kind Sel kept pointing at was fuchsia, Hello Kitty pink

– that she'd let her choose as long as it was any other colour, so they ended up with yellow. It hadn't worn all that well. Harriet said they had to buy new bedding too; she said Minny must choose the colours for Ash and Selena because she wanted to have the room all done and nice for the first time they all came. Minny picked out a very pale green paint, and pale pink for the edges, like window-sills. Selena would like that. She said she didn't like pink any more but she really did. 'And pink blinds?' Harriet asked, slurping peppermint tea. 'Have you ever tried herbal tea?'

'I don't know,' Minny said doubtfully, 'maybe green. Pink might be a bit . . .'

'Much? Do you know what herbal tea is less disgusting than?'

Minny giggled. 'No.'

'Herbal cigarettes. My mother used to smoke them – they were supposed to help her give up the real ones. I stole one from her pack once and tried it and I thought I would die. Ugh, shouldn't have thought about that while I still get morning sickness. Hurry, hurry and get dressed.' She pulled the clasp out of her hair and ran her hands through it. 'Quick, let's go.'

They drove out to a retail park. Harriet was good at shopping. She knew exactly how much paint she wanted and got the counter man to get the pots carried out to the car. Then she whipped Minny into a big home-furnishings place, which had racks of duvet covers and sheets stretching to way above their heads. Minny chose green and blue for Ash, orange and blue for herself, lilac and yellow for Selena. Harriet was standing longingly in front of the nursery stuff, and Minny looked at the blankets because when she did a rundown of her family she ended up at Raymond. There was a nice blue and yellow quilt he would have liked, with fish and an octopus on it. Harriet said she wasn't allowed to buy any more baby stuff yet because it was bad luck, but she ended up getting a Moses basket because she couldn't resist it. The cloth parts were all white and lacey. Then she said she couldn't possibly stand up any more and needed cake so they went to the café.

'I'm sorry, Minny,' she said, when they'd sat down with the tray and she'd prised off the top layer of her cherry Bakewell slice with a fork, rolled it up and stuffed it in her mouth. 'Sorry about that basket. Today was supposed to be all about you girls and getting ready for you.'

Minny hadn't minded at all. Nita had been the same when she was pregnant with Raymond, excited all the time she wasn't deathly tired. And no one could not like a white lacy basket for putting a baby in.

'You like your little brother, don't you?' Harriet said.

'Yes.'

'That's nice. God, that's nice. Go slow with the milkshake – after all that ice cream last night you'll be having some kind of reaction.'

'Sorry,' Minny said, wiping her chin. 'I don't get this kind of stuff much because of Ash being dairy-intolerant.'

Harriet drank her juice. 'It must be hard on you, having an older sister like Aisling.'

Because she didn't say it judgementally, or with too much sympathy, Minny felt like she was right and that perhaps it was all right to admit it. 'Sure,' she said, and shut her inner eyes on the picture of Nita looking at her.

'Is it rough at school?'

'It can be.'

'Dessie told me something about what happened last week, with her clothes and all.' She scraped some more icing off the plate with the edge of her fork. 'And he said something once, or maybe it was your mum, about you getting into trouble for something . . .'

'The time I was suspended? Yeah. For pushing David Fletcher down the stairs.' She licked her fingers and saw Harriet's expression. 'Oh, I didn't really push him down the stairs.'

'Oh good.'

'Yeah, of course. I just pushed him, and he fell down the stairs.'

'Minny!'

'Well. I was only eleven and he was massive. He was picking on Ash and I came along and I lost my temper and shoved him; he was twice my size. And he did this really dramatic fall and roll, and he happened to have been quite near the top of the stairs, so he slid down; he barely hurt himself. But they said they had a zero-tolerance policy for violence, so I got suspended. It was only for a day.'

'I must remember not to get on the wrong side of you.' Minny got the sense she was treading carefully. 'Tough for you though, isn't it, having to think like that? I mean, she's your big sister. I think you seem to handle it incredibly well, when you're not hurling boys down stairs, but it's a lot. Of course, I don't mean to say it's not super-hard for Ash herself . . .'

'Sure,' Minny said.

'But I hope you look after yourself too. I mean, in a way it's none of my business. But – I hate to bring this up because it sounds, well, a bit of a cliché, maybe – but it's not actually that long since I was your age. And it was tough, but I didn't start off with anything like the baggage you have to deal with. Do you mind me talking about this stuff?'

'No. It just feels a bit weird. I mean, I don't normally. And, you know, I haven't known you very long. I don't mean to be rude at all, and I'm just saying – that it feels strange to talk about it. Not bad though.'

They went home. It was only twelve o'clock by the time Harriet had got the man downstairs to 'help' carry the paint, which actually meant him making three trips while Minny brought the towels and duvet covers and Harriet put the kettle on, so they got started on the painting. She found

Minny an old grey shirt of her father's to put on, and lent her a blue scarf to tie around her hair, as if they were painting a room in a film. It was fun. Minny found herself talking a lot, not just about Aisling and Selena but Raymond too – Harriet seemed curious about him, which made sense seeing that she was about to pop a baby out herself. Minny told her stories about Babi and Gil as well, and a bit about Penny.

'But you've been friends since primary school?'

'Yeah. But she's always been really annoying. It's just that now – she gets a boyfriend, who's a real tosspot . . .'

'Been there,' Harriet murmured, shaking her head.

'So I never see her except when she wants to talk about him and how much she *lurves* him. And then as soon as there's someone new at school and I happen to know him and hang out with him just a little bit she's all offended and feels abandoned. She doesn't actually want to spend any time with me, she just doesn't want me to have any other friends. Or even to do more stuff with Aisling actually. It's pathetic.'

Harriet was painting carefully around the windowsill. 'She doesn't like Franklin? This is Franklin we're talking about, right?'

'Yes.'

'Does she give a reason?'

'She says she thinks he's a bad influence on me.'

Harriet raised her eyebrows at the window. 'And is he?'

'No, not at all. Honestly, I haven't done a single bad thing while he's been around. She's crackers – she thinks that because he smoked weed once he's making me do it now. I've never done it in my life, but what's weird is that even if I had, I wouldn't have expected her to think it was such a big deal, like the end of the world.'

'Maybe she's jealous.'

'Yeah, I think she is. She doesn't want me to have any friends.'

'Actually, I meant jealous because Franklin is pretty cute.'

'Oh.'

'You like him?'

'Yeah, he's cool.'

'But you *like him* like him?'

'No. I mean, I'm not – it's not like that.'

'Not yet, anyway.'

She was joking but Minny felt uncomfortable. It really wasn't like that. She didn't see why it had to be like that.

Her father came back, not too late, just when they were finishing up sandwiches while the first coat was drying; the whole flat smelled of paint, even though all the windows were open. He had a bag of fancy fruit and a newspaper and he loved the room. 'It's like a sunny afternoon.'

'It *is* a sunny afternoon, Dad,' Minny pointed out.

'A sunny afternoon in a wild mossy garden. I think I hear a bird singing.'

'Come on, Blarney Rubble,' Harriet said, pulling the scarf

off her head. 'What have you got planned for us this afternoon?'

Minny had her homework so they set her up at the big wooden desk with the fancy white computer and all the stationery in the world, which was overkill since she only had a French comprehension and some reading for history. Her father pottered about in the background while Harriet slept on the sofa in the sun. Then in the evening they went out and roamed around Ladbroke Grove and Notting Hill till they found a restaurant they liked the look of – it felt like being on holiday – and stuffed themselves again, with Indian food. It was easy. Going back to the flat afterwards was not unlike going home.

She left the next morning after giving the bedroom walls a second coat. She felt a little bit sad, but on the other hand eager for Raymond and a Sunday afternoon at home, homework done for once. 'So what do you think?' Des asked, as if he'd been nerving himself to it, while they were standing saying goodbye. 'Would you be up for bringing your sisters here when your mum goes to Edinburgh?'

'Sure,' Minny said, shrugging. She didn't want to dwell on the fuss she'd kicked up, or why she felt better about it now.

'Great. That's really great. Of course, I'm hoping I'll get to see you again before then,' he added. 'That's weeks away.'

'See you later, Minny,' Harriet said, hugging her again. 'Thanks for all your help.'

She felt dozy and content on the Tube, but, after changing at Hammersmith, more and more impatient to be home too. She wondered for the first time what it would be like to have a new baby brother or sister. She wondered if he might look like her. Because she looked like her father.

It was especially nice to get home. Everyone seemed pleased to see her, even Selena, who was full of questions about what she'd done and what the new bedroom would be like and what she'd had to eat. 'He took you to restaurants?' she asked wistfully. 'Were they fancy?'

'Er – not especially.'

'What makes a restaurant fancy, Sel?' Nita asked.

'Fans on the ceiling,' Selena said with certainty. 'And red velvet tablecloths.'

Aisling sat next to Minny on the sofa and kept asking her where she was going every time she left the room. When Raymond got up from his nap he was so delighted to see her she spent five minutes disentangling his fingers from her hair. 'So you had a good time?' her mother kept saying. Minny told her she had, and that it was OK for her to make her arrangements for Edinburgh. Selena got overexcited and went zooming around the house doing handstands in inappropriate places. Ash said, 'Oh, OK,' and ten minutes later went on the computer and started writing out a timeline of American presidents, which was one of the things she did when she was nervous. Babi said since everyone was going away she might go on holiday with Gil – not to Paris because it was overrated; perhaps to Seville, or Riga, somewhere where he wouldn't be expecting too much. Then Nita reminded her that she still had to look after Raymond, and she looked relieved.

Gil turned up a bit later. Minny had been feeling all tolerant; not even Babi had tried to wind her up yet, but Gil managed it instantly by just looking so annoying. He had his hands behind him and leaned back and said, 'So, Minny, how was your trip?'

'Oh, fine,' Minny said.

'Not as bad as you thought then?'

'No,' she breathed, rictus-grinning.

'So. He behaved himself then, your dad?'

It might have been just a throwaway remark if Gil hadn't been part of the last row they'd all had. But he had. She said, 'Mmmm,' imbued with as much 'and what possible business is that of yours; you are not a member of this family' as she could manage. Then he suggested a walk by the river, and somehow almost everyone went: Ash and Selena, and they took the pushchair. Nita asked Minny if she'd help with dinner.

'OK,' Minny said, following her warily into the kitchen. She got handed a paring knife and a bag of potatoes, while her mother whipped up Yorkshire-pudding batter – Minny decided that Ash or Selena must have had a difficult weekend; they didn't normally have roast dinners on a Sunday.

233

'I'm so glad you had a good time,' Nita said. 'You see, being brave pays off. It's a nice flat, is it?'

'Yeah, it will be. They're doing it up.'

'Oh good. Right. Well, it's nice to have you home.'

'Mmm.'

'There's actually something I need to talk to you about. Don't cut those too small, they'll be mush.'

'That's when they're nicest.'

'The thing is, something rather . . . odd happened yesterday.'

'What?' Minny turned the hob on.

'I got a call from Cora. Penny's mum.'

Minny looked up and put the knife down.

'Yes, I was surprised. I wondered for a second if she was going to start talking about how you two were rowing, but it wasn't really that. Not exactly. She said that Penny was devastated and had been crying all day and finally it had come out that she was upset about you. Worried because, er, you'd changed so much lately and you've been taking lots of drugs and, er, hanging with a bad crowd. But, yes. Drugs.'

Minny actually shook her head, as if she was in a cartoon, though whether to check that her ears were not full of water or to help compose her ideas she couldn't say.

'Minny?'

'She must have gone mental, Mum. It's the only possible explanation.'

'So, you haven't been—'

'No, of course not. Cross my heart, honestly.'

'Oh good.'

'I think this is all because of Franklin. Or – I don't know.'

'Yes, his name came up.'

'He told her that he once got expelled for having . . . weed, but that was ages ago. I've never heard him even talk about it, much less do it.'

'Really?'

'Yeah. I mean, she got a thing straight off about him smoking cigarettes, as if speaking to him was going to turn me into a nicotine addict. And then she did have a go at me last week in the park and accuse me of being stoned, but I thought she was just sort of making it up for the sake of having a go at me. I didn't think she could really possibly believe it.'

'Well, it seems she does.'

The thing was, even if she did, which Minny couldn't get her head around because there was no evidence of Minny doing anything like that whatsoever – even if she did believe it, why on earth would she tell her mother about it, knowing full well that Cora would tell Nita?

'It sounds as if she's in a very strange place, poor kid,' Nita said, when Minny put this to her. 'Either she is really, genuinely worried about you, which would suggest she's lost quite a lot of proportion—'

'– or she just wants to get me into trouble and is making up lies about me,' Minny finished. 'What did you say to Cora?'

'Well, I told her my instinct was that Penny was mistaken. Of course she thought I was kidding myself. She said she'd ring back this evening when I'd had a chance to talk to you, as if she needed to check that I was going to bother raising it with you at all.'

'So what will you say to her?'

'I'll tell her that Penny is wrong, and perhaps gently suggest that she try to have a chat with her about what's going on with her rather than with you. I don't expect it to go well. I wouldn't be pleased with that if I were her.'

'Penny's never going to talk to Cora about what's going on with her and Jorge,' Minny said. 'Which makes it even weirder that she'd tell her something about me. Maybe she was just trying to distract her.'

'Distract her from what?'

'I don't know.' She fell silent, wondering.

Her mother looked at her. 'You wouldn't consider maybe making up with her?'

'No, Mum.'

'OK.'

'You want me to make up with her now, after this?'

'It's just, whatever's behind it all, it sounds like she could do with a pal right now.'

'Well, it's not going to be me.'

'OK. But try not to be too angry with her, all right? Don't start any fights over it – that's all I ask.'

She was a fine one to talk; her conversation with Cora

that evening degenerated into an extremely frosty exchange of advice. Minny hadn't been allowed to stay in the room, but they all heard Nita, just before ringing off, say rather loudly, 'No, I don't have my head in the sand. No, actually I don't. Look, one of us has a daughter who's trying to distract us from her own problems by pinning something on her friend, and let me ask you this, Cora – whose daughter has a history of fantasising?'

'Who's Mum talking to?' Aisling whispered, coming out onto the landing where Minny was leaning over the banister – and from where she could see that Babi was standing just inside the kitchen door, also listening.

'Cora Grey.'

'Penny's mother?'

'Yes.'

'Oh.' She went back into her room.

Nita came out of the back room, slamming the door, and walked past Babi into the kitchen.

'Lesbians are neurotic,' Babi remarked.

TEN

Minny found that week curiously intense. She really didn't want to get into some kind of feud with Penny so she tried hard to avoid her, but they had all their science and maths lessons together so it was a question of not giving her dirty looks – which turned into trying not to look at her at all, which was ridiculous. Penny never said a word to her. She seemed to spend most of her lunchtimes snogging Jorge outside at the side of the football pitch, under a horse chestnut tree. On the other hand Minny found that a lot of people were suddenly talking to her who never had before, a few from her year but mostly from the year above. She put it down to being friends with Franklin, who seemed to have had less trouble than they'd all feared finding people to hang out with – and maybe they were feeling bad over Aisling too. Anyway, it was exhilarating but exhausting, trying to think of things to say to people like Veronica Sedgwick, who sometimes came to school dressed entirely in yellow right down to her home-decorated sandals, and Luis da Souza, who you occasionally saw around town in the evenings dressed as a girl.

Then at home her mother was hardly around, and when

she was she'd be in a fret of organising her Edinburgh trip, on top of the usual end-of-term rush of events and reports – and making sure Aisling was all right. Nothing had been sorted out for her yet for next term; Nita barely had time to set her work to do. Ash was strange and silent, and kept following Minny around when she got in from school. Minny tried to put up with it, but it drove her mad. On Thursday evening Franklin rang up to ask if Minny wanted to go to the cinema after school the next day; there was a film on they'd been talking about seeing. 'Can I come?' Aisling asked.

'You hate the cinema.'

'Can I come anyway?'

'No. You'll just want to leave in the middle and make loads of noise moving about.'

Aisling didn't say anything, she just went upstairs. Selena looked over from the corner where she was trying to build a Jenga tower before the baby could knock it down.

'Well,' Minny said. 'She would. I'm not her babysitter. I can't give up my social life entirely just because Aisling's bored here all day.'

She did go to the cinema with Franklin, but she didn't feel great about it, especially when he asked how Aisling was before the trailers had even started. 'You're always worrying about my family,' she snapped, without meaning to. 'I mean, I would have thought you'd have thought our problems were kind of small-scale.'

That sounded terrible, she realised. Franklin took a couple

of Minstrels from the bag she was holding. 'Not really, you know. You're just all going through some . . . stuff, aren't you?'

'I suppose so. But I feel guilty,' she admitted, suddenly putting a name to her irritation. 'You have to live away from home and everything – and stuff has happened to you – you know what I mean? I mean, what makes you such a saint? Why are you worried about my sister, or my mother of all people?'

'I like Ash. She used to be nice to me when we were kids, and everyone just ignored her all the time. Anyway –' he took another Minstrel and looked at it as the lights went down – 'I just always liked you. All of you. It was nice coming round your house, I looked forward to it. You always had music playing, and you weren't stuck-up round me like everyone else, and your mum talked to me like I was real. Even your dad – he wasn't there usually, but you all looked forward to him coming home. You just seemed like a . . . a really nice family.'

Minny didn't move but the bag still crackled. 'I can't believe you remember so much. We were only little.'

'I know, but . . .'

'I don't know if we are that nice a family.'

'Yeah, but you'd all do anything for each other, wouldn't you?'

'I don't know.'

'Course you would.' He was staring at the screen. 'The

last thing I asked my mother to do was come to the hearing with the social worker. She didn't make it.'

Minny passed him the Minstrels.

After the film – which was unimportant – she invited him to come back to their house because Ash would like the company. Only they walked into the beginning of a tremendous row. Her father was there, in the front room, shouting at her mother, who was holding Raymond while Selena stood beside him trying to interrupt and trying not to cry, and Aisling sat on the stairs.

'What's going on?' Minny asked her in dismay.

'Des is angry about you,' Aisling explained. 'Hi, Franklin.'

He raised his hand in silent salute.

'Oh, he's here!' Her father strode into the hall. 'Oh great! You chose not to mention, Nita, that Minny was out with him. That's just marvellous.'

'Shut up, Des, and let me explain things to you before you make even more of a fool of yourself,' Nita shouted. 'And don't pick on anyone in this house, this isn't your house.'

'What's going on?' Minny asked again.

'What's going on is that I received a phone call at lunchtime which necessitated my dropping everything including client meetings and panting across London because I thought I might get more sense out of your mother, and you, face to face.'

'What was the phone call?' Minny asked helplessly,

looking at her mother, who tried to speak but was shouted down by Des.

'The phone call was from Cora Grey, whom I had to rack my brains even to remember, yet who apparently has more interest in keeping me informed than anyone in my family when one of my daughters – at least – is going to rack and ruin.'

'Now, stop it, Des.' Nita stepped in front of him. 'Minny has just got in the door of her own home. Even if there was something to worry about, this wouldn't be the way to handle it and you don't have the right.'

'It's not a right, it's a responsibility . . .'

'Long ago delegated by you, and you haven't got it back yet,' Nita said. 'Which is why you didn't know about this situation last week when it first came up.'

'This *situation*?'

'Yes. Minny and Penny have been arguing a fair amount lately, and for some reason Penny handed this tale to her mother.'

'I don't believe this,' Minny whispered.

'None of it is true – not what Penny says Minny has been doing, nor the kind of influence she says Franklin is exerting.'

Minny didn't know where to look, even if she hadn't been about to cry.

'All right, let's calm down,' said Des. 'Could we talk about this, just the three of us?'

'No.' Minny held onto the doorknob.

'Well. Let's look at this for a moment. Minny, your best friend, Penny—'

'No, she isn't.'

'Your best friend has told her mother that you've been hanging around a good deal with . . . Franklin, and some other types at school that you've never been friends with before, who are into drugs –'

Minny sagged.

'– and that you've been smoking a lot of pot, maybe trying out other kinds of drugs too, and acting very strangely altogether. This is very worrying for me, Minny. I would have thought it would be for your mother too.'

'It would be,' Nita said, 'if I believed it for one second.'

'Perhaps you've lost your sense of proportion. Minny?'

She couldn't speak without wailing, which she would have done if Franklin hadn't been there.

'Perhaps Franklin should go home now,' Nita suggested.

'Oh, home? Or back to my mother's house, where he's exploiting another member of my family?' Des shouted, losing it again.

'Shut up, Des!' Aisling screamed.

'It's OK, I'm off,' Franklin said. 'Minny hasn't been taking any drugs though, you should know.'

'And what about you?' Des snapped. 'I don't trust you, son. I don't know what you're doing living with my mother.' He strode right towards where they stood in the doorway, and Minny backed away in alarm, keeping Franklin behind her, but Des was headed for the train blackboard. He whacked it so that chalk showered lightly over him. 'Life is like a bloody train!' he yelled. 'You don't get to ride for free!'

'Jesus *God* you've changed, Des,' Nita said, holding the front door open for Franklin and patting him on the elbow as he slipped past.

'I've just grown up, Nita. You could do with it yourself. This is just great.' He paced up and down the hall.

Minny hadn't been able to say goodbye. She could see Selena sitting in a frozen heap on the sofa in the front room, Raymond pulling at her knee. Aisling was crying.

'Des, I think you should leave,' Nita said calmly. She was still holding the door. 'If you can't be reasonable, then this is pointless.'

'I just don't believe you, Nita. I never picked you for a head-in-the-sand type, ignoring what's in front of you, or I never would have—'

'You never would've what, Des?'

'Never mind.'

'You never would have abandoned your daughters to my sole care?'

'Look, Nita, don't turn this into a personal attack on me. This isn't about us or your anger, it's about Minny, and the fact is, because of your policies—'

'Oh, which policies are those?'

'Your obsession with helping lame dogs, to be frank. Apparently Penny's been worried for a while because of Minny being under undue pressure to look after Aisling at school – fair enough, I'm not saying anything about that, but I don't see why you need to extend it to every misfit who crosses your path. Now she's suddenly dropped her former friends in order to hang out with a boy who has a known history with drugs – Minny herself told Harriet that.'

'Yes. She told me too. I already knew, because your mother had told me.' Nita stretched out an arm to pull Aisling towards her.

'Oh great, and you thought it a good plan to encourage Minny to get involved with him?'

'They're not involved, Des.'

'Really? Once again you're proving unable to see the obvious, Nita. Maybe Minny finds it difficult to talk to you. She told Harriet, on the other hand . . .'

Minny saw her mother's eyes narrow.

'Yes, she did, Nita – she told Harriet that she had a crush on this boy.'

'No, I didn't,' Minny cried.

'And that Penny was jealous because they were spending so much time together. Well, I ask you, Nita, what do you think a fifteen-year-old boy has on his mind when it comes to hanging around with a young girl who has those kinds of feelings for him?'

After that the conversation became, briefly, rather ugly. Minny lost track of what she was shouting herself; she could scarcely hear anyone else over the baby, who'd started screaming when she did, but anyway it didn't last long, because her mother kicked her father out. He was yelling things about lawyers and seeking his rights if no one else was going to be looking after his daughters when she slammed the door in his face and pushed everyone through into the back room.

It took Minny all evening not to feel shaky. The first thing she did was send Franklin a text:

So sorry. He is mental and Penny has been making all this stuff up. Don't know why. Think she has gone nuts.

His reply came quickly but it just said:

Don't worry about it.

The worst part was when Babi got back just as they were going to bed and demanded to be told what had happened. Their mother tried to take her aside, but they could all hear Babi's reactions. Minny sat next to Selena, who had been frankly overacting during the whole situation – crying and stuff, and looking all traumatised, when it wasn't about her at all.

'I told you,' Babi said loudly, in the kitchen. She sounded triumphant. 'I told you this is what would happen, but you had to be so civilised, and urge the girls to give him another chance straightaway, and this is the result – he thinks he can still treat you and them however he pleases and do whatever he likes. You're going to end up needing a lawyer again, I tell you now.'

'Shut up,' Selena screamed. She ran to the door. 'Shut up, shut up, shut up. You're not our mother! And he –' she pointed at Gil, who was standing by the fridge – 'he isn't anything.'

'I'm worried about Selena,' Nita said on Sunday evening.

It hadn't been that bad over the weekend. Selena had seemed more or less her usual self on Saturday morning – she didn't apologise and it was a bit weird and awkward, but it seemed they all, including Babi, had agreed just to forget about it. Sel did have a screaming fit at four o'clock on Sunday morning when Aisling turned on the light in the bathroom and hence also the extractor fan (and turned the hot water off, but at least that didn't make a noise). They found her standing on the landing with her hair on end still yelling, even though Ash had gone back into her bedroom and shut the door. And she had cried over her maths just that evening, even though she only had about eight sums to do and she was good at maths.

Aisling was upstairs watching *The West Wing* for the millionth time on her computer because no one else could stomach it any longer. Babi was out with Gil; Sel and Raymond were in bed. Their mother was lying on her spine on the sofa glugging white wine because it had been a rough couple of days. She'd spent her Saturday afternoon driving out to a college miles and miles away to see if it might be at all suitable for Aisling, only their angle had been to ask her why she was so keen to force a person with a learning disability into doing academic exams. 'That was why they dragged me out there, so they could share their philosophy with me. Open my mind.'

'Ash doesn't have a learning disability.'

'I know.'

'Do they not understand what the autistic spectrum is?'

'Apparently not.' She took a swallow of wine.

'It's not the lessons that are the problem, it's the teaching. And the other kids.'

'I know. You and I can understand that, and your grandmother, but it seems no one else in the entire world.'

Minny wriggled into a more comfortable position; her Hello Kitty pyjamas had seen at least three summers and were on the snug side. 'So what are you going to do?'

'I don't know. There are still options, but the trouble is everything will be closing down for the summer soon. I'd really like to get a plan in place so that Ash knows what she'll be doing come September. But I'm so bloody busy with this play, and the end of term – I'm already neglecting you all shamefully.'

'We're all right,' Minny said. Everything was relative.

'I don't even know what the hell's going to happen when I have to go to Edinburgh.'

'Well, you know what's not going to happen.'

'I could murder your father.' Nita refilled her wine glass. 'He just had to go and make such a spectacular arse out of himself that not even Selena will consider going to stay with him.'

'You wouldn't want us to, would you? After that? And *she's* even worse.' Minny really felt that. That Harriet should, in an inflammatory context, start talking about what Minny had told her during a confidential conversation – let alone start making stuff up – was desperately bitter. It made her feel like an idiot. So they'd decided that Penny – completely unknown to Harriet and virtually so to Des – was more trustworthy than Minny. That was fine. She could exist in a state of mutual lack of trust as far as they were concerned.

'I'm sorry you feel so let down, honey,' Nita said now. 'Things have gone wrong, haven't they?'

'You could say.'

'And now I have to leave you all.'

'It's only for five days, Mum. We'll be fine.'

'I hope so. You know I have to rely on you, don't you?'

Minny sighed. 'Yes.'

'Even more than usual though? Babi does her best, but she can't always . . . concentrate. And with Raymond in particular, you know . . .'

'I'll keep an eye on him.'

'Just . . . be there at bathtime, always? And don't stay out any nights, will you? And at mealtimes – make sure she cuts the grapes in half.'

'I will, Mum.'

'I know. In a way he's the one I'm least anxious about; he's not going to crack up. Try to keep Ash talking, won't you?' She twisted her glass. 'I'm worried about Selena.'

249

'Why?' Minny had found one of her grandmother's emery boards sticking out from under the sofa. She started filing her nails.

'She looks beside herself most of the time.'

'Well, you know. She doesn't sleep well, does she?' Sel had always had patches where she got a lot of nightmares. She used to sleepwalk sometimes.

'I know, but normally she comes in to me. She hasn't appeared at my bedside in weeks. I think she's struggling to – I don't know, I think grow up. Be more independent. Consciously, I mean. And all this Bible obsession – she keeps reading the Old Testament. I didn't mind the Jesus stuff, but there are some nasty stories earlier on. Poor kid. It's hard for her to process all this about her father – you were so angry when he left that I think you got some of it out of the way. She was very little. Maybe she still has to go through it. She said something very negative about Harriet this morning.'

'Selena did?'

'Mmm.'

'Well, you can't blame her. Harriet's a cow.'

Nita pulled a face. 'I don't like saying this because it makes me sound like a bitter ex-wife, but I think she's just very *young*, you know? She just got it wrong – both what you said, and what she did about it. I mean, look at it from her point of view: your father was ranting and raving about how worried he was; she was trying to help, I think.'

'It was a power thing.'

'Well. Possibly.'

Minny wriggled again. 'She's massive now.'

'Oh yes? It's not long to go, is it? You might like having another baby in your life. Would you rather a boy or a girl, do you think?'

'Girl.'

'Why?'

'I've got a baby brother already.'

'I expect Harriet's hoping for a boy,' Nita said, refilling her glass again and leaning back. Minny thumped up her cushion and leaned against her. 'Your father won't care – he always got on better with girls anyway. But Harriet will be wanting a boy, I would think.'

'Yeah?'

'Yeah. To give him something different.'

It was dim in the room because the bulb had broken in one lamp a couple of weeks before and they hadn't replaced it yet. Her mother was twisting a strand of Minny's hair into a rope so Minny lay still. 'It's not really different though, is it?' She could suddenly feel every place her body was bent. 'It's not as if Dad's really only got girls, is it?'

She waited, without turning her head; there was a long pause when nerves thrummed along the length of her stretched-out legs.

'I don't know what you mean,' Nita said, wrenching her fingers out of Minny's hair and sitting up to put her glass down.

'Yeah, you do. I've always kind of known, Mum.'

'No, you haven't. Isn't anything to know. How?'

'Come on, Mum – Raymond. He looks just like me, everyone says it. And I look like Dad.'

Her mother rubbed her face, all over, with her fingertips and sat still with her eyes shut. 'I was always amazed that no one else noticed it. He was the image of you from the moment he was born. Have you really always known?'

'I don't know. Sort of. I didn't . . . think about it. I never really bought your secret short relationship though.'

Nita made a face. 'I know. I felt so puerile – a made-up boyfriend, for God's sake. But I thought it was better than a made-up wild night of sex with a man whose name I never knew.'

'I suppose so. I didn't know what was wrong about it, but it just never sounded right. And then he was born, and he looked like me, and he felt like he'd always been here, and it felt right. So . . .' So she hadn't needed to ask any questions. 'I still don't really get it though. I mean Dad had been gone two years, nearly, when he was born.'

'A year and a half. Yes. I won't give you too many details.'

'No, don't.'

'But do you remember when I went away to that conference in Glasgow?'

'Yes.'

'Well, I didn't. I went to New York. We'd just had that really tough year – obviously – Ash was having a hard time

252

settling at Raleigh, and you'd been in trouble and were still miserable, and I was panicking about money. The lease was up on the flat and I didn't know whether to renew it or not. He was sending us money, but I was all in a haze about whether we could rely on that lasting because I couldn't really tell what state he was in, just over the phone when all we did anyway was argue. And I hoped I might even persuade him to come and see you three, because I knew he'd be rolling in guilt and self-loathing and would never make it if I left him to it. So I just decided it was time to see him face to face and talk things through – the future.'

Minny had started peeling the label off the wine bottle while she listened. 'Why did you tell us you were going to Glasgow?'

'Well, for God's sake, things were fraught enough, and I was scared that you would think I was trying to bring him back. I honestly wasn't – not that I didn't have a fantasy that things would be wonderful and he would have a revelation, but I knew it wouldn't happen really, we'd come too far. Anyway –' she topped up her glass – 'I went. And I'd honestly thought I was over it, I'd thought we could just have a calm discussion. But it didn't happen like that.'

'Ewww,' Minny said, putting the cushion over her face.

'Grow up, Minny, we're having a conversation here.' She batted her with the other cushion. 'I won't go into detail, but suffice to say we got extraordinarily drunk. We rowed almost the whole time, and I finished up with the conviction that I wasn't the right person to pull him out of what he was going through. So I pulled the plug. I told him that we, he and I, were truly over and I'd been seeing someone else – that was where the imaginary boyfriend first showed up, but he mightn't have believed it otherwise. And I came home and moved us to Babi's house where I knew we'd have a roof over our heads whatever happened with your father.'

'And what about when you found out you were . . . ?'

'Ah. Well, that was a few weeks later. And I was very happy.'

'Even at first? How could you be?'

'Well, I loved your father, Minny. I still do in a kind of way. Raymond was the seal, for me, the conclusion. An end and a beginning. I could never regret him.'

Minny was still behind her cushion, thinking. 'Was he with Harriet already?' She didn't know what she wanted the answer to be.

'No, not really. He knew her, he mentioned her actually, but they weren't together.'

She came out for the most serious question. 'Does Dad know?'

'No.'

'How can he not know?'

'I never told him I was pregnant. I don't actually know how he found out, but a few months in, just after I'd told you actually, he was on the phone gibbering one night.'

'And?'

'I told him the baby wasn't his. I told him I knew conclusively that the father was my imaginary boyfriend.'

'Why?'

'Oh, I don't know, Minny. Try having the most complicated life you can possibly imagine and then this. I've told you, I didn't want your father after that weekend. He wasn't ready to come back here; he certainly wasn't ready to be part of my life again. On the other hand he was already miserably guilty over abandoning us. What would have happened if I'd told him we were having another child? And if he did come back, for this one, what would that do to you girls?' She poured out more wine. 'Also, can you imagine what my mother would have said?'

'So if he believed you, why was he looking so goggle-eyed when he turned up here and saw the baby?'

'Why do you think? He knows what he looks like. He knows what *you* look like.'

'So he knows?'

'No. I fobbed him off again. I told him you must take after me more than we'd ever realised. We didn't have time to argue about it, not in the front room with the rest of you in here, and anyway, why would he have argued? He wanted to believe me, so he did.'

'He can't really believe it. Not looking at him.'

'Well, he's choosing not to think about it, just like you did for a while. I don't much blame him – it would be devastating to a lot of people if it came out now.'

Minny thought, fiercely, about how anyone could look at Raymond and not want to be his father.

'So don't stir it, Minny, all right?'

'Fine. What? I don't stir things.'

Nita let it go. Minny could see in her mother's face that she felt guilty about giving her even more to deal with, and she was worried about the secret being out to the tiniest degree, but that she was also glad. That kind of secret, kept to yourself, could make you feel like you were going mad. Minny was glad herself. She would help her mother keep the baby safe.

ELEVEN

Term ended on Thursday. Minny was dying to be shot of school, but apprehensive because, currently lacking a normal structure of friends who made telephone calls and things like that, she didn't know what she was going to do with herself for six weeks. Franklin said he'd have to get some kind of job.

On Wednesday night when she got home from school there was a letter on the kitchen counter, for her. Not a library reminder or a postcard, an actual letter, with scruffy slanty inky writing on it. Babi pointed it out to her without comment. Minny went up to her room to open it, and scrambled up onto her bunk in case Selena came bursting in.

It was from Harriet. It was quite hard to read, being handwritten, and it took her a while to plough through it. It went on about being sorry and all that, and how much Harriet had enjoyed their weekend and getting to know Minny and how much she regretted that it was spoilt. Then she said: *'The thing is, I appreciate I was probably wrong because I've never even met the girl, and when I reflect on the fact that her mother called up Des after she'd spoken to your mum, and didn't even tell your mum she was doing it, it sounds as if she might be a tiny bit crazy all right. Des is so sorry about the way he handled it – I think he lost his temper because he was so worried and so guilty, that his leaving might have had a really bad effect on you, you see – and he'd been so impressed with you before that. Because he thought you'd handled it so well and grown up so well. Anyway he feels now that he definitely went the wrong way about things with accusing you like that, and that after all perhaps your friend Penny wasn't telling the truth. He was just worried about you, Minny. It's scary being parent to a teenager, not that I know – yet! – from personal experience but I can see he's always thinking about it. If he phoned you, or if maybe you phoned him if you'd rather, would you talk to him and let him apologise? Anyway I've got to apologise because I guess I did betray your trust and I can see that it might be hard for you to trust me again. Would you think about forgiving me? I'd love it if we could sort things out so that we'd all be ready for your little brother or sister – you, and Aisling and Selena, are going to be so important to him – or her!'*

Minny lay still on the bed, thinking about it for half an hour. She was wondering with a certain level of detachment how long she would keep up being angry this time. Also, if it was up to her at all. It was like a collective thing, this deciding how the relationship with their father was going to be, and it was all getting away from her a bit. All these people in her life were so unmanageable. Just as she was going to give up thinking about it for now and arise from her sweaty pillow, her mobile rang in her pocket. Of course it was Des. He was the most impatient man in the whole world; he couldn't leave well enough alone.

'Darling, thank you for answering. Are you all right?'

'I'm fine.'

There was a pause. 'Did you get Harriet's letter?'

'Yes, Dad, about five minutes ago. Do you have someone watching the house?'

'No – your post comes late. Have you read it?'

'Yes.'

'And?'

'Dad, I'm thinking about it still, OK?'

He paused again. 'How's Steinbeck?'

'All right. I finished *The Grapes of Wrath*.'

'So what next? Are you onto Jane Austen now?'

'No,' she said slowly.

'I thought you said your mother was pushing her hard? You've got to tell that teacher about what you read,' he rattled on. 'Jesus, I hope you get a good one next year, it's about time.'

'Dad.' She grasped the rail of the bed. It made her hand hurt. 'Have you been reading my emails to Uncle Kevin?'

There was a long pause. Her nails were digging into the wood.

'Why do you say that?'

'Just answer the question, Dad.'

'Minnymouse, there were years when I wouldn't have

259

been in any touch with you at all, you wouldn't talk to me – understandably – and it was driving me crazy not knowing anything about you . . .'

'Did you WRITE those emails? Was that you?'

'No – some of them . . .'

She turned her phone off, so hard she heard it crack, and dropped it over the side of the bed. Half of her felt like banging her head against the wall, but it submitted to the other half, which was just deeply confused.

She hadn't figured it out by the next day. She hadn't told anyone either; it felt terrifically personal, perhaps because that was how she had felt about her relationship with Kevin. And because she felt like an idiot. Having to have physics with Penny giving her glances from across the lab didn't improve matters, however hilarious the teacher's last-day experiment was. When she met Veronica Sedgwick in the corridor on her way to history she grinned at her in a particularly friendly way, because Penny was nearby. Veronica stopped to ask after Ash.

'Yeah, she's fine. Still not doing any work – she's been on holiday for weeks already.'

Veronica walked backwards away from her. 'Listen, I've got some people round this evening. Franklin's coming.'

'Oh, right.'

'Do you want to come?'

'OK, sure.'

'Good. Bring Aisling if she wants to come. See you later then.'

There was a furious tut from the other side of the corridor as Penny also walked off, tossing her hair.

It was nothing major. Franklin said there probably wouldn't be many people there, it wasn't a party or anything. Still, Minny took unusual care sorting her hair out. The house was very quiet; her mother was onto her last week of rehearsals now and had a bunch of arrangements to make which meant she wouldn't be in till late, and Selena had gone for a sleepover at Victoria's house. She had been freakishly excited about it. Aisling wandered in while Minny was considering which eyeshadow of her mother's to borrow.

'Why are you putting make-up on?'

'I'm going out.'

'Where to?'

'Veronica Sedgwick's house. She's having a thing.'

'What thing?'

'People round, I mean. What's the matter with you?'

Aisling had sat down looking despairing on Nita's bed, right in the light from the bedside lamp. 'I don't want to stay here on my own with Babi and Gil.'

Minny pulled a face. 'Is Gil here?'

'Yes. He just arrived.'

It really was a terrible thought. Even Raymond was about to be put to bed; Minny reflected that she'd better not appear

261

downstairs until she was ready to leave, or she might end up entertaining Gil solo while Babi bathed the baby. She looked at Aisling and winced. 'Do you want to come with me?'

'Mm . . .'

'You can if you want. Veronica said you could come.' She flicked the eye-shadow brush to shake the loose stuff off; usually she managed to get flecks in her eye and then her eye would water till there was black smeared down to her jaw. Aisling was still sitting limply. 'Well, what do you think? Hurry up and decide. Look, I don't think anyone's going to be there who was bullying you. Veronica's pretty sound. And you can always leave. Or we can.'

'OK,' Aisling said in a bright voice. Minny wasn't at all sure about this really. She hadn't taken Aisling anywhere with her socially since they were both so young that their mother would have been there as well.

'Well, seriously, hurry. We're meeting Franklin on the corner in fifteen minutes.'

'What do I have to do?'

'Oh, for God's sake, Ash. Brush your hair. Put your black vest on, and a skirt. And some mascara.'

'Will you do it for me?'

'Only if you hurry up.'

They barely had time to tell Babi that Aisling was going too – she raised her eyebrows, but since Minny had cleared her own evening with Nita – 'She's just a sort-of friend,

Mum, she's cool. You'd like her. I'll walk home with Franklin. NO, no drugs.' – she said it was fine.

'Have you got a taxi number in case of emergencies?'

'Yes,' Minny said, rolling her eyes. She didn't feel comfortable leaving Raymond in the bath, but luckily Babi was raring to get him out so she could hurry downstairs to Gil.

'Don't be late, or do stupid things.'

Franklin was already there, leaning on the corner by their street sign. Dusk was beginning to fall, the purple kind you get in summer. He had a bottle sticking out of his jacket. 'Should we be bringing booze?' Minny asked him, when they were on their way. She felt unprepared.

'No, not unless you're planning to drink it.'

'Well.'

'Are you?' he asked.

'I don't know. Will everyone else be?' He shrugged; how would he know?

'I like booze,' Aisling announced. It was true, she did. Their mother said she'd been stealing gulps of wine since she was a baby. Minny wasn't a fan; it wasn't the sourness of the wine so much as the way it coated your teeth, like flat Coke. She'd had beer once or twice and that was even worse. It made your nose tickle. She decided that this probably wasn't the right occasion to try out public drinking, at least not in a quantity that would require her to bring her own alcohol. She was responsible for Aisling, and she

263

had to go home afterwards, so if she was drunk her mother would know. Anyway, at least she had a cast-iron excuse for leaving if it was too awkward; Ash was certain to be ready to go any time she was.

Veronica lived less than a mile away. Her street was familiar because it was the most direct way to the river from school. If it wasn't a party, it wasn't the intimate gathering Minny had rather been expecting; there were a lot of people spilling out of the front door as Minny, Ash and Franklin came up the street. There was a nice cat sitting on the wall opposite, watching, and Minny and Aisling crossed the road to stroke it first.

Someone random waved them in. Minny felt uneasy, especially because Franklin looked so amused while she hovered, so she pushed Ash ahead of her up the hall. Veronica popped out of the kitchen and was welcoming and friendly to all of them, talking to Aisling for at least three minutes and actually concentrating. Then she lifted Franklin's bottle out of his jacket, put it on the kitchen table with lots of other bottles and got them each a beaker of something that looked like Coke and smelled like lighter fuel.

Minny recognised a lot of people, from school and just from round about. Some of them were older but not all. She saw Linnea Jessop on the stairs talking intensely to a sixth-form boy and turned away, rolling her eyes. Another girl she didn't really know, called Karen, from the year above, summoned Franklin to an argument she was having with a group of people in the corner of the patio outside the back door, all of them waving cigarettes about; every now and then there was a puff of mauve smoke against the dusk. It was quite blary; Aisling kept putting her hands over her ears, and in the end Minny moved them both outside, past Franklin's group. At least they could sit down out there, and it was pretty dark so not so many people would see them being a pair of complete losers. Aisling was in a quiet mood, as usual gulping her drink as fast as possible so she didn't have to worry about it any more.

'Be careful of that,' Minny warned her. It tasted really strong – she had to not breathe while she was swallowing it. 'You don't want to get hammered.' It was nicer outside. It was a big garden with tangles of bushes round the outside so that there was a channel of light up the middle, cast from the kitchen. Minny found she was getting close to the end of her beaker, and wondered if she had the cojones to stay sitting in the middle of this unknown garden with her autistic sister if neither of them had a drink and no one else was talking to them. Fortunately Veronica came wandering out with a jug and refused to give any to the group Franklin was still with before she'd refreshed Aisling and Minny. Minny liked Veronica. She liked her crazy hair; she had a violet curl on each side of her face, so entirely distinct from every other curl that not a single violet hair could be seen anywhere else. Minny didn't want Aisling to keep on drinking, but she could hardly say so.

'Watch that,' Franklin said unexpectedly in her ear, sitting down beside her. She nearly spilt it on him. 'It's really strong, didn't you say . . .'

'Oh, shut up, Franklin.'

People kept coming up after that; some of them said hi to Aisling, which was nice. There seemed to be a lot of people around them, almost having the same conversation. Someone else gave Minny a drink. She had slyly passed Aisling's cup to Franklin, who started drinking it with an innocent expression; Ash didn't seem to mind. Minny talked to a boy called Dylan who was in her French group for a minute, and when she turned back round Linnea was squished in next to Franklin with her arms wrapped round her knees, her skirt shining white in the evening and her head on one side. Minny gulped at her drink. Dylan had drifted off and she had no one to talk to for a second. She heard Aisling saying, 'Franklin. Franklin. Excuse me, Franklin.'

'Hang on a sec, Ash.'

'What is it, Aisling?' She tugged Ash a couple of inches towards her. 'Don't keep talking to Franklin,' she hissed in her ear.

'Why not?'

'We don't want to look like we're tagging onto him. Look, I'll tell you later. Just don't hang around him too much, OK?'

'Who shall I talk to then?'

'I don't know.'

There were other people available; Veronica was sitting near them. Aisling looked reflectively over at the lit-up kitchen; there was a gang of kids squashed onto the sofa there. 'That girl goes to my youth group.'

Minny looked at the one Ash was pointing out; she was crammed in between two boys, looking from one face to the other and smiling faintly. She had long glossy thick brown hair with blonde stripes and a pouty pale-pink mouth. 'You mean she's autistic?'

'Shush.'

'What? I was quiet.' Maybe she hadn't been, or maybe Ash's hearing was veering between super-sensitive and a bit deaf, like her own. 'Really?' Minny couldn't not be interested; the girl didn't look autistic at all. 'What's she like?'

'I don't know. She doesn't talk much to me.'

Minny wondered what it would be like being her. Could you get away with being autistic, as a girl, if you were good-looking in a certain way and never opened your mouth? And if so, would that be a good result? She wanted to ask Aisling, but she had moved, which was just as well – Minny nodded wisely to herself; it might upset her maybe. She thought about asking Veronica, who was beside her instead, but realised it wasn't very cool to out someone as autistic in case it wasn't generally known, so instead she asked if she knew where Ash had gone.

'I told her there was a bunch of weirdos playing Cluedo inside,' Veronica said cheerfully. 'I throw the best parties.'

That was perfect. Aisling wouldn't win, she never won Cluedo, but she would enjoy it so she would be fine. Minny beamed.

'You look happy,' Franklin said, breaking straight out of what he'd been saying to Linnea, who seemed to have turned into Susannah Pitcher.

'Yeah, I am.'

'Good, you don't need to drink any more then.'

'Franklin,' Veronica chided him, 'don't be such a bossy git. You sound like . . . You two aren't even going out, are you?'

'No.'

Minny blushed.

'Well, you sound like a controlling boyfriend.'

'No, this is more like a bloody relative or something. I live with her grandmother and I promised—'

'Yeah. You still sound like him.' She nodded towards the kitchen. Minny turned round and saw Penny in there, looking fragile against the background of Jorge's T-shirt.

'Oh, bloody hell,' she said, turning back again.

'Oh yeah, that's your mate, isn't it, Minny?' Veronica started getting to her feet.

'Not so much any more.'

'I'd better say hello. I'll get some more drinks out.'

Minny checked on Aisling a bit later because she had a sudden panic that it might be Strip Cluedo or something, but it wasn't and she seemed fine. There were two boys playing the game with her and a scared-looking girl watching. Veronica's house was nice; Minny went on an expedition. She felt the slightest bit wobbly and thought perhaps she wouldn't drink any more; the fuzzy bright head was pleasant enough but she didn't want to fall over or anything, or spill things on the floor, especially upstairs because there were carpets there and they were very clean. Once upstairs, she decided to go to the bathroom; it all felt a bit of an epic adventure, what with the size of the house and the heaviness of all the big white doors and the way you didn't know which way they opened. Minny thought she must be drunk, after all, but it was nice, you didn't worry about being on your own. She got a dark bedroom where there were voices, and backed out as quick as she could because she realised one of them was Penny. 'Can't you just stay with me a little while?' she was saying.

'I want to go downstairs. It's a party.'

'You never want to just be alone with me any more.'

Safe outside, Minny found an airing cupboard full of coloured sheets and then a bathroom, which was a mess. She still looked all right in the mirror. On her way back down there were girls all over the stairs, it was like a dream. 'Hiya,' she said to Linnea. Linnea went on talking to a girl Minny didn't recognise. 'Hiya, Linnea,' Minny said, tugging a lock of her hair.

'Hello, Minny.'

Franklin was at the bottom, talking to Damon, that boy from his year. Minny was so delighted to see him she tripped

269

on the last step. He caught her and propped her against the wall. 'You think I'm drunk,' she accused him.

'You are drunk.'

'I am not. I am socially able.'

He laughed down at her. 'I'll tell Judy that, shall I?'

They went back into the garden. Minny found the fresh air helpful, and rubbing her hands through the dew-wet grass. 'What are you going to do when you grow up, Franklin? You're so good now, and everything.'

'I don't know. I don't know if I'll get to university, so it depends. I'm going to Texas sometime, soon as I can.'

'Texas? Like a cowboy?'

'No, like Steve Earle. Or Townes Van Zandt. Only without all the substance abuse – like Aisling said, like a good addict's child.'

Minny yawned into the grass. 'You've lost me.'

'It's where all the best musicians are from. I'm going to live there. What about you, Minny Molloy?'

'I don't know.' She half rolled over, and looked up at the sky. 'I used to think I'd do English and be brilliant, and maybe write books, but I suck at English now. I'm not good at anything any more.'

He snorted. 'Who told you that?'

'I don't know. Mrs Lemon.'

'Mrs Lemon is a fool. Anyway, I bet she didn't. Why would you let one bad teacher make you think you aren't good at something? That's ridiculous. Don't be stupid.'

'All right. Blimey. I won't then.'

'You were always brilliant at English. God, you're frustrating.'

'OK . . .'

'You shouldn't need me to tell you this stuff.'

'I don't.' She rolled her dew-wet fingers over her face. 'Actually I don't.'

He went off after a while, maybe to get a drink. There were different people out there now. Someone said hello to her through the dark; it was Alex Traves, which gave her a flutter for a quick second because last year she had sort of had a crush on him, mostly pretend, to have something to talk about. She stopped when Penny started going out with Jorge, because it was either that or start pretending to be terribly in love with him. He didn't seem anywhere near as cool all of a sudden, but in a good way; he was drunker than she was. For some reason they were talking about fruit, and which was the best fruit.

'You'll probably take this as evidence that I'm gay,' Alex said, 'but I like bananas.'

'I like bananas too,' she said. 'Are you gay?'

'No.'

'Why would I need evidence that you were gay?'

'I don't know. I like pineapple as well.'

'Oh. I think I like plums best.' She felt pleased with the inspiration.

'Really? That's weird.'

'No, right, because I know, you take a fruit like an apple, or an orange or something, right? And most of the time it's nice. I mean, sometimes it's really nice, but mostly it's fine, you don't often have a bad apple, for instance. And you don't see plums all that much, I mean it's not like they're in the shops all year round, and even when they are they mostly aren't that great. But when you do get a good one – mmmm. It's special. You forget in between, you see. You've forgotten. But I . . . remember. Have you read *The Grapes of Wrath*?'

He hadn't, he said. Minny thought that Franklin might have done – she'd been meaning to ask him – and if he hadn't then he should read it now, so she got up and went to find him. Also Aisling. Just as she got to the kitchen door there was a big bustle and a whole stream of people poured in through the front door, so she waited; some of them split off into the side rooms, and others pushed past her into the kitchen and through to the garden. When there was space she went to find Aisling, who had been through the second door playing Cluedo, only she wasn't now; she was standing by the bookcase with someone in front of her. It was Georgia McDonald. Who had been suspended after the thing with Aisling's clothes. And, now Minny looked, she was flanked by Maria Hoyle and Matty Dent, who was sort of Georgia's boyfriend possibly, and a couple of others. They were all twice Aisling's size. And Ash looked miserable and terrified. In fact, Minny could hear her saying, 'Leave me alone.'

'No, why should I? You think you can try and get us expelled and expect us to be nice about it?' Before Minny had gathered herself together, Georgia McDonald pushed Aisling, and Aisling, who hadn't been expecting it, staggered back into the bookcase.

'Leave her alone.' It wasn't Minny's own voice, though it was so much what she had been about to shout that she squeaked in agreement before looking round. Jorge was standing in the other half of the room, by the other door as if he'd just come in. There were a lot of people sitting down in there, though she couldn't see Penny. He walked over. 'Leave her, Georgia.'

'Oh, rod off, Jorge.'

'Leave her alone.'

'Or what?' Matty Dent was massive.

'I'm not talking to you,' Jorge told him. 'I will, if you want, but I'm just asking Georgia nicely to leave Aisling alone.'

'Yeah? Why should I?'

'Because she was invited,' Veronica said from the doorway. 'And you weren't, so you can leave.'

Minny used the pause to step across the gap and take up a place next to Ash, between her and Maria Hoyle.

'You're trying to kick me out?'

'Yeah. And you lot as well,' Veronica said to all the people with her.

'What?' Maria started. 'I haven't even done anything.'

'But I don't like you.'

Jorge continued to stand where he was until they had left, laughing and kicking stuff on their way out, and then walked out of the room without catching anyone's eye.

'Thanks for that, Veronica,' Minny said.

'S'my absolute pleasure. Are you all right, Aisling?'

Ash was white. 'I want to go home,' she said to Minny, as if they were alone. Veronica backed tactfully away.

'Why? It's fine now.'

'No, I want to go home.' Her hands clenched and unclenched. Minny, who felt like they ought to stay since a bunch of people had just been thrown out for their sake, and who wanted to stay, tried to soothe her but couldn't. Finally she said, 'Well, fine, if you can convince Franklin, we'll go, but not for a few minutes or we'll just bump straight into that lot again outside. Fifteen minutes, OK?' It was ten o'clock. 'Quarter past ten, yeah? Why don't we go into the garden.' But then she got held up herself in the kitchen because there was a scene going on, which Ash could walk straight through but she couldn't.

A lot of people just seemed to be watching Jorge be angry with Penny, which was odd; they were really rubbernecking. Penny was trying to put her arms around him but he was shouting at her. 'Christ, stop being so bloody needy and leave me alone for a single second.'

'OK, I'm sorry, I just wanted to—'

'God, it's pathetic. Just go and talk to someone else.'

'Don't—'

He put his arms up and shrugged hers off.

She started crying.

He went outside.

She fled, sniffling, past Minny – gave her a scared look – and up the corridor. Minny heard her thumping up the stairs. She hovered, glancing round to see if anyone else was going to follow, and then looking outside after Ash – Ash was probably with Franklin. She ran after Penny.

She was sitting on the bathroom floor, back against the bath, but she hadn't shut the door properly let alone locked it. Next morning Minny would reflect that she had probably hoped to be followed, although possibly not by Minny.

'Are you OK?' Minny asked.

'Fine.' She sobbed. Minny went and sat down beside her, and considered what to say.

'He shouldn't treat you like that,' she offered in the end.

'He doesn't normally. Not often. I think I drive him mental.'

'Why are you going out with him then?'

'I don't know. I love him.'

'I mean, why is he going out with you if he doesn't like you?'

'I didn't say . . . Of course he likes me. He loves me. Oh, shut up, Minny. What do you care anyway?'

'I don't, I just . . .'

'You just hate Jorge.'

'I don't, actually, he was—'

'You just hate me then.'

'I don't.' All her anger came bubbling up suddenly. 'I could though, why shouldn't I? Your mother told my dad I was taking loads of drugs and practically in a gang or something with Franklin, and he believed it. Now we have to stay with my bloody grandmother when my mum goes to Edinburgh . . .'

'I don't understand a word you're saying. You're drunk.'

'Oh, why not say I'm bloody high as well? Hooked on drugs, me.'

'I don't have to listen to this,' Penny muttered, gathering up her bag.

'The point is, you're a liar.'

'Oh, leave me alone, Minny! I'm going home, I hate everyone!' She was off again, leaping over Minny's legs and galloping down the stairs.

'Wait, Penny, you can't go on your own,' Minny shouted over the banisters after her. 'Wait, we're leaving now too . . .' but the front door banged.

She hurried down, thinking that if she could find Ash and Franklin in time then they might catch Penny up. Her mother had rubbed it well into her that you didn't walk around on your own after dark. She found Franklin all right, but not ready to leave – he was on the sofa under the window in the sitting room with Linnea on his lap.

She stopped dead in the doorway. He looked up and saw

her before she could back out, if she'd been going to. And she was mortified that he must have seen her expression, and furious and anxious that she could not be on her own right then, immediately, so she dashed out to the garden, to a gap in the blackberry bushes where there was a wall to lean against for a second.

'Minny.' He was calling her, almost instantly. She stayed silent and didn't look round. 'Minny.' He was close now, ignoring the people who greeted him, and she knew he must have seen her. The breeze blew against her as he came and stood beside her. 'Minny.'

'What?'

'I don't know. You ran off.'

'I've got to go home.'

'OK, well, I'll come . . .'

'I didn't want to disturb you.' She wasn't going to just not mention it.

He sighed. 'Sorry about her. Linnea.'

'Why are you sorry?'

'She just came and sat there.' Silence. 'What, you think I seized her and said, "Come and sit on my lap, petal, you're everything I desire"?'

'I don't know. Why not. She's pretty. Got nice hair.'

'She's OK, but . . .'

'But what? I thought that's all you were interested in.'

'Why are you so angry?'

'I'm not.' She had stupid tears prickling the backs of her

eyeballs, like the brambles were prickling the backs of her legs.

'Minny . . .'

'What?'

He didn't answer so she turned towards him and he was leaning. At her. His arm went round her waist and his face was so close suddenly that she had a sense that they were sharing air. And for a moment the skin along her arms and back was all tingles and she felt her eyelashes sweep her cheekbones like something out of a perfume advert.

But then she recoiled, so that the brick wall scraped her shoulder blade, and put up her hands to actually push him away.

'What? What's wrong?'

'Nothing, just don't.'

He looked helpless, he looked embarrassed, even in the dark. 'Sorry, I thought you wanted—'

'I didn't! I don't. I just didn't want you to kiss her.' She gave a miserable, horrified sob and ran away, back into the house, looking round for Aisling. She couldn't see her, but there was Veronica. 'Have you seen Ash?'

'She left.'

'What? When?'

'Only a couple of minutes ago. You could catch her.'

'Oh God.' She ran for the front door. 'Thank you for having me,' she called over her shoulder.

This must be a dream, she thought, running up the dark

street, which felt much narrower than it had earlier, and almost misty; she felt like someone in a film, or a Simon and Garfunkel song. She was already out of breath when she reached the corner and stared so anxiously ahead for Aisling that her legs almost couldn't keep up with her head and she staggered for a second. It wasn't anywhere near as dark on the main road and there were a few people in sight. One of them, more than two blocks ahead, was probably Aisling, and Minny called her. Not that she answered, of course, and Minny scared herself by how loud her voice was. She kept on running, pretty slowly by the time she got near Ash, who had at least stopped and waited for her. 'We weren't supposed to walk home alone,' Minny gasped.

'I know.' She was crying, not loudly but her chest was going up and down too fast. They walked on together, Minny's knees trembling; she didn't often run. She was grateful not to be drunk any more.

'Why are you crying?'

'I'm not crying.'

'Yes, you are. Are you worrying about those silly cows?'

'No.'

'Well, don't. That was just bad luck, seeing them tonight. They can't do anything to you now, can they?'

Aisling sniffed. 'Where's Franklin?'

'I don't know. Linnea Jessop was after him so – with her, I suppose.'

'Linnea Jessop?'

'Yeah.'

'He wouldn't like her,' Aisling said.

'How would you know?' Minny was aggravated. 'He's a boy, isn't he? She's got big boobs and long hair, hasn't she? Anyway, he didn't seem to be hating it, with her sitting on his lap. I don't care.'

'OK.' There was a long pause. 'Roger Ram is up and Roger Ram is down . . .' she whispered. Minny had never heard it so quiet. 'Matty Dent hurt my nipple,' she said suddenly at normal volume.

'What?'

'He pinched my nipple at the party.'

'What?'

'When he came in with Maria and Georgia and Simon,' Aisling explained. 'I'd just put the Cluedo away and I heard them. I should have gone away. I heard them laughing at me and then he came up behind me and pinched me on the breast, and they all laughed.'

'What a moron,' Minny burst out. 'Did – does it still hurt?'

'A bit. He twisted it. Why did he do that?'

'Power,' Minny said. 'Just more bullying. It's not just you though, you know. Someone did that to Penny when she was walking down the street last term, and I got my bum pinched in assembly a couple of weeks ago, I don't even know who it was. It's boys. They're disgusting.'

'All boys?'

'Most. Things are so rubbish,' Minny burst out again.

Aisling rubbed more tears away. 'What things?'

'Penny being so mad. She had another go at me – and I wasn't very nice to her, but she deserved it, only Jorge had just been a right sod. I thought for a second he was OK when he told Georgia off, but then he had to go and be a git to Penny. I don't get it. And I don't get why she puts up with it. People seem to put up with such crap from people, some people can get away with anything – boys. And men. Dad being such a prat. You can't trust anyone, not even Mum – she's a liar too. She thinks it's OK because everyone knows, really, everyone who matters knows who Raymond's father is. Probably even Harriet knows, but no one admits they know and no one says it so it's not the same thing, is it? It's still a lie. Because Raymond won't know. And the whole thing is just her giving Dad an excuse not to take any responsibility for his child, and protecting him from getting into any trouble, like she always does. And Harriet's another one. And Kevin, you can't trust him either – I don't even know him. Maybe he had nothing to do with it, but then all that means is that he doesn't care about us at all and never got in touch with me – and that it was Dad the whole time. And that would be . . .' She thought about it, and shuddered. 'Even more creepy.'

'It's all right, Minny,' Aisling said. 'Everything passes.'

Their mother wasn't home yet, which Minny was glad

about in case she still seemed at all drunk, even though she wasn't. Babi's bedroom door was shut. When she came out of the bathroom Minny peeped in at Ash's door, but she was already in bed with the light off. She went into her mother's room and tucked the light blanket around Raymond, who always kicked it off before he went to sleep. She checked Selena was asleep too before she climbed up into bed. Everyone else had been defecting on her lately. You couldn't rely on anyone not to start lying or to have been lying all the time, except her sisters and her brother, who wouldn't bother.

She felt pretty rough the next morning, so it was just as well she didn't have to get up before her mother left. Babi shouted outside the bedroom door at nine o'clock because she needed help with the baby; when Minny limped downstairs she looked at her with raised eyebrows and then brought her a glass of water. 'Aisling is mysteriously not feeling so well this morning either,' she said. 'Peculiar. Take some ibuprofen and eat some breakfast. I have a meeting in an hour.'

The school reports were lying, opened, on the kitchen counter. Normally Minny might have sneaked a look at Ash's or even Selena's, but she wasn't even up to reading her own. Instead she took a plate of toast into the back room, where Aisling was lying on the sofa with Selena sitting on her legs complaining that it wasn't fair for one person to take up so much space. They were watching very noisy cartoons. Minny collapsed hastily into the armchair and shut her eyes to eat her breakfast.

TWELVE

The next few days were hardly any better, even though she'd recovered from her hangover. It rained a lot, and even when it wasn't the sky was grey and low. She felt as if the whole holiday had been ruined and wasted and only despair lay ahead. Nita was so busy with her play: almost every evening if she was in at all, she'd put Raymond to bed and then have to go out again to extra rehearsals, or meetings, or at least sit hunched over the computer looking at figures or catching up on reports. They had Babi cooking their dinners, which was fine, but she was around most of the day too, which was less fun. So they all got away with trailing wretchedly around the house, likely to be on the verge of tears any moment. Selena was almost the worst; she absent-mindedly picked up the phone, which they'd all been avoiding doing, on Saturday afternoon, and it was their father. She listened to him for a minute while Minny considered grabbing the phone from her, then she said, 'No, I can't talk now, Daddy,' hung up and burst into tears. Minny took the phone off the hook, but she wasn't allowed to leave it like that in case Gil rang.

Then, when it rang again in the evening, there was no

one else in the room so Minny picked it up to save Selena's nerves, and it turned out to be neither Des nor Gil nor a cold-calling insurance salesperson, but Uncle Kevin. 'Is that you, Minny? Listen, your dad's just been on the phone to me and I wanted to tell you – well, tell you how it all happened.'

'Right,' she said.

'You remember back when you were nine or ten and we started emailing each other. Mam was over with you of course, and you never came here so I only ever got to talk with you when I was visiting and I hadn't been for a long time, remember? And then when your dad left and I didn't feel like – I thought it might be too much for your mother if I came over – I was thrilled to still be in touch. I loved getting your messages, Minny.' He paused, but she didn't have anything to say. 'But then after a while your dad started calling me more. I think he was very lonely over there and he was feeling terrible. He's my little brother, Minny, it was hard to hear how low he was, and the worst part was being so alienated from you girls. I started reading him out little bits of your emails, funny things, just snippets to prove that you were doing OK and what a grand girl you were. Only it was a lifeline for him and it got to where he was just pestering me all the time until I'd read out whatever you'd written most lately and there didn't seem any point in not forwarding the messages to him so he could read them himself.' Minny changed the receiver to her left hand and sat down. '. . . shouldn't have done that. Then in the end, and I still don't know how the bugger did it, he hacked into my account somehow and started sending you replies. I don't suppose he meant any harm, Minny, he was just trying to forge a relationship with you when he was desperate.'

'I don't—'

'Right, right, I didn't mean to be defending him. The thing I feel most bad about isn't him or his chances with you now, it's that you're feeling like I betrayed your trust and so did he, again, and you've got nowhere to turn. I would hate that.'

'Well.' She rubbed her eyes. 'Tough.'

'Will you talk to me?'

'No.'

'Never?'

'I don't think so.'

'Why not?'

'Because I don't know you.' She was dying to get him off the phone; this was literally painful. 'I don't know which emails were from you and which from Dad, I don't know anything about you.'

'Can we not start again?'

'No. Don't you get it – you're . . . a made-up person. I don't even know for sure I'm talking to you now – how can I? – to Kevin Molloy, I mean. You could be Dad. You probably are. I'm not doing this.'

'OK.' There was a silence.

'So – I'm going now.'

'OK. Look after yourself, Minny.' There was a click. After a minute she hung up too. There was too much confusion. She didn't understand anyone any more or why they did what they did, and how the good things fitted with the bad ones. Everyone should just pick a line and stick to it.

They did have one outing with Nita – she seemed to feel she was neglecting them terribly but she only had one day, which meant one half-day as she was rehearsing again from four o'clock. She picked the Science Museum. It wasn't really a success; it was packed, for a start, with people who didn't know what to do with their school-liberated children, as well as with tourists from all over everywhere. Raymond found a few buttons he liked. Aisling stood and looked at the rocket for ages. Selena dragged her feet and whined until they ate their sandwiches, and then it was more or less time to go home. The Tube was jam-packed too: Nita shoved Minny on, passed her the baby, then lifted Selena on – she had to actually push her past the threshold because people on the train weren't getting out of the way for a timid seven-year-old; then she got on herself and by sheer shoving managed to make enough room to be able to drag Aisling on by the arm, through three other people who had pushed past her in the meantime. Then of course the doors tried to close three times before Aisling could be tucked in enough to let them. Minny would have been more in a position to admire her mother's toughness if she hadn't been stuck holding the baby till the train emptied enough at Hammersmith for her to pass him over; her back was breaking.

That was the 'fun' day. Then they were on their own again and stumbled along, Minny thought, like they were blindfolded and couldn't touch each other. It felt like it was going to be a very long summer, even though Nita had promised they'd go away somewhere for a week late in August – she hadn't had time to organise where yet, and Minny thought they'd be lucky to get Wales, though Selena was fantasising about one of the sunny places with water slides that she'd seen on adverts. The only bright spot was that Minny had, in despair one morning over back-to-back *Charmed* reruns, forced herself to start reading *Jane Eyre* and it was excellent. She felt ashamed of her ten-year-old self. She couldn't read it all the time – it was too intense, and she had to help with the baby a good deal – but it made things just about tolerable.

Nita left for Edinburgh the following week. She was all excited. She'd been leading up to this day for months and months. Minny thought she was probably happy just to be getting away from home for a few days too, though it sounded like it was going to be manic. Only someone with her mother's life could see putting on a play starring nine children with special needs three hundred miles from their homes and looking after them at night in rented accommodation in a strange city as a getaway. She was nervous too though, and not just about the play. She kept making Minny promise again and again to keep an eye on things, and on everyone, and to try to make sure no one went missing or got horribly burnt or drowned in the bath. 'And don't be away for the night or for completely whole days, OK?' As if she hadn't noticed that the only times Minny had left the house since school finished she'd had at least one sibling in tow.

Her actual leaving, running out the door into the drizzle laden down with bags, was a bit like the scene in *Little Women* where the telegram comes about their wounded dad and Marmee has to leave them all alone and they're bereft. Selena's face was shaking. Aisling had gone silent again. Minny picked up Raymond to give him his morning milk, and hoped no one would get scarlet fever.

Babi was in a foul mood that day. She hated being in real charge. Minny had to admit that Nita was right, her grandmother did do a lot for them, maybe especially for Nita herself. She always agreed to look after them when Nita needed her to. And even though Nita knew that half the time she might not be knocking herself out to do it tremendously well, Babi always managed to convince her that they'd all be OK. Minny was glad Babi could do that for her, because otherwise she didn't know how they would manage.

It got worse in the evening, when Gil came round. He'd been steering mostly clear since Selena had shouted at him, hovering on the doorstep or at most in the hallway to wait for Babi to go out with him. He turned up that day after dinner and Babi brought him straight into the back room. Minny and Selena were sitting around watching TV while the baby played with his magnetic numbers on the floor. 'Here's Gil,' Babi said.

Minny finished watching the scene, then looked up. 'Hello.'

'Hello, Minny. How are you?'

'Oh, fine.'

There was a pause.

'Selena,' Babi said loudly. 'Here is Gil.'

Selena muttered a hello.

'He's come round so that you can apologise to him for being rude.'

Minny looked up again, with wide eyes, and then at Selena, who was sitting forward so that her hair hid her face. Her ear was scarlet. She picked up two little magnetic threes, one yellow and one purple, and Raymond squawked in protest.

'Selena?'

Selena muttered something and ran out of the room.

Gil sighed.

'She had to apologise, Gil. If no one makes a child apologise then they will stop knowing when they have done wrong.'

'You're not big on saying sorry yourself though, are you?'

Minny said, gathering Raymond up and taking him into the front room.

Later she passed the back room and heard them talking about holidays. 'I would not dislike seeing Copenhagen.'

'Or Reykjavik.'

'Or Reykjavik, certainly. But can we afford it, Gil? These are very expensive.'

'Well. Not if you go last minute, you see. Right now, anyway, there's this deal on – but we'd have to go by the end of this week.'

'But I can't. Nita isn't back until Sunday, or possibly Saturday.'

'We'd have to go by Friday at the latest.'

'Then we cannot go.'

'What about the father? That's no go?' Babi must have shaken her head. 'And what about his mother? I thought they all got on well with her. Couldn't she have them for a night?'

'She is an old woman, you see, older than me. And of course she has this child, this boy living with her now.'

'Yes, but just for one night . . .'

'And she is not the baby's grandmother. You see. Nita doesn't feel able to send him to her, or to have her babysit, since he arrived.'

'Yes, I suppose. So not even for one night.'

'I cannot, Gil. If Nita hadn't left already I might ask her

to consider these things, but I promised her to take care of them. We can go later, perhaps in September when everywhere will be less crowded.'

'Of course. Only it will be getting colder.'

'Well, then we will go to Bologna instead.'

'What's at Bologna?'

'Or wherever you would like.'

'Bologna sounds nice.'

Minny aimed the baby at the back room, watched him crawl in and then went upstairs. Selena was lying on her bed sobbing. Minny pushed the giant rag doll off the chair and sat down.

'Don't cry,' she said after a while.

'Why not?' Selena shouted into the mattress.

'It's not worth crying over.'

'Yes it is. I want Mum back. Why does she have to be in Edin-berg?'

'Edin-borough. It's not for that long.'

'She shouldn't have gone. Can we go there?'

'No, of course not.'

'Why not? We could help.'

'No, we can't. It won't be long.'

'It's already long. Can we go and stay with Granny?'

'No.'

'Why not?'

'Because we've got to look after Raymond and Granny's not his granny, is she?'

'I could go. Just on my own.' Selena rolled over and looked at her eagerly.

'No, we should stay together. And anyway she's got Franklin to look after, hasn't she?'

Sel's face clouded again and she began to sob.

'Oh, don't, Selena. I don't suppose Gil will be round that much. Tell you what – you could call up Victoria or one of your mates and ask if you can go and stay there one night again. That would be OK, wouldn't it?'

'But Mum said that Victoria would come here next because I've just been to her house. She said I could have a sleepover next week maybe.'

'Right. Well. That's something to look forward to, isn't it?'

Selena quietened down. She lay still watching Minny tidy up a bit – stuffing some scrunched-up papers into the overflowing bin and throwing the Sylvanian Families back in their box. 'Couldn't we go to Dad's?'

'No.'

She was completely silent and in the end Minny looked up from the bin. 'I just can't, Sel. Not yet anyway. And – this is our house, it's where we live, we shouldn't leave it just because . . .'

'I know.'

'He's not – we couldn't take Raymond there either.'

'I know.'

'They're so . . . untrustworthy. You don't know what they're

293

going to do next, and I don't want to owe them anything. I know Mum wouldn't want us to either.'

'Yeah, I said.'

'I mean. I suppose you could go. On your own, if you really wanted to.'

'No, I CAN'T.'

'OK.'

'As if they'd want just me.'

'What do you mean?'

'They don't even know me. They don't love me like you two.'

'That's a funny thing to say.'

'No, it's true. I was only little before Dad left. He doesn't know me and he didn't like me very much even then.'

'Selena, what do you mean?'

She gave a great sniffle and a shrug. 'He left because of having too many children, didn't he? So it was me, because he didn't leave when he only had two.'

Minny gaped. 'You don't really think that.'

'Why not?'

Minny didn't know what to say; she wondered if it might be best to laugh it off. Instead she pulled a sensible face. 'Sel, that's ridiculous. First of all you were four years old, how's it going to have been your fault? You were probably the least of his worries. Secondly he was depressed, like mentally ill, and none of us was to blame for that. Thirdly it probably had a lot to do with him and Mum, their marriage and all.' She felt she had put it well. Selena didn't look convinced. They gazed at each other. 'Listen, of course it wasn't our fault. It probably had nothing to do with us, personally, at all, except that maybe he wasn't ready for the responsibility of us and in that case he'd been fighting it since way before you were even born and he just bolted when he bolted. But if it was anything about any of us, Sel, it's hardly going to have been you, is it?'

'What do you mean?'

'Well, if there was – is – one of us who's more trouble and makes life a bit more stressful than the rest and is going to send him off to America, it's Aisling, isn't it, not you.'

There was a noise and they both whipped their heads round. Aisling was standing at the door. She looked at them for a few more seconds before her face crumpled and she went away.

'Oh crap,' Minny said. She felt almost too terrible to go after her, but she couldn't not. She'd gone into her room and shut the door. 'Can I come in, Aisling? Ash, I didn't mean it like that. Honestly. It's not true, what I said. Can I come in?'

'No.'

'Don't be upset. I was just . . . talking rubbish, I didn't mean it. You know that, right?' Her phone bleeped in her pocket and she glanced at it in case it was her mother. Penny.

You might be pleased to know me and Jorge broke up.

Minny rolled her eyes. She texted back – *Good* – and knocked again. 'Ash, please let me in so I can say sorry properly. I didn't mean it.'

'Go away.'

She did in the end. Not that there was anywhere to go to.

Minny didn't begrudge this Edinburgh trip to her mother, or to her drama group – obviously it was really important and empowering and all that – but things had gone downhill quite fast already; the house was full of sulkiness, and Gil, and the baby was missing Nita and crying a lot more than usual, and for the summer holidays it really sucked, especially as there was practically nothing else she could actually be doing – if she could look forward to next week when her time would be her own again it would be one thing, but she seemed to have no friends at all right now, one way or another. Penny's text had sounded totally unfriendly, and her own reply probably wouldn't have helped smooth things over. Besides she was still angry herself and not keen to make up and that more or less cut her off from the other girls in their year who were sort of her mates, because she didn't want to have to talk about Penny. She hadn't heard from Franklin since Veronica's party. The other people from his year she'd been chatting with were only really acquaintances. The whole summer stretched ahead, looking as friendless as it must look to Aisling.

She did try, next day, with her family. During the rainy

morning she played the guitar for at least half an hour, trying to lure Ash out of her room; she only stopped because the baby kept taking the pick away and posting it inside the guitar. She didn't even put in her stock complaints about having to schlepp to Babi's Weight Watchers meeting at lunchtime – again. Babi insisted that she couldn't leave Raymond and Selena at home, and so Minny had to go too to look after them while she did her weighing and her inspiring words of wisdom. She didn't want to, partly because it was so tedious, but mostly because she didn't want to leave Ash on her own. Minny put her head round her door before they left, expecting her to be watching a film or TV or something on her laptop, but she was just sitting on the bed.

'What is it?'

'We're off to Babi's meeting now. Do you want to come?'

'No.'

'Are you sure? It's not that bad – we can laugh at the fat people.' Aisling didn't smile. 'It doesn't take too long.'

'I don't want to.'

'Why not? We get to eat the horrible snacks and everything. Please come. You're not doing anything.'

'I am.'

'And I could do with the help watching Sel and Raymond.'

'I don't want to,' Ash said. She was gearing up for a meltdown. 'I don't want to talk to you. I want to stay here. So leave me alone.'

'Fine,' Minny said, and stomped downstairs.

'It's probably just as well,' Babi remarked, when they were all finally installed in the car and on their way. At least Ash not coming meant Minny could sit in the front again, not jammed in the back with Raymond's car seat digging into her thigh and Selena elbowing her on the other side. 'I don't really want the place filled up with skinny teenagers. It would put my women off.'

'Every cloud,' Minny said sourly.

She sat and fretted, reading stories to the baby at the back of the church hall while everyone queued up to get weighed. What she'd said the other night – it could be a really bad thing for Aisling to have overheard. Mainly because, being Aisling, she might believe it. In the same way that Sel could apparently believe that it had been her fault Dad left. Or, even if she didn't believe it – she might think that that was what Minny believed – that Minny blamed her. She might very well think that. And it wasn't true, not now, not ever really. But she didn't know how to get that through to Ash.

It couldn't have been more boring: women – almost all – coming into the church hall looking timid and ashamed, various degrees of fat or in some cases quite thin, but mostly pretty lumpy, standing on scales talking to Babi of all people and her little old ladies. You would think nothing could be worse, but actually the first couple of times Minny had been she'd found it interesting how Babi became a different person the moment the first weighee stepped through the door.

She made them laugh, exhorted them to be positive, even grabbed handfuls of flesh at her own hips to wiggle at them if she was talking about how she used to be large. When the actual meeting began and everyone sat down in their circle of orange plastic chairs Minny let Raymond play with the buttons on one set of scales while she weighed herself on the other. She weighed a pound more than yesterday, which seemed impossible. Then she sneaked a minute speed-reading a page of *Jane Eyre* so she missed what happened next, but it seemed Babi must have paid the price for living her life on four-inch spike heels; the floor was wet from feet, she slipped and the heel of her shoe broke and pitched her down onto the wooden floor on her derriere.

Of course she was surrounded in seconds by elephant legs, and Minny had to look after the baby and stop Selena running to add to the chaos. The next time they saw Babi, a minute later, she was easing herself down onto a chair. 'Shall I ring for an ambulance?' one old lady quavered, the one who sat behind the table and took half the meeting to figure out how much change to give someone from a fiver when they bought a one-pound snack.

'Don't be ridiculous,' Babi snapped. She was obviously in pain – it seemed to be her ankle that was the trouble – but she was in danger of losing her jolly reputation during the next few minutes, while they all wittered on about what to do and threatened vaguely that this was the kind of thing that turned you into an elderly person.

It ended up with Minny, Selena and Raymond being crushed into the hot back seat while Letty, the oldest woman in England, drove them home at five miles an hour and then took Babi on to the hospital. 'Make sure to feed the baby,' was all she said through the window once they had been decanted onto the pavement outside the house, 'and give him enough to drink.' Then they drove off.

It was a dull afternoon. Hours passed. In the end Minny thought she'd better get everyone out for a walk, but Ash wouldn't come. 'Please,' Minny said. 'I can't manage the two of them without help.' She could barely get Raymond into his pushchair on her own, he hated it so much.

'Don't go then.'

'You haven't been out of the house in days.' Minny hesitated. 'Are you worried we might bump into someone from school?'

'No. Leave me alone.'

'Because we don't have to go to the park. We could walk the other way up to the river.'

'Leave me ALONE,' she shouted, and kicked the door shut in Minny's face.

Minny went downstairs and, to improve staying in the garden, spent a sweaty twenty minutes emptying buckets into the grubby old paddling pool while Selena followed Raymond around and shouted at Minny every time he put a pebble in his mouth. She was incapable of stopping him herself without choking him or making him cry. Clouds closed in and as Minny grimly topped up the pool with a final bucket, rain pitter-pattered gently into it.

They stayed outside because there was nothing to do inside. When the shadows were getting longer and the paddling pool was filling up with floating specks of dirt at the top and swirling dirt at the bottom, and the sky with darker clouds so that even though it was warm you shivered sometimes, Ash came and stood at the French windows. She slid one of them back and forth. 'I'm hungry.'

'Sandwiches for dinner, I suppose,' Minny said.

'There's no bread.'

'Well, you'll have to go and get some.'

'Me?'

'I can't go, can I? Unless we all go, I suppose.'

The phone rang. Selena was quick as a fish and got to it before anyone else, ignoring the fact she was dripping thin mud onto the carpet, but once it was obvious it was Babi – you could hear her voice from the other end of the room – Minny wrenched it away from her.

'Give it to me – oh, sod off, Selena. What?' she said into the receiver.

'I have not died, thank you for your kind concern, nor am I about to lose one of my limbs.'

'Well, I knew you wouldn't be,' Minny said, exasperated. 'So what is happening?'

'I have a severely sprained ankle.'

'Just a sprain?'

'Which, as the twelve-year-old doctors and adolescent nurses here have been eager to point out, at my age is a serious situation. Sorry that I didn't break my neck.'

'Right,' Minny said, running a hand up through her hair. 'Are you coming home?'

'Yes. Gil has extremely kindly come all the way to the hospital and we are on our way back now.'

'OK.' Great. 'The thing is, we don't have any food.'

There was a heavy sigh. 'I will ask Gil if he would mind stopping to get something.'

'Thanks,' Minny said sharply, and replaced the handset.

Selena hadn't got past her embarrassment with Gil, Aisling was still surly, the baby was tearful, Minny found herself in a foul mood and Babi was shouting at anyone who ventured within two metres of her foot, so dinner was awkward. Even though it was nice Lebanese food from the café by Gil's shop. Minny thought about the Lebanese meal she'd had with her father. Perhaps pleasantness under false pretences was to be preferred to honest horribleness after all.

The actual trouble began when Gil ordered Minny to wash up and Aisling to make a coffee for Babi and himself. Of course if their mother had been there she'd probably have made them do it and they wouldn't have minded too much. But as it was, even Ash looked resentful. 'What about the baby?' Minny muttered. 'Who's looking after him?' She'd already realised that, with Babi having an excuse to sit on the sofa not moving, her own workload was significantly increased.

'I'm sure Selena can keep an eye on him for a few minutes,' Gil said, offering Babi his arm and picking up her glass of wine for her.

He would have done better, if he actually wanted his coffee, to get either of the others to make it or to make it himself. Minny had finished clearing the table and washing the plates by the time Aisling had it ready. She took it through, a mug at a time, while Minny made tea.

'Oh, but.' Aisling was suddenly lathered with indecision. 'Isn't it too late for tea?'

'Oh, yes,' Selena said. It wasn't quite seven o'clock, which was when Sel had her pre-bedtime drink of water. Aisling left hers till half seven. They had once read that you shouldn't drink anything two hours before you go to bed, lest you get woken up in the night by a full bladder.

'Have tea for once instead,' Minny said, pressing her lips together and marching them into the back room. Babi and Gil should not have it all their own way the whole time Nita was gone; her mother would never be able to fight a battle against lines already solid. This was their house now too. She picked up the remote and switched on the TV; it was *Emmerdale*, which Babi watched but never with Gil, because he wasn't a big TV fan. She wanted to see her grandmother's eyes trying not to slide towards it.

As it happened Babi was in the mood for dealing with

things more directly. 'Minny,' she said in a voice which grated so much that Selena looked round in alarm. 'Turn it off.'

Minny settled herself into the chair beside her, because it was closest to where the baby was playing with a pack of cards. 'Why? You like *Emmerdale*.'

'Turn it off.'

'Why?'

'Because she said so, that's why,' Gil said.

'That's not the way this house works,' Minny said. Her cheeks were beginning to burn. 'We haven't been brought up to obey unquestioningly, Gil.'

'Is that what it is? I thought you were just extremely rude.'

'She's not rude.' Aisling was watching the baby.

'Minny,' Babi said, leaning heavily on her crutch to stand up, 'turn off that television.'

'Do it yourself,' Minny said, placing the remote on the arm of the sofa and folding her arms. Babi snapped the button and the TV flickered to silence.

'What is the matter with you?' She was still standing there, right in front of Minny. 'Why are you being a spoilt brat?'

'I'm not. I just came into the living room of my home to watch some telly. I don't see why that's unreasonable.'

'You are being deliberately obstreperous and unpleasant.' Minny sometimes wondered if her grandmother would be even meaner in her first language; there was never any shortage of critical vocabulary. 'You wouldn't be acting like this if your mother was here.'

'I should hope not,' Gil said.

Minny snapped. 'No, probably not, because if Mum was here you wouldn't be inflicting your horrible mood on us just because you made a tit of yourself at your stupid meeting and now we've all got to put up with him sitting around like he owns the place—'

Her grandmother, swaying on her crutch for extra force, slapped her across the face.

Minny flung all the tea in her cup over her grandmother.

Selena screamed. Aisling backed into the corner. Gil leaped up and in front of Babi, which put him looming over Minny; for a second she thought he might hit her as well, she was so shocked.

'That's enough,' he said. 'That's more than enough. Milena, are you all right? Are you burnt?'

'Of course she's not burnt,' Minny shouted, 'it was half-drunk milky tea, not steaming acid.'

Gil was helping Babi away. She wiped her face. Her hair was dripping at the front. 'That's it,' she said. 'I have done all I can, but that's it. If you were a little older or I had not a sprained ankle I would throw you out of this house, you little . . . ingrate. I have had enough disrespect. I will go instead. You can go to your father's and deal with him as best you can, and when your mother gets back we will go into this.'

'I want Mummy,' Selena wailed.

'Where are you going?' Aisling asked.

'Away from here.'

'Yes, I'm taking her away,' Gil said. 'She gave up a holiday to stay here and look after you girls.'

'And this is what I get.' She picked up the house phone and the address book. They all watched her dial. She listened for a moment and then crashed the receiver down. 'I refuse to speak to his fancy-piece, and really I don't see why I should speak to him either. Minny, you can explain the situation to him.' She hobbled out.

Aisling stood in the corridor, twisting her hands, while Babi was getting a bag together, helped by Gil. It didn't take long. A lot of her stuff must have been at his house by now anyway. Minny could hardly speak but she stood up stiffly, pushing away Selena, who didn't know what to do with herself, and dialled the correct number. By the time Babi appeared again everything was settled.

'You have spoken to him?'

'Yes.'

'He will take the baby too?'

'Yes. He's coming to get us in the car.'

'Fine.'

'But I don't know what Mum's going to say about it.'

'Shall I tell you frankly, Minny, I don't care. I would rather your mother have her few days away without feeling she must dash back because of your bad behaviour, but I am

306

beginning to be indifferent even to that. She is after all your mother, and responsible for you, since your father is not able to be. I am in a great deal of pain and I am very angry. I think a few days away for me is called for.'

They were gone. Minny was high – she didn't know what to feel except that enthralling danger was here. Her mother . . . her mother might think she had been wrong to sling tea over Babi, but she was pretty sure she would be furious that Babi should slap her, Minny, and she would find it hard to forgive their being abandoned. Why, Babi hadn't even hung around until Des showed up. Which was just as well.

'Shall I pack to go to Dad's?' Selena asked in a small, tinny voice.

'No,' Minny said, not rubbing her face though it tingled. She wanted to go and look in the mirror to see if it was red. No adult had ever hit her before in her life. Selena didn't know what to say; Minny could feel that without looking at her. Not even Ash . . .

'Is your face all right?' Ash asked.

'I don't know. It smarts a bit. How does it look?'

'Red. Why?'

'Why what?'

'Why not pack to go to Des's?'

'We're not going.'

Selena gasped. 'Didn't he want us?'

'I didn't ring him.'

307

'I heard you ring him.'

'That was acting, dimbo. No, we'll just stay here.'

'On our own?'

'Why not?'

Neither of them seemed excited at the prospect. Minny was excited, partly; another part was scared, and the third was saying firmly that there was no reason to be scared or excited. They were only staying at home, after all. She'd done everything she would have to do tonight a million times without anyone watching; come to that, even if Babi was still here a fat lot of good she would be, either in a pinch or in the normal run of things, with a sprained ankle.

'I think we should go to Dad's,' Selena said, interrupting her thoughts.

'No,' Minny and Aisling said together.

'I think we should go to Granny's,' Aisling said.

'No.'

'Or get her to come round here.'

'We're not doing that, Ash.' Her reasons were obscure but she felt them strongly. It wasn't only that she hadn't seen Franklin since Veronica's house. Or heard from him.

She didn't exactly manage to persuade them, that is stop them looking sceptical or troubled, but as long as they stopped arguing and didn't threaten to pick up the phone themselves, she was happy. She sweetened the deal by pointing out that there was quite a lot of ice cream in the freezer, and that the shopping was booked for delivery tomorrow, so right now they could tag whatever they wanted onto the order. 'You see,' she said, clicking to add garlic bread to the basket, 'it's just going to be perfectly normal, and Mum's back the day after tomorrow. A nice ordinary night tonight, only with extra ice cream and chocolate sauce, and the lights off.'

'The lights off?' Sel squeaked.

'Yeah. Just in case Babi comes past or anything. I don't suppose she will. You can have your nightlight on and everything. But, till we go to bed – you've got a torch, if you need it, don't you? It's not as if it's really dark yet anyway.'

It did make everything different. She read the baby's story in the bathroom, which faced the back of the house, and then tucked him up in his cot. He lay looking up at her – she could see in the twilight peeping in through the curtains – with eyes that seemed reproachful. 'Look, it's not my fault Mum's in Edinburgh,' she told him. 'Anyway she'll be back the day after tomorrow. It's not long to wait. And I'll sleep in her bed tonight, so I'll be here if you need me.'

Selena wasn't very pleased. 'It's like the Book of Job,' she said when Minny went in to fetch her pyjamas. Sel was sitting up in bed with her torch lit. 'Bad things keep happening, Minny. I don't like it.'

'Oh, rubbish. I bet it's not like the Book of Job at all.'

'It is. Maybe I'll get boils next.'

'Don't be silly, Selena. It's just a row. OK, a few rows, but it's going to be fine. Mum will be back soon. Go to sleep.'

The baby moaned and complained for quite a while, and Minny couldn't get properly to sleep until way after one o'clock when he seemed to settle a bit. Then just before four a little white ghost appeared at the door. 'My torch has gone out.'

Minny shut her eyes again and moaned into the pillow. 'You've still got your nightlight.'

There was a pitter-patter and a breeze and Selena scrambled in beside her. 'I can't sleep. And there was a spider.'

'Oh,' Minny said, turning over, 'why not a werewolf?'

THIRTEEN

The morning was unpleasant – Aisling had been woken by Selena's journeyings, too early even for her; it was dark and lashing with rain outside, and they were all starving by nine o'clock when the shopping arrived. They had ham and cheese sandwiches and Wagon Wheels for breakfast. And then they drank supermarket Coke and played on the Wii for a while. And then hung around waiting for lunch.

'I'm bored,' Selena said.

'Me too.' Aisling never did anything but this kind of stuff. Minny didn't know what she was whinging about.

'Read a book,' she snapped, reminding herself unnervingly of her mother. The baby was bored too.

'Can't I have Victoria round?'

'Of course you can't have Victoria round, idiot.'

'Why not?'

'Oh, shut up, Selena, for God's sake.'

'Well, can we go to the park then?'

Minny took them in the end, in the middle of the afternoon, when it had more or less stopped raining – the grass would be sopping and so would everything in the playground, but they needed air. She would buy them an ice cream, why not, so what if there were three full tubs in the freezer. She was too exhausted to argue. Aisling wouldn't come, even though she hadn't been out in so long and even though Minny begged her to. The baby wailed about having his rain jacket put on, threw his hat off and screamed all the way there so that people stopped and stared after them; he hit new heights in the queue for the ice-cream van and only settled down when Minny shoved quarter of a flake into his mouth.

'Mum says we shouldn't bribe him to be good with food,' Selena remarked.

Minny squatted down to let him lick the ice cream. 'Yeah? What about you? Does she say that about you too? Shall I have that 99 back?' A fat drop of rain hit her right in the eye. 'Oh God, why does it have to be raining on top of everything else?'

Selena looked smug. 'Job. I told you.'

They went to the playground. Minny pushed Raymond on the swing with all the other babies while the mothers and fathers chattered around her, and thought about Penny. She should probably call her. Perhaps her having texted at all meant that she wasn't still angry with Minny; perhaps she was just really upset about Jorge. Maybe her own one-word reply had been a bit abrupt. Although they were probably back together by now.

Then Selena got into a fight with another little girl over whose turn it was on the monkey bars, which was unlike her anyway, and the other little girl somehow fell off them and bashed her head. Minny had to drag the baby out of the swing, retrieve Selena from an angry mother without getting involved and run away, Raymond stuffed into the pushchair bottom first and screaming again. 'I don't know why we're all so bad-tempered,' she said aloud as they left the park.

'Because it's a terrible summer and there's no one looking after us.'

'I'm looking after us.'

'Well, you're rubbish at it.'

She ran on ahead and Minny followed, shoving the pushchair right through puddles. She was wet up to the waist anyway. Halfway home the rain suddenly tripled in volume and soaked the other half of her. The whole top of Whitsun Road was underwater; she almost caught up with Selena, who was goggling at it till she saw Minny coming and pranced off ahead again.

Minny was gasping from the rain by the time they got home. The front door was open so Aisling must have let Sel in. She stood with water pouring down her neck, battling with the pushchair rainhood and hauling the baby out, then stripping him on the doormat. He scampered off while she wearily removed her own cagoule and sodden trainers. All of her was sodden. She followed Raymond into the back room just to make sure he was safe before she went upstairs and got dry clothes, but unfortunately Franklin was sitting in there with Aisling, tuning the bloody guitar again.

They looked up. Minny had hair plastered flat to her head and neck. Her face was actually dripping. Her T-shirt and skirt were sticking to her.

'Hi,' she said. Her heart gave a great knock of mortification, right against her chest wall.

'Aisling called and asked me round.'

'Oh. She did.' She wiped her face. When she sneaked a glance at Franklin, he was flushed and looking in the opposite direction.

'You're really wet,' Aisling said. 'Raymond's got no clothes on.'

'Yeah. I'd better go upstairs and sort that out.'

She went up, shaking her head in disbelief. Selena was locked in the bathroom. 'Hurry up, Sel.'

'Why should I?'

'Because I'm soaking wet.'

'Well, so am I.'

Cursing, Minny fetched a towel from under her mother's bed, and a T-shirt and shorts for the baby. She was freezing. 'Selena, let me in.'

'No.'

'Unlock the door!'

There was silence. Minny beat on the door with the side of her hand. 'Let me in NOW! Oh, I'm going to kill you, Selena.'

She went down in the end, in disgust, afraid the baby would have frozen to death. He was still with the musicians so she had to go in to dress him. Franklin and Ash were singing 'Desperados Waiting for a Train'.

'I don't understand this song,' Ash said, breaking off in the middle of the chorus, which was just the title repeated several times.

Franklin played another chord. 'What do you mean?'

'Why are they like desperados? He never says. It's just about an old man and a little boy being friends, Mum says.'

'Well . . .'

'Have they broken the law?'

'It's a simile,' Minny growled, pulling the T-shirt over the baby's head.

'Oh.'

'You're never very good with similes, are you, Aisling?'

'But – so what's the train then?'

Minny pulled Raymond's shorts up. 'He's just making an image, like an old film with a couple of cowboys getting chased and being all tense waiting around to hop on a train or something – and they depend on each other. It's them against the world.'

Franklin looked at her.

'Yeah. So what's the train?' Ash asked.

Franklin's phone rang. He went off into the kitchen to answer it.

'Aisling, what are you doing calling up Franklin and making him come round?'

'I wanted to sing.'

'You can sing on your own.'

'I wanted to see Franklin.'

'You can't just make people come and see you, and you should have asked me. It's really awkward for me with him, right now, you know.'

'Why?'

'It doesn't matter.'

'Why does that mean I can't see him?'

'Leave it. Anyway, it looks pathetic, like you're proper googly-eyed over him.'

'What does googly-eyed mean?'

'Oh God, never mind.'

The baby crawled off again, through the legs of Franklin who was coming back in. 'That was your gran.'

'Oh yes?'

'She was just checking I was here, and it was OK for me to be . . . here.'

'Why wouldn't it be?' Minny asked, not looking at Ash.

'She's at the airport, waiting for a flight,' he explained.

'What?'

'She had to go to Ireland,' Aisling said, looking up. 'Uncle Kevin broke his leg.'

'Oh.' Minny frowned and sat down on the arm of the chair. How ridiculous to feel guilty. Anyway, people broke legs all the time. 'How long's she gone for?' she asked Franklin.

'She said she'd be a couple of days.'

'So what are you going to do?'

He shrugged. 'I'm not really meant to stay there by myself, that's the only thing. So, I mean, if you can't have me, then maybe I'll head back to my mum's or something.'

'I think we should go to Dad's.'

That was Aisling. She had stood up, laid the guitar aside and was sounding unusually firm.

'No.'

'I think we should go to Dad's.'

'So do I,' Selena said, darting in under Franklin's elbow and over to the window.

'We've settled this. We're staying here.'

'It's not safe.'

Minny stared. 'Of course it's safe, don't be ridiculous.'

'It's against the law, with Selena and the baby and everything.'

'Er – where's your other granny?' Franklin asked.

'Oh, Aisling.' Minny rubbed her face. 'It's safer than trekking across London with them when it'll be evening soon, for one thing.'

'But Dad would come and get us,' Sel pointed out.

'We don't know that. We don't even know he's there, remember? We haven't actually spoken to him in ages, they might have gone away or something.'

'We should ring him,' Aisling said, sticking to her main point with even more stubbornness than usual.

'Aisling, we're staying at home till Mum gets here

317

tomorrow.' She sat down again and picked up the book lying near her feet. 'We've had this conversation.'

'But I didn't agree with you.'

'I don't care,' Minny shouted. 'You're being stupid and we are going to stay here, not spoil everything ringing Dad when we've made it this far.'

'I'm not being stupid.' Ash's voice wobbled but she stepped towards the phone and picked up the receiver.

'Look. I'm in charge, right, aren't I? Put that down and I'll explain again.'

'Why are you in charge? You're not in charge.'

'You weren't saying that when I was looking after Raymond all night, or getting dinner, or breakfast this morning.'

'You always think you're in charge,' Ash said. Tears were leaking out of her eyes. 'But I'm the oldest.'

'So what? You don't act like it.'

'Why can't we do what I want for once?'

'What are you talking about, "for once"? Our whole bloody lives are lived because of what you want, Aisling, when do you EVER not get what you want?'

'All the time,' she said to the floor.

'You have your own room even though not even Mum does, you have your own computer, you don't have to go to school any more. I get all the crapness of being the oldest, having to look after everyone and do everything, and now you want to take the credit and start making STUPID decisions. Everything we do and everything about how we live is about you, so shut up.'

'I won't shut up,' Ash shouted. There was a sob in the corner and Selena dashed out again, nearly knocking Franklin over. Minny became aware that he'd been umming and making *calm down* gestures for a moment or two, and that he looked horrendously embarrassed.

'Sorry, Franklin,' she said, her voice cracking. 'Look. Sorry, Ash. I just don't want to phone Dad. We've made it this long, we can last till tomorrow night.'

'I'm not stupid.'

'No, I know you're not. Sorry. Sorry, Franklin.'

'OK, but I still don't know what's happening. Do you want me to go?'

'No, you might as well stay. We're all adult-less at the moment – Babi went off in a strop with her boyfriend last night, you see, after smacking me across the face—'

'What?'

'After smacking her across the face,' Aisling said, enunciating clearly.

'She thought we were going to go round to Dad's, but she didn't bother checking so we just stayed here. Mum's back tomorrow . . .'

'You could have rung Judy.'

'Yeah. Well, we could have. But anyway we didn't, and it was fine.'

'Yeah, only . . . the baby.'

'I look after the baby all the damn time anyway, Franklin.'

'It wasn't fine,' Aisling said. 'We had Wagon Wheels and Coke for breakfast.'

Minny sighed. 'Yeah, well. It was pure rock'n'roll when you put it like that.'

She decided to make them all a cup of tea. Aisling had stopped crying. It was still hammering down outside, water streaming down the windows and the sky dark grey. Minny switched on the lamp on the way out to the kitchen.

'Er . . .' Franklin said from the corridor. 'Should the baby be getting out the front door?'

'What? No.' She pushed past him. 'Raymond, come back here. Where do you think you're going?' She dragged him back in and slammed the door. 'Jesus, good thing you spotted him.' She looked back uneasily. 'I'm sure I didn't leave the door open.'

'It wasn't me,' Aisling said immediately.

'I know. I was last in. Selena!'

There was no reply.

She ran round the house first, all the rooms upstairs and even under beds and in wardrobes, though she knew Selena wasn't old enough to have left the front door open just to scare her.

'Shall I check outside?' Franklin shouted up the stairs.

'No, you'll get soaked,' Minny said irrationally, flying down again and towards the front door.

'I've got a jacket, Minny. Calm down. You look out the front. I'll check round the side of the house and the garden, OK?'

She wasn't anywhere to be seen. Aisling had put Raymond into the front room, shut the door on him and was putting her jacket on.

'We can't all go out,' Minny called, her mouth filling up with rain. 'Someone's got to stay with the baby.'

Franklin appeared behind Aisling in the doorway. 'Do you want me to cycle up to the park?'

Minny hesitated. 'The thing is, Selena doesn't like you much.'

'Oh.'

'You stay here,' Aisling agreed.

'Well. Take my bike then.' It was leaning against the side of the house, locked to a drainpipe; he came out to unlock it.

Minny hated riding bikes. She hadn't been on one since they went to France the summer she was eleven and she fell off the first time she went round a corner. She seized its handlebars. 'Don't watch.'

'Just don't get killed, all right.'

'Ash – you go down the street and up Milsom Road and down the next one and just keep looking, OK, and calling her.'

She was horribly afraid, especially on the main road, almost too afraid of falling under a car to keep checking the pavements for Selena. She wasn't there anyway. There was rain flying into her face so hard she had to keep shutting her eyes; it was better when she got to the park because the wind wasn't blowing right at her, but worse because there were millions of trees she couldn't see behind. Anyway she didn't find her. Nor at the playground. She was going to ride back by way of the river, just in case – Selena liked the river – but the towpath was under water. She stopped the bike for a second, looking at it, then turned sharply and set off again. The wind was really getting up, pushing her so hard she felt as if she might take off. Lightning split the sky, but the thunder was a comfortingly long time after it.

Her bum was killing her by the time she got back to her own road. She couldn't bear to go on further. Her calves were murder too. She disembarked delicately outside the house and pushed the bike up. Franklin appeared. He must have been watching out. 'Any sign?'

'No. Is Ash back?'

'No.'

'Is the baby OK?'

'Yes.'

Minny turned. Aisling was padding, slower than a walk, up the pavement. 'Did you find her?'

'No,' Minny said, and her middle gave a sharp lurch. 'I'll call Babi and see if she's around.'

'She's not,' Aisling said. 'I passed Gil's house and the car wasn't there.'

'Oh Christ. They must have gone on that holiday then.' They stood looking at each other. Minny dashed rain out of her eyes. 'Maybe I should call the police.'

'You can't.' Franklin had stepped out, shivering, to join them. 'You don't have anyone looking after you. How's your mum going to explain to the police why you were all on your own? You'll have social services right on top of you, all of you, even if your mother doesn't get prosecuted or something.'

'But –' Minny could feel her heart beating in her face. On the other hand she couldn't feel her legs at all. 'I read something once about the golden hour, how if you don't find them at once then—'

'Don't be stupid,' Franklin said bracingly. 'That's if they've been abducted. Selena left the house on her own, she took her raincoat, she's run away. That's completely different.'

'She might have been taken by now.'

'She's not going to get in someone's car, is she? She's sensible.'

'No, she's not.'

'And she's not going to get run over. We've just got to figure out where she's gone. Who are her mates?'

'Victoria.' Minny's heart bounded. 'I'll find the number.'

The carpet would never be the same again after they'd all pounded over it with wet feet, but she couldn't care about that now. She had to scoop up the baby, who was virtually hysterical to see her, and shush him as she waited for

323

Victoria's sensible parents to answer. The problem was they didn't.

'Maybe they're on holiday too,' Aisling said helpfully.

'But Sel wanted Victoria to come over for a sleepover. They can't be.'

'Do you know where she lives?' Franklin asked. 'I'll go round and check she's not there while you call her other friends.'

'I don't know her other friends,' Minny said, and burst into tears.

Aisling found the address for him, in the phone directory. It was a couple of miles away, on the other side of the primary school. He went off, after a final worried look at where Minny was sobbing into Raymond's hair. 'I'll make a cup of tea,' Ash then said, and went off to put the kettle on.

'Ash.'

'Yes?' She reappeared at the door.

'What are we going to do?'

'I'm going to make tea.'

'I'm so sorry, Ash. I've been being a cow. I haven't meant any of it – you know I didn't mean Dad left because of you. You know he didn't, don't you?'

'I suppose.'

'I'm a jealous awful person and I was horrible to you and now I've made Selena run away.'

'It's OK.'

'No, it isn't. What are we going to do?'

'I think we should call Dad.'

Minny looked at her in amazement. 'Of course we should call Dad. Of course we should. I'm going to call Dad.'

'OK.'

'I should, shouldn't I? I mean, he's going to go proper nuts with us. With me. And with Mum, and this could cause all kinds of kerfuffle, but I think I have to, because, you know, it's Selena. And then he can decide if he should call the police.'

'Yes.'

Minny found the number on her mobile. 'Yes?'

'Yes.'

'Dad? Where are you right now, Dad?'

'Minny, oh, I'm so pleased to hear from you. How are you, darling?'

'Where are you, please, Dad?' she asked again, in a trembling voice.

He was in Kingston about to see a client, he said, so he'd better call her back in an hour if she didn't mind, unless she wanted a chat with Harriet, who'd come with him for the shopping; he'd ditch the client, only it was an important one . . .

Minny's heart gave a painful thud because Kingston was only twenty minutes away unless the traffic was bad. 'Dad, I've got to tell you something. Listen – I've got to tell you now.' There was a pause.

'I'm listening, go ahead.'

She told him, she knew, in a scattergun way – she couldn't seem to marshal the story at all – but the gist of it got across. He cut through her telling him about the row with Babi. 'The traffic's awful. Give me fifteen minutes.'

He thought he was the best driver in the world, her father. She pictured him driving on the pavements like a car chase in a film, and almost smiled as Aisling handed her the tea. Then she jumped up. 'We can't sit around drinking tea. We need to be ready.'

'Ready for what?'

'Whatever. Come on, let's go outside. Get your jacket on – we need to be looking. Bring your phone.'

'Aisling,' Minny said as they manoeuvred the pushchair out again, baby squawking, a few minutes later. Both of them had winter boots over bare legs. The puddles were getting deeper all the time.

'Yes.'

'You don't think she ran away to Scotland, do you. To Mum.'

Aisling gazed at her. 'She kept saying she wanted her.'

'Did she?'

'Yes, all yesterday, and today.'

'I wasn't listening.' She pulled the rain hood over the baby, who roared and batted at it. 'I don't know. If she was really upset she might have meant to, but I don't know if she really would – because Mum's coming back tomorrow, she knows that. Once she'd calmed down a bit, wouldn't she come home, not try to make it all the way to Scotland? She didn't have a ticket.' She might have had her Zip card though – that would have got her to King's Cross. Would she know that it wouldn't work to travel out of London? It was too hard to think when the baby was crying, her eyes and ears were both full of rain and it still kept hitting her. 'Maybe that's what we should try. But . . . we're ages behind her. If that's what she's done, she's in town by now.'

'We can tell Dad,' Aisling remarked.

'Yeah. That's the best thing. Maybe he'll ring the police and tell them she might be on the Underground. When he gets here. Ash, I'm really sorry.'

'You said that.'

'Do you forgive me?'

'OK, Minny. There's Franklin.'

'Where?' He came hurtling up on the bike, shoulders hunched and eyes squinting. 'No sign?' she yelled.

His brakes squealed and he shook his head, sending raindrops flying in all directions. 'No, there was no one there. No car.'

'Maybe they are away then.'

'The road's flooding,' he said. 'I think they're going to block it off to cars – that bloody burst pipe's finally overflowed properly. *And* the park's flooding.'

'What? It wasn't when I was there. That's not even an hour ago.'

'Yeah, well it is now. All the middle's under water. I guess it must be high tide, or a flash flood or whatever they call it. Don't look like that,' he said sharply. 'It's shallow. It wouldn't be over her knees.'

'It would be by the river. I *have* to call the police. No – when Dad gets here . . .'

'She could have gone to Granny's,' Aisling said.

Franklin stopped with his bike halfway up the kerb. He and Minny looked at each other, then at Ash. 'But Judy's away.'

'And Selena knows it,' Minny said, 'doesn't she?'

'Oh.' Ash was despondent. 'I thought she didn't.'

'But she was in the room when you guys told me, wasn't she?'

'I thought so,' he said.

'No,' Aisling said. 'She came in just afterwards.'

'Are you sure?'

'Yes.'

'She's sure,' Minny said to Franklin. 'That might be where she's gone. Could you bear . . . ?'

'I'm on my way.' He wheeled the bike around. He looked frail in his soaking green jacket in the rain, but he got up on it without wincing. He must be fit. Minny's own coccyx still felt very worn.

'Sorry.'

'Don't be silly. I'll ring you when I get there.'

They watched him till he was out of sight, his bony back beaten by the weather. Then they followed him up the street.

Minny was wondering if they should split up and go in different directions or if she would just worry that Aisling wasn't looking properly, so for a moment she didn't register what she was seeing as she looked down and up the main road. Then Aisling gasped beside her. It sloped fairly sharply at that point; their street was halfway up the short hill, and below them, up to the middle of their their block, water was being rippled violently by the rain. It couldn't be that deep: at pavement level the ground was still clear. Still, in the gathering dusk and the rain it was eerie, particularly as there were no cars moving.

'She'll be OK, won't she, Ash?' Minny said.

'I expect so.'

'I mean, this isn't going to be a proper flood. We'd have heard. They tell you stuff like that.'

'Selena can swim,' Aisling said.

Minny wiped the rain off her face for the three thousandth time. 'Bloody, bloody Job. Right. We'd better stick together, I think. And go down.'

'We'll get wet.'

'Aisling, we could both have been stood in the shower for the last forty-five minutes and we wouldn't be wetter than we are now.'

They heard a car crunch against the kerb behind them and swung round; their father leaped out of the passenger seat. Minny almost expected him to vault the bonnet. 'Have you found her?'

'No.'

The driver's door opened and Harriet's hair began to struggle out.

'No ideas at all where she might have gone? Jesus, girls, you're soaked. Is the baby OK?'

'Not really – he's fed up and it's his nearly his bedtime. Oh yeah,' Minny remembered. 'We haven't had any dinner.'

He had reached them and suddenly she found herself crushed against him. He was dry. She relaxed, just for a second. Aisling's face was inches from her own, on the other side of his chest; she looked very white.

Minny pulled away and wiped her face again. They all had to lean together to have a conversation; the wind was getting up. 'We think maybe she might have gone to Granny's house, so Franklin's gone back to check – he was here helping us look . . .'

'But Ma's gone off to Kevin. She's not there.'

'I know. But Selena didn't.'

'Right. Is he on foot? When did he go?'

'He's on his bike. He's fast – he's probably nearly there by now. Or . . . she might have tried to go off to Edinburgh.'

'What?'

'She's been missing Mum,' Minny said. Her chin began to tremble and she took hold of the pushchair handle. Aisling was holding the other one.

'So. Would she be at King's Cross yet?'

'Probably not, but she might be getting near.'

'Well, that's something to go on. We'll wait a few minutes to hear from Franklin and if he hasn't found her I'll ring the police and tell them to look round King's Cross.'

'I think you girls should come back to the house,' Harriet said. 'You're soaking and you look shattered.'

'No,' they said together, and Minny added, 'but if you'd take Raymond that would be great, and give him something to eat – some bread and butter or something, or toast, and there are bananas, or baby-food pouches in the cupboard . . .'

'It's all right, Minny,' her father said as Harriet took the pushchair and the keys she was holding out. 'We'll find her.'

'But it's so wet everywhere. What if she went down to the river?'

'Now why would she go down to the river?' He had his arm around her.

'And it's getting dark, anything could have happened.'

'Nothing's happened, and we'll find her any minute, you'll see, and it's not really dark; it's only the storm. The baby's off your hands now, you don't have to worry about him. Can you think of anywhere at all she might have gone apart from what you've already said?'

They went through it again, then he said the two of them should head up the road checking each street and he'd go down. Minny's phone hadn't rung yet. 'Tell you what – why don't you ring him and see where he is? He must have got there by now.' He raised his sleeve to protect her phone from the elements.

Aisling, who had set off in the correct direction, shouted something.

Minny looked up.

Half a block away, crawling towards them in the battered light from the street lamps, was a curious shape. Minny squinted. She might need glasses. She set off running. When she caught up with Aisling she could see what it was – Franklin, bruised by rain, wearing only a T-shirt, pushing his bike, Penny holding its saddle from the other side. Selena astride it, wrapped up in something which didn't fit her and with her hair streaming.

Minny flew past Ash and right at them, so that Penny let go of the bike in alarm, Franklin staggered and Selena tipped on top of him with a squeak. Minny pulled her off and nearly crushed her. She felt tiny, and as if she'd never be dry again. Franklin's jacket fell off her.

Then Ash was there, grinning and squeaking, and their father, who lifted Selena right up and didn't put her down again. 'What happened? Where have you been? I ought to murder you – we were petrified. Minny's been crying.' Minny didn't even deny it. She tried not to hold onto Selena's leg.

'Where did you find her?' she asked, handing Franklin's jacket back to him.

'I found her,' Penny said.

'I went to Granny's house, but she wasn't there,' Selena said into her father's shoulder. She'd started back in the direction of home, but there weren't any buses and the rain

332

was getting harder and harder; and she didn't want to go home. 'I thought you'd laugh at me,' she muttered to Minny. 'So I walked up to church.'

'Oh God.'

'I thought it would be nice – but it was cold and there wasn't anyone there. And the chapel was locked. I could see the Jesus lamp was lit, but I couldn't get in.'

Her father squeezed her, and Minny leaned her head against Selena's side. The poor scrap. She'd been standing in the car park trying to decide what to do when Penny happened to come past, and Sel's raincoat, which was sulphur yellow and had once been Minny's, caught her eye. Penny had just been bringing her home when Franklin saw them and pulled up so hard on his bike that he sent a spray of water over their heads – according to Penny. From what Minny could work out, both she and Franklin had refused to leave Sel to the other. And she was tired so Franklin put her on his bike. 'Why didn't you ring?' Minny asked, laughing for sheer relief.

Penny looked embarrassed.

'Come on,' Des said, shepherding Aisling away and still carrying Selena. 'Can you manage that bike, Franklin? You look done in. Let's get back to the house and get everyone dry.

Left on the corner, Minny and Penny stared at each other. 'I deleted your number,' Penny said, snuffling in the rain. 'After your text.'

'Oh, Penny.'

'So I couldn't ring.'

'Look, I'm sorry about that. I thought you sounded like you were still arsey with me though – your text. And it just came at a really bad moment and I didn't have time to answer properly.'

Penny snuffled again. 'You never rang me though.'

'Yeah. Sorry. I've been busy, but I should have done. Are you OK?'

She thought about it. 'Yeah, I think so. We just weren't good for each other, you know?'

'Minny,' Des shouted from over the road. 'Come on, you'll freeze. Penny, come on.'

'Come back to the house,' Minny invited her.

'I can't,' Penny said. 'I've got to go home, there's a thing. My mum's birthday.'

'Sure? OK. Well. Thanks for finding her.'

'Will you ring me tomorrow?' Penny asked hesitantly.

'OK.'

'Because, you know – I can't ring you.'

Minny sighed. 'Yeah, I will.'

'And – you can tell me what's new with you.' She grinned. 'Because it's obviously much more interesting than what's been happening to me.'

Minny's own grin froze because a cheerful voice behind them suddenly called, 'What on earth is going on?' She turned round and Nita was just getting out of a taxi. 'What are you doing out here in the rain? Is that . . . Des? What's happening? Just let me pay the man . . .'

FOURTEEN

Nita's theatre in Edinburgh had been flooded as well; it was an underground one. 'I'm beginning to think I'm a Jonah. But it didn't matter because the big show was last night and it was packed out. It all went incredibly well. I didn't ring because I wasn't sure if we'd get a train, and then I thought I'd surprise you. Now, tell me . . .' She had the baby hanging onto her with all four of his limbs and his head as well, and Selena clinging around her waist. They had to detach Sel to get her into a hot shower before she froze to death; she didn't want to go, partly because of wanting to hug her mother and partly because she didn't want to miss what they said. Minny was keen to send her upstairs so that her mother didn't have to control her reaction when she first heard what had happened.

While the story unfolded people got showers, and put their pyjamas on, and fetched a bottle of milk for the baby. Franklin had to be cajoled into a pair of tracksuit bottoms Nita never wore for the runs she didn't go on – and a jumper of Minny's. 'I can't wear that.'

'Franklin, it's a boy's jumper.'

'It doesn't smell of boy.'

By the time their mother was over the worst of the shock, everyone was feeling quite friendly to everyone else. Des even thanked Franklin for all his help and cycling during the panic, and they had a rather manly conversation about bikes. Nita kept bringing more and more toast and biscuits into the back room where they all sat round, half of them in heaps of tiredness on the floor since there weren't enough chairs.

'I don't know how we're going to sort all this out,' Nita said.

'It'll be fine,' Des said. 'You've got to let me help.'

'I know.'

'This just seems to me like a problem of management, in that everyone's been under stress, a lot of it due to me, and people have been taking it in turns to take too much on and so everyone snapped within a couple of days.'

'You're right.'

'What this family needs is a management consultant. Or some goodwill and determination. Mind you, I wouldn't blame you for having a few sharp words with your mother.'

'I will, I will.' Even Nita looked more relaxed. She leaned her head on the back of the sofa.

'I should be going,' Franklin said, starting to get up.

'Don't even think about it,' Nita answered. 'Don't look at me like that, Franklin. First of all, the weather is far too wild for you to be cycling out again and I can't be bothered driving you, and secondly there's no one at Judy's. I doubt that's even a legal situation, especially in your particular case. And after all your help today there's no way we're sending you away. You can go home as early as you want in the morning and pick some stuff up so you don't have to keep wearing Minny's clothes. But you're staying nights here till Judy's back. You can sleep on the sofa, it's comfortable.'

'Is it?' Harriet said, struggling to change position in the big white chair.

'Not for you right now – most of the springs have gone,' Nita told her.

Harriet sighed.

Minny wandered past the kitchen a few minutes later and heard her father apparently having a conversation with himself. She pushed open the door. He was moving around the kitchen making yet more tea and talking to his mobile, which was sat on the counter, set to speakerphone.

'The bar sounds very quiet tonight, Kevin.'

'I'm not in the bar, Des, I'm not let be in there for the next few days, I'm told.'

'Hello there, middle daughter,' Des said, seeing her.

'Is that Minny? Good girl, Minny.'

'Will you forgive your poor old uncle now?' Des asked her, in a not very low voice.

'Don't be at her, Des.'

Minny rolled her eyes.

'Ah, go on. He has enough to put up with.'

'Mmm. Sorry about your leg,' she told the phone.

'His leg nothing, Ma has him driven mad already and she only got there an hour ago.'

'An hour and a half,' Kevin said tragically. 'There's a pot of stew on the stove already and it smells revolting. I'm going to get fat and I'm not even going to enjoy it.'

'All right,' Minny said.

'You mean you'll talk to me again? Honest now?'

'It was all my fault anyway,' her father pointed out.

'True,' Minny and Kevin said together.

'That means the world to me, Minny,' Kevin carried on. 'I'm going to open a new email account just for you, so be sure not to tell your father the address.'

'Very funny.'

'How is the leg?' Minny asked, pointing out the box of herbal tea to her father.

'Not as painful as my ears, listening to Ma. It'll be fine. I only stepped off a rock the wrong way, it's ludicrous.'

'Aha,' Des said suddenly. Minny looked round and saw him pounce on the school reports, which had got crowded into a corner of the counter, behind the olive oil. 'What are these little beauties? Now this is interesting. The school report of one Miss Minny Molloy, Kevin.'

'Read out the one for English,' Kevin said instantly.

'No, that's not fair,' Minny protested. 'I haven't even read it yet.'

Her father held it above his head and squinted up. 'Let's see now. Chemistry, physics – that's your mother's business.

338

French – boring. PE – who cares. English. Ahem. *I have enjoyed teaching Minny this year.'*

Minny scoffed to herself.

'She is very bright and has it in her to be an excellent student. Once she acquires some discipline and learns to challenge herself as a reader, and edit herself as a writer, I think English may really be her subject.'

'Pah,' Kevin said, after a pause.

'Load of nonsense,' her father agreed.

'You're an extremely intelligent reader, Minny.'

When I'm not wallowing in old books I've read hundreds of times, Minny admitted to herself.

'And a vivid imaginative writer,' Des declared.

Mmm. But I do go on a bit.

'She underestimates you,' Kevin said.

Minny shrugged, forgetting that he couldn't see her.

Des dropped the report beside her. 'When are you going to stop underestimating yourself?'

Kevin said goodnight after that. He said he wanted to get into bed before Granny came up from the bar so he wouldn't have to talk to her. 'Sounds as if my mother will be back in a couple of days, if Kevin has any say at all,' Des said to Franklin, handing him a mug of tea. 'You won't be on the sofa here too long.'

Minny collapsed back onto the floor next to her mother's legs. Nita leaned over and brushed back her hair. 'You need a haircut. How are you doing down there? Tired?'

'Yeah.'

'Busy day. Do you think you'll make it up with Penny?'

'Yeah, I suppose so.' Minny yawned. 'I still can't understand what went on though, really – all that with her mother. I'll just have to not think about it.'

'Well –' Nita passed the digestives to Harriet – 'she always did have a bit of trouble not exaggerating things. You don't know where the lie came from – perhaps she was in a difficult situation and it snowballed till she couldn't take it back.'

'Like, her mum sort of asked questions she had to lie to?' Selena mused.

'But if she didn't expect her to, it wasn't her mother's fault exactly,' Minny argued. 'It wasn't like she knew Penny was going to lie, not like Mum says.'

'What are you two on about?' Franklin asked.

Selena sighed. 'Mum always says, don't ask someone a question if you know they're probably going to lie. Or it's like you want them to lie, and then it's partly your fault.'

'Mum does always say that.' Minny nodded. 'It's her theory of parenting. You do say that.'

'You do,' Aisling agreed.

'Well. I didn't know I *always* said it, but—'

'Yes,' Aisling told her. 'That's why we never asked you about Dad being Raymond's father. Because we thought you'd probably lie about it, and there wasn't any point since we all knew anyway.'

There was a sudden silence. The fuzzy yellow light in the

340

room seemed to harden. Minny looked first at Harriet, since Nita and Des were behind her. Her face was blank.

'Aisling,' Nita gasped. 'What are you . . . ?'

'How did you know, Aisling?' Des asked. He sounded like stone.

'I always knew. Minny did too, she told me.'

'I didn't!' Minny gasped too.

'You did, after the party at Veronica's.'

'Oh,' Minny said in a small voice.

'Did you know?' Harriet asked, her words dropping into a well of space between her chair and the sofa, where Des sat next to Nita.

'No. I didn't. I asked her – I asked you, Nita. When Minny – when her email said you were pregnant I got in touch specifically . . . and then, when we first got back and I saw him, I asked again and you said no way.'

'You forced her to lie,' Aisling nodded, as if this were a normal conversation.

Harriet was sitting perfectly still. So was Franklin, as if, if he didn't move, he might become invisible. The baby finished his milk and crowed, grabbing for Nita's fringe.

Everyone was very calm, but every speck of jolliness had gone out of the room. Nita said that she had to put the baby to bed, right now, because he was so tired. Des and Harriet went, unhurriedly, into the front room, which emitted no raised voices or anything like that. Minny, Aisling, Selena and Franklin were left staring wretchedly at each other.

'Should I not have said that?' Aisling asked after a while.

Minny closed her eyes. 'Maybe not tonight.'

'I thought everyone knew.'

Minny sighed. 'I think probably everyone did. They just weren't ready to talk about it.'

'*I* didn't know,' Franklin pointed out. 'You never said.'

'Sorry.'

'Don't be stupid. It's just . . . interesting.'

'I suppose. Ash, don't worry; it was going to come out. It had to.'

'Yeah.'

'It's not that interesting,' Selena piped up, stretching her legs out over Franklin. 'Not to us. I mean Raymond was always our brother anyway.'

'Did you know too?'

She sniffed. 'Sort of.'

A few minutes later the three adults appeared in the doorway, Nita shuffling not to get in Harriet's way. Harriet wasn't looking at either of them. 'Girls,' Des said, 'your mother and I are just popping out. We need to have a conversation and we don't want you to have to listen to it.'

'In the storm?' Aisling asked. The rain was still battering the window.

'Just up to the Fox, not far. Pretty sure it won't be too crowded on a night like this. Love,' he said to Harriet, 'are you sure you don't want to come with us?'

'Completely sure,' she said in a clipped voice. 'We'll talk afterwards. At home.'

'OK.' He paused. 'Girls, Harriet's going to stay here with you till we get back. We won't be long. We really won't.'

'Take as long as you need.' Harriet walked into the room and sat down with her back to them.

'Girls,' their mother said. 'Kids, I mean – don't you think you should go to bed? You've had a tiring day and everything. Selena?'

'No.'

'She can watch TV with us,' Minny said. She could see that Selena was not going to go willingly to bed while she was still afraid the world might end, so she might as well be allowed to stay up till their parents came back from the pub.

Harriet seemed to be taking it pretty well, though Minny was cautious about looking at her; she even smiled at Aisling when Ash was debating what to watch. Minny said she'd do the washing-up before she settled down. Selena came with her, she was feeling clingy and Minny was the best option left. Ash was all right staying in the back room; this wasn't the kind of thing to phase her. Franklin came in at a certain point and started to dry the dishes. They couldn't talk normally at all, it was all significant glances and low voices, even when they were just passing clean cutlery.

Then, when they filed back into the back room, trying to act naturally, Harriet wasn't in there. 'Where's Harriet?'

Aisling looked up from the cushion she was squashing. 'I don't know.'

Minny peered into the front room. Harriet was there, leaning against the window. Her face would leave a smudge, not that they were fussy. 'Are you OK?' she asked.

'Mmm. Yeah. No, not really. It's sort of ironic or something, Minny,' she said, pressing her cheek hard against the glass, 'but I think the baby's coming.'

'Don't worry,' Minny said in a voice that sounded eerily calm to her own ears. 'It takes ages. It took Mum eight hours with Raymond and he was the fourth.'

'Mmmmm,' Harriet said, but Minny didn't know if she was agreeing or not; her eyes were squeezed shut and she pushed against the glass so hard Minny was afraid it might break.

The others were crowded into the doorway, looking terrified. 'It's a bit early,' Ash said. 'There's meant to be still four weeks to go.'

'Oh, that's nothing, these days. Put the kettle on, Aisling,' Minny said. 'You'd like some tea or something, wouldn't you, Harriet? Do you want to sit down? Shall I ring Dad?'

'Yes,' she said breathlessly. 'I think you'd better. Interrupt the talk about one baby with another. Tell him it hurts already.'

Minny dialled her father's number. A moment later they all heard the theme tune to *Match of the Day* start up next door. Selena ran after it and came back holding the phone. 'It was down the side of the sofa.'

'It must have fallen out of his pocket,' Minny said. She hung up numbly.

'He's always had that for his ringtone,' Harriet whispered, sitting very straight on the sofa. 'It reminded him of home, when he was in the States.'

'Lovely. No worries,' Minny said. 'I'll call Mum.'

'Ask if I can speak to him,' Harriet said. 'I'm OK now.'

Minny would have done, but her mother's phone had gone straight to answerphone.

'Oh God,' Harriet said feebly.

'Why don't we call the pub?' Franklin suggested.

They all crowded round the computer. Minny couldn't type properly, she kept looking at Harriet, who surely shouldn't be having another contraction already. 'There,' Sel yelped, pointing at the right 'Red Fox', halfway down the screen. Minny seized the phone and dialled.

'Come on,' she said, turning her back on all their anxious faces, 'come on.' There was no answer. It was perfectly obvious there never would be. She dropped the phone and said a quick prayer. 'No answer there. Franklin – I'm really sorry to ask but . . .'

'I'm going,' he said, relief written all over his face. 'I'll be as quick as I can.'

'Yeah, but don't get killed. Have you got lights?'

'Yes, Mother.'

'Cycle carefully,' Harriet said, upright and calm again. 'Could someone get me some sheets just in case and could I have some herbal tea, please?'

They fell over themselves, all three girls running upstairs and pulling sheets out from under Babi's bed where they lived, then downstairs again, grouped round the kettle. 'Should we call an ambulance?' Selena asked.

'She hasn't said to.' Minny handed her a mint teabag. 'I don't know – she's still the adult, isn't she? She hasn't suddenly gone mad.'

'We could ask her,' Aisling suggested.

They all trailed back in, Sel carrying the mug. Harriet was in the throes of another one, hunched up in a ball, rolling on the sofa. 'Oh. Fuuuu-nnn. Me.'

'Selena,' Minny said abruptly, taking the mug from her, 'you go next door and put the TV on, OK?'

'But I want to help.'

'Please, Sel, that's the most helpful thing you can do right now. I tell you what – fill the kettle up first, full to max, and turn it on, all right?'

She actually went. Obviously everyone was as petrified as she was herself, maybe including Harriet. Minny waited respectfully until she stopped swearing and then bent over her. 'Harriet. Don't you think we'd better call an ambulance?'

'No,' she choked into the back of the sofa, then rolled over and looked up. 'There's no need yet. If Dessie just gets back in the next few minutes, he can drive me in, no problem.'

'Are you sure? It's twenty minutes from here to the hospital.' Her heart sank a little. Even with no roads blocked off.

'It doesn't happen that fast, it's not like TV. I've got plenty of time. I'd like to be in hospital, but not on my own, and I – you're not meant to call an ambulance except in an emergency.'

Minny sat beside her, until another contraction started and she jumped up nervously and went over to the window. The rain was still lashing outside. Just as she was picturing her father tearing up the road, perhaps her mother walking glumly behind with Franklin, the phone rang.

'It's shut,' Franklin yelled, over the rain. 'Bloody pub's shut. Where else would they have gone?'

'I don't know.' Minny's brain had shut down; she stared straight ahead, trying to think.

'Well, they're not walking the streets on a night like this.'

'There's the Crown . . .'

'Yeah, but it's downhill. Where it's flooded. I think they'd have gone up.'

'OK, well, you're the one out there. There's the Anchor, on the corner of Rosemount Road.'

'I'll try there, and ring you. Minny, call an ambulance.'

'Harriet says—'

'I think you should call it. It could take a while to come. The water's still going up. There's some in your road.'

'Holy God.' Minny rubbed the window, but it was too wild to see. 'OK. Go carefully.'

'I'll find them.'

Harriet was pale and sweating, Aisling just pale. Minny told them about the pub. 'I think we should call an ambulance, Harriet. Because driving anywhere's going to take longer tonight; some of the roads are blocked off because of all the water.'

Harriet immediately went into another contraction. Minny was beginning to find them irritating, they made business impossible. She knew perfectly well that Selena was in the corridor, not watching TV at all, and she went to try to move her.

'You don't want to be part of this,' she said, flapping her onto the sofa. 'I'm telling you, if I could hide in here, I'd turn the telly up so loud nothing would get through. Although –' she frowned at the TV, which was showing a clearly unsuitable police drama where people were buzzing around a dead girl in a ditch – 'let's put a DVD on, shall we?'

It was all a distraction from the panic which probably set in any time someone suggested you call an ambulance, a *NOW NOW NOW* kind of panic that said every second counted . . . She straightened up and tossed *The Magic School Bus* DVD box at Selena. 'I've got to go back next door, but you watch this, OK?'

'Call me if you need me,' Sel said.

Minny went purposefully next door. Aisling was chewing her hand, standing against the window.

'I'm calling 999, Harriet. Look, this might or might not

be an emergency, but I'd rather have it and not need it than need it and not have it.'

'OK,' Harriet said weakly. 'Sensible. I wish I'd thought of that eight and a half months ago. I never thought it would be like this, Minny.'

'No, I know.'

'It hurts so bloody much.'

'Then we need to get you to a hospital so they can stuff you full of drugs . . . Ambulance, please.'

They asked her, after all the details had been given, and they had talked about if there were spaces between contractions, if she would like them to stay on the phone. Minny looked doubtfully at Harriet, who was crouched with her bottom squeezed between the bookshelf and the mantelpiece. It was such a ludicrous thought that she, herself, might be called upon to do something at the birth of a baby that she couldn't consider it right now. 'No, I don't think so. I can call back, can't I?'

'Of course.'

She didn't want to tie up the line either. And sure enough there was an answerphone message from Franklin. Her heart was beating painfully as she pressed buttons. 'Minny, they're not at the Anchor either, but I can see another pub up the road so I'll check that one and then I'll go back to the Crown. And if they're not there I'll do something else. Don't panic. I hope it's engaged because you're talking to the ambulance people.'

Ash was now in the corridor, squeaking quietly. Minny went out to her and took hold of her wrist. 'Ash,' she hissed, 'what am I going to do? I can't deliver a baby . . .'

'Of course you can,' Ash said in a surprisingly normal voice. 'You can do everything.'

'What are you talking about, I can't even be in the room with her. I've never even done first aid . . . I'm weak and pathetic, I quit things all the time, I've got zero faith in myself and I'm panicking.'

'You can do everything,' Aisling said, patting her on the elbow.

Minny gazed at her for a second, then took a deep breath and went to put a saucepan of water onto boil. She had no idea what all the boiling water was for, but they always did it in books. She breathed deeply all the time, so that when she'd done it she was ready to go back in.

The corridor was empty, which surprised her. Ash wasn't in the front room, where Harriet was lying on her back, but not writhing now. 'Has Aisling . . . ?'

'She said she was going out.'

Minny couldn't believe it, even though it was so typical. '*Where?*'

'I didn't ask.'

She couldn't go after her; she had Selena and Raymond to think about as well as the situation here. God knows what was in Aisling's mind – perhaps she meant to try the Crown since Franklin had gone the other way. She wouldn't go into deep water. There wouldn't be deep water – just a bit too much for cars. And ambulances. Minny patted her phone to make sure it was still in her pocket. Honestly, what a stupid thing to do, when you had a fiancée eight months pregnant, leaving without your phone. Perhaps he'd realised and was even now roaring back from wherever they'd been; or maybe Nita had noticed her phone was off. She knelt on the carpet beside Harriet, who had begun to moan again, and took out her phone to try her mother once more. No luck. She left a message, trying to sound calm. Then another deep breath.

'The ambulance will be here any minute. I'm sure Franklin will have found Dad by now too,' she said. 'Can I do anything for you?'

Harriet gripped both her wrists for a few seconds; her fingers were like iron. Then she slumped back again. 'No,' she said. 'I'm going to kill Dessie.'

'Me too.'

'If he misses this – no, I'm going to kill him anyway. Pillows. And more sheets. I don't want to . . . have to worry about . . . bleeding all over the carpet.'

Minny flew up and gathered so much bedding she nearly fell down the stairs. She arranged layers of sheets and towels and Harriet had just rolled over onto her face on top of them when the front door opened. Minny's brain clicked over into joy. 'Here they are,' she said to Harriet, rushing into the corridor. But it wasn't her father, or her mother either. It was Gil. He whipped off his jacket, dropped it on the floor and moved straight past her. 'What are you doing here?' she stammered, following him.

He was crouched down beside Harriet, holding her wrist. 'Aisling came to see if we were back. She's just helping your grandmother; they'll be here in a few minutes. I came on ahead. Throw a sheet over this sofa, that's a good girl.'

'But we thought you were on holiday.' Minny felt sluggish.

'I took Milena to a hotel last night, to give her a break. We got back a couple of hours ago. I think Ash spotted the car.'

'But . . .'

'Now, Harriet, let's get you turned over,' he said firmly. 'That's right. I know it hurts, lovey. I just need to take a little look and see how far along you are.'

'You can't do that,' Minny whispered, scandalised, as he flipped Harriet's skirt up to her chest.

He looked up. 'Yes, I can. I'm going to help her, Minny. Shush now, everything's going to be fine.' He pushed Harriet's knees up. 'I used to be a nurse.'

FIFTEEN

Of course the baby was a girl.

Her father told her, later, that he'd been convinced it would be a boy. Running along the street, yelling questions at Franklin cycling in the gutter beside him, heads nearly torn off by the wind and rain, he'd sworn to himself it would be a boy. 'You know, Minny – you wait sixteen years for a boy and then two come along the same night.'

Minny rolled her eyes.

Anyway, he was wrong, it was a girl, which was just as well. Everyone was pleased, even Harriet. At least she looked pleased – you could have counted every one of her teeth – once it was all over.

Des, and the others, got there about the same time as the paramedics; too late to be useful but in time to say he was there. And hold her hand for the last two minutes, which Minny supposed counted for something. She was glad to be displaced – Harriet had squeezed the bones in her hand to mush and it was all far too gory now in the front room – and to huddle in the corridor with Aisling and Selena, trying to keep out of the way of the paramedics and anyone who could do anything helpful. Babi was still in the front room, leaning on her elbows on the floor beside Harriet, hoarse with all her encouragement, but she got up and dusted herself off once the baby was out, and came straight to them. She put her arm round Nita, who still had her raincoat on.

'Make some tea,' Babi ordered Minny. 'Where are you going, Nita?'

'Just – to see Raymond a second,' their mother said. She leaned over the banister for a moment and put her hand on Minny's head. 'Well done, sweetie,' she said.

Minny stood with Babi at the bottom of the stairs, watching her trudge upwards with her head down. Then they looked at each other.

'I'll go,' Babi said.

'I'll come too.'

'No. Stay down here.'

Minny looked doubtfully towards the door of the front room. Ash was standing there, Sel peering round it. 'To look after the others?'

'No, to rest. It does seem that you have done very well today.'

Minny felt like protesting; it had been a day of complete disaster. There was also something else she wanted to say, but she was too tired to think of what it was, let alone what words to use.

'Don't argue with me, Minny. For a change, hey? I will look after your mother. You have done well today. And I would rather not talk about yesterday at all.'

Minny was happy to go along with the last part. The rest – 'Anything good about today was Aisling as much as me. I would have been stuffed on my own.'

'Have you told her that?'

'No.'

'It's all she would want, your approval. Selena too. Leave your mother to me.'

Minny went towards the front room, to stand between Selena and Ash just inside the doorway. Her mother was hurt right now. She was bound to be; she could say till she was blue in the face that she didn't love their father any more; it might even be true. But he was the father of her son. He'd just found that out and they'd probably been having a huge row, then before he had the chance to feel pleased at all about Raymond, here he was having a new baby, with his soon-to-be new wife. It wasn't a nice evening for Nita.

Minny knew all that, in her tired brain, and also knew she couldn't do anything to help her tonight. And that here was her new sister to go and greet. None of it was Nita's fault at all, really, and yet here she had to be hurt. But Minny came to the conclusion that there wasn't any point in punishing anyone for it, not this new baby or Harriet, or even her father any more. Or herself. If you loved people you just were going to get hurt by them, sometimes.

Meanwhile, here was a new person in the family that she might have to look after one day. A person they would all have to relate to, if only because they were related to her.

How messy things were, honestly. 'Granny won't like it that you delivered her granddaughter,' she murmured to Gil, who happened to be standing on the other side of Selena.

He raised his eyebrows. 'Why not?'

'Well. You being Babi's boyfriend – being the hero . . .'

'I daresay she'd rather I'd done it than that you had to,' he suggested. 'And all I did was what I've been trained to do.'

'I never knew you were a nurse.'

He nodded. 'In the army.'

'And they trained you to deliver babies?'

'It's proper training, young lady; you're supposed to be prepared for every situation. I stopped when I left the army, but you don't forget. Anyway, if anyone round here was a hero it was you lot, coping with the situation like you did, and staying with her.' He shook her hand, then Ash's, and then Selena's. Then he clapped Franklin on the back, nearly making him drop the tea tray he was bringing in. He was so cheesy. But Franklin had turned pink.

She stood between her sisters. Selena, who was holding Minny's non-sore hand tightly, had tears streaming down her face. They were all three still wearing their pyjamas.

'We did do well,' Minny muttered to Ash. 'You did. Did you know Gil was a nurse?'

'No.'

'Then why did you go and get him?'

'I went to get Babi. You said you didn't want to do it on your own.'

'I wasn't on my own, you were there. You called all the right shots, all day.' She squeezed Aisling's hand. 'You're going to be fine, you know.'

Aisling nodded.

'Come in,' Des called them, 'come in and meet the newest Miss Molloy.'

He was sitting on the floor holding the blue-wrapped baby; the sheets had all been rolled away so it didn't look so much like a battlefield. The paramedics didn't seem to be in a massive hurry to take Harriet to hospital, they were getting tea from Franklin at the table. Minny picked up a cup for Harriet, who had after all been doing the hard work. 'Thank you, as well,' she said to Franklin. 'This is what you get when you hang around us.'

'So I bloody see.'

'You're part of the family now.'

'No chance. Find another sucker.' He passed her the milk. She poured a cup out for her father too.

'A new life,' Selena said, with awe, kneeling on the floor. 'Right at the beginning.'

'Life is like a train,' Aisling remarked. Their father, his face gleaming with sweat and tears, grinned.

'How is it like a train this time, Ash?'

'Life is like a train,' she said, passing him the sugar. 'You just have to make sure you get everyone on board.'

Look after me

Aoife Walsh

'But we don't know the first thing about looking after babies.'

Phoebe's mum and dad are foster parents, and they're having a tough time. Her dad's moved out for bit, and her little foster brothers are playing up. So when Phoebe and her brother Adam find a baby abandoned in their den, they decide to try and look after her themselves . . .

'A delightful and moving story'
'Booksellers' Choice',
The Bookseller

'Enormously engaging, funny, and thought-provoking'
Booktrust

9781849397131 £6.99

When You Reach Me

REBECCA STEAD

Miranda's life is starting to unravel. Her best friend, Sal, gets punched by a kid on the street for what seems like no reason, and he shuts Miranda out of his life. Then the key Miranda's mum keeps hidden for emergencies is stolen, and a mysterious note arrives:

'I am coming to save your friend's life, and my own. I ask two favours. First, you must write me a letter.'

The notes keep coming, and whoever is leaving them knows things no one should know. Each message brings her closer to believing that only she can prevent a tragic death. Until the final note makes her think she's too late.

Winner of the John Newbery Medal 2010

Shortlisted for the Waterstone's Children's Book Prize

'Smart and mesmerising'
New York Times

9781849392129 £6.99